THE A

Terry Newman was a researc̲h̲_____, _____ __ _____ ____
lung function, who one day found himself in the BBC's Broadcasting House writing comedy. He is still rather vague about how this happened, but afterwards he decided that writing was more fun than sitting at an electron microscope in the dark. He has gone on to write award-winning films and plays and also writes for TV, radio, New Media, animation and games.

His first novel, published by Harper Voyager: *Detective Strongoak and the Case of the Dead Elf* introduced the well-dressed, axe-wielding, Master Detective Nicely Strongoak and was a #1 Kindle Bestseller in the USA. Nicely's adventures continued in *The King of Elfland's Little Sister* and *Dwarf Girls Don't Dance*.

Camelot Noir is a new series featuring the world-weary Sword-for-Hire and investigator Chaucere in King Arthur's Camelot.

Terry now works in a nice bright room with a view of the Sussex Weald, where he also writes musicals and songs, but he does sometimes still miss his microscope.

Other books by this author

Detective Strongoak
Detective Strongoak and the Case of the Dead Elf
The King of Elfland's Little Sister
Dwarf Girls Don't Dance

The Resurrection Show: Who Wants To Live Forever?
(co-written as Dalter T Newman)

For children
The Duke of Delhi
Tarquin and his Troop
(with Tarquin Taylor)

CHAUCERE
&ᴏ CAMELOT NOIR ᴄꙅ

TERRY NEWMAN

ᴍB
MONKEY BUSINESS

MONKEY BUSINESS

An imprint of Grey House in the Woods

This paperback original 2023

Copyright © Terry Newman, 2023

Terry Newman asserts the moral right to
be identified as the author of this work

A catalogue record for this book
is available from the British Library

Paperback ISBN: 978-1-909295-27-8
ebook ISBN: 978-1-909295-28-5

This novel is entirely a work of fiction.
The names, characters and incidents portrayed in it are
the work of the author's imagination. Any resemblance to
actual persons, living or dead, events or localities is
entirely coincidental.

Set in Garamond

1 2 3 4 5 6 7 8 9 0

For Jane, with many, many thanks.

CONTENTS

Chapter 1. Camelot   3
Chapter 2. Emald   11
Chapter 3. Steam   18
Chapter 4. An Old Career in a New City   25
Chapter 5. Gipp   37
Chapter 6. Cat and Mouse   43
Chapter 7. Wellan   52
Chapter 8. The King's Return   59
Chapter 9. The Hardening   75
Chapter 10. A Departure   80
Chapter 11. Timothy   92
Chapter 12. Aiden the Carter   98
Chapter 13. The Errand   103
Chapter 14. Sir Dace   112
Chapter 15. Rachel   119
Chapter 16. The Big House   128
Chapter 17. The Field of Penitence   135
Chapter 18. The Lady   143
Chapter 19. Merlin   150
Chapter 20. The Word from the Forge   162
Chapter 21. The North Country   165
Chapter 22. The Oath   171
Chapter 23. Hecuba   184
Chapter 24. The King's Parade   190
Chapter 25. Merlin Again   199
Chapter 26. The Round Table   203
Chapter 27. The Shepherd's Hut   207
Chapter 28. A Wedding   215
Chapter 29. Westward   225

Chapter 30. The Other House on the Hill   233
Chapter 31. Avalon   247
Chapter 32. Good Broth   259
Epilogue   264

CHAUCERE

ଈ CAMELOT NOIR ଔ

I
CAMELOT

Camelot is always crowded at this time of year: harvest time. Crowded and flyblown, smellier than a pig's arse and a lot less attractive. That's unless you have gold in your purse.

I didn't even have a purse.

What I did have was a knot of hunger in my belly and an empty ale horn in my hand. Oh yes, and a sword hanging by my side. The sword stayed sheathed by order of the Great King and nobody crossed him or his fancy Round Table, not unless they wanted to be found swinging from the very imposing New Gates in the early morning autumnal mists.

I looked around at the great unwashed, pledging their allegiance to the recuperative powers of beer, wondering, yet again, why exactly I had come back here. I had reached an age where surely I should have known better. Except some people never really do learn, do they – the dreamers, the schemers and the what-might-have-beeners? All hoping that there might be some of that Camelot magic still around to rub off on them – the magic that had helped save a people, the magic of a land they hoped to call Britain.

So which one of them was I?

I was fresh out of dreams and I had never had a scheme that wasn't holed below the water line. Was I the last of the great might-have-beeners then? There could be some truth in that, but the greater truth was that I was worse than all of them: I was a man with a mission. I just didn't know what it was yet – apart from getting the next drink.

'More?' asked the alewife, proffering her beaker. I nodded and put down a coin, my favourite coin, my last coin. It had been with me a long time – it was a shame to see it go. She must

3

have liked it as well, as she made sure my horn was full to the brim. Or maybe she liked me. It happens sometimes, but not for a while now. With her flaming red hair, honey-coloured eyes, fair freckled skin, good teeth and pleasingly plump figure, I am sure the alewife was not short of more convivial company.

She'd called the ale *cuirim*, which marked her down as one of the Northern Celts. She was a long way from home, but weren't we all, one way or another?

I nodded my thanks to her and sipped appreciatively, making it last. As ale went, I'd drunk a lot worse. I'd drunk a whole lot worse, to be honest, but that's mainly because I'm not fussy. Fussy people don't get to live long in my line of work. If there was one piece of advice I would happily pass on to the next generation, it would not be to do with brotherly love, or the foolishness of desiring gold too much, or even to beware of green-eyed women with strong sword arms. It would simply be this: never drink the water. That was all I had that passed for wisdom – or at least then it was.

I'd done all right by this rule up to that point. If sitting in an alehouse full of sweaty men in the fastest growing city this side of Avalon, having just handed over your last coin, can be considered doing all right. At least I was better off than many of my old associates and comrades, in that I was at least still drawing breath. Mind you, none of them had died from water poisoning, not unless the blade was wet.

This was not the time to get maudlin. There was work to be done.

The ale stake over the door had been good news, as I had made my way through the crowded numerous backstreets earlier that evening. It was just the right sort of alehouse, nothing too fussy, but not too cheap either; the sort of alehouse that attracted the right sort of customer – customers with money in their purses but no irritating bodyguards.

I had a real thirst coming upon me; the kind of thirst that can end up with you losing a kingdom or gaining one. With my wealth exhausted I sat quietly and made the drink last. I'm good at that, I've had plenty of practice. On balance, though, I'm probably better at downing a dozen and banging someone's head through the wall. I've had plenty of practice of doing that as well.

There was a good-sized fire burning in the red-headed woman's alehouse and it kept the autumn chill and the flies away. I wasn't fond of either, but the cold can kill you quicker; the flies just make more of a meal of it. The night was beginning to close in quickly, as it will at this time of year. The torches had been lit and the stink of tallow was making me thirstier still.

The room had filled up. An occasional scuffle broke out, but nothing to get excited about. Just young men drinking and liking to pretend that they were 'real men' and not boys any longer. The real men didn't scuffle at all and most had forgotten that they were ever young. I had as well, until recently at least, and I wasn't too sure how my remembrances were sitting at the moment. An old friend of mine once said, 'never go back, the places will be smaller, the women uglier and the smell worse. The only thing you'll ever find there will be regrets'. And he never did go back, not even in the shroud he was wrapped in. Of course, I never listen to good advice. I'm always far too busy acting on the ridiculous recommendations.

I spotted him coming in before he spotted me. You could say he never saw me coming, good old Honest Jack. I judged him to be one of the new Freemen of which Camelot was so proud, a property owner – a small farmer in his case – who paid his taxes directly to the King with no other Overlord in between. It wasn't just farmers either, many tradesmen, like smiths and ostlers, were now also judged to be Freeman of Camelot. It had been a clever move by the King and had made him many friends amongst the common people of his new capital. It had been less popular amongst many of the aforementioned Overlords, but as the King now had himself a whole new group of well-armed Knights around his fancy table, I judged he was not too bothered.

So here was Honest Jack, still stinking of cow shit – bless him! The trulls and coin girls saw him as well, but I got there first.

'Hello Jack,' I said, waving him over. 'Come sit here, near the fire, and warm yourself up! The chill's coming in early this year.'

It was no coincidence that I had the seat nearest the fire or that I had been scowling at anyone who came near the free stool next to me.

'I don't mind if I do,' said Honest Jack. 'It's been a long day. A right long day, I don't mind telling you!'

He had 'country' written all over him, mostly in shit and cow-spit. A simple farmer, an honest 'Jack' up to the Big House for the autumn run, bringing in the flock or herd – or whatever it was he kept to provide for him and his family – for the big autumn market. He looked pleased with himself, he'd done well, and now wanted to get his fill of the Big Burh lights and I was just the boy to show him.

I knew all the bright lights and was best friends with the type of men who lit them.

'The ale is excellent here and I recommend the deer stew as well – proper meat in that stew! Something that walked around proper like, not scuffled about on the floor.'

Honest Jack was glad to hear this. So glad he had the alewife top up my horn for me. Of course I had no idea what the stew was like as I hadn't eaten in two days, but the stew was all there was to eat here anyway, and the flame-haired woman had the looks of a good cook, if I was any judge.

By our third horn Jack and I were new best friends. A shared plate or two of the venison stew and another horn later we were practically related and by the fifth, or maybe sixth, I think I had agreed to marry his eldest daughter.

'A marvellous girl, our Agnes – good strong thighs, proper hips for childbearing. Quite a catch you know!'

This was perhaps more than I needed to know and Honest Jack sounded more like he was discussing a prize heifer than his eldest girl – which indeed he might as well have been. I was not impressed by the fact that her face had not got a mention.

'Great teats! No problem with teats like Agnes has!'

Now that was far too much knowledge to be sharing with a stranger in a market day tavern. But I sat there smiling, to all intents and purposes absolutely spellbound by the stories of the exciting life he led. Taking out the cows and bringing them home again and … taking out the cows and bringing them home and … my eyes never strayed from his purse and the coin that tumbled across the trestle table as the alewife walked by with her beaker.

I told Jack about a little place I knew, a good clean place – he liked the idea. He liked the idea of Helewidis, 'hale and wide', naughty Jack. Truth be told, by this time even I liked the idea of Helewidis and I had made her up. Jack needed to get to see Helewidis with some urgency, as there were other folk interested in Jack.

We emptied our horns and left.

The Big House loomed high above us in the night, as it now loomed above everything in the lives of the people of Camelot. As it had loomed above me, ever since I had returned to this place I once swore I had left forever.

We showed our deference to the King and his Knights by pissing up against the castle wall: two streams steaming in the moonlight, two streams of gold. For is it not the way of men to take the gold from their purses and to water the meadows and walls with it later?

'I do swear that from here I could piss in the King's cup tonight!' said Honest Jack, laughing as he relieved himself.

'He'd need a big cup!' I added, with genuine admiration for Jack's bladder capacity.

'Then maybe I could fill that Grail he's always looking for,' Jack mentioned without concern for the religious sensibilities of many of the locals – not that the lower reaches of Camelot were renowned for their piety. The Grail was a very different matter to the business we were about tonight.

After our communal making of water, my farmer friend was beginning to run out of steam as well. So we decided to leave Helewidis for another night and I walked him back to his lodgings, which were nearby – or so he thought – though those unused to the Big Burh ways were liable to get lost quicker than a maid's virginity on the first day of spring. I made sure that we went the way I desired.

I had watched them closely in the alehouse, slipping my sword out a finger and catching their reflections in its well-polished surface. I knew the look in their eyes – mean and hungry. Didn't I see the same far too often when I looked down into a quiet pond to drink? It was the look that I hoped would never be permanently etched into my features. For them it was far too late. They were mean and they were hungry and nothing was going to change that now.

For all their doggedness they were following us far too closely, not even trying to be quiet. One had the red hair that seems much more common these days, not the red of the alewife but a darker and somehow more threatening hue. He was carrying no spare flesh and had a wolfish look. The other of the pair had hair so thick and black it looked more like an animal's pelt. I imagine it covered him like the bear he closely resembled in his mass and muscles. He'd looked smaller sitting down, that's for sure.

Merrily they rolled along – just two more 'good fellows' who had supped too much ale. They hadn't touched their drinks, though, for at least an hour before we had all left the alehouse, because their horns were empty and the alewife was shooting them dirty looks for the space they were taking up.

As we stopped just before Honest Jack's lodgings they made their move. I was ready for them and waiting to see what they had planned. Let them try their best.

'Chlann Aoidh!' shouted our red-headed attacker in a thick accent that spoke of many long weeks on the road away from his birthplace. He swung a cudgel that was carved to do some damage. The pelted fellow made less fuss, looking for a way in with his dagger while we were distracted by the bellow.

Fortunately, the redhead went for Honest Jack. The cudgel clipped my drinking partner with a sickening 'thud' even as I pushed him out of harm's way. I hoped that farmers still came with thick skulls. They certainly always used to. I can adjudge to that.

My sword was already out and it broached the first man nicely in the meat of his belly as he recovered from his swing, leaving me to knock aside his friend's blade with a quick parry of my long knife and to thrust with that in my turn. This caught him full in the throat just above his leather collar and below the look of surprise that was now all over his face. He blew red bubbles from his neck, which quickly became a torrent of life's liquor and then he dropped like a stone.

Unfortunately, I hadn't anticipated that they had also invited a third member to the party. Which really isn't creckett as they say. Smaller and weasel-like, with a shaved head and rotten teeth, but still armed with a mace that had probably tenderised a lot of meat in its day. Not expecting any contest, weasel wasn't paying attention to the way the performance was playing and was already on one knee, searching for Honest Jack's purse as he lay sprawled. We couldn't have that, mostly because the purse was already safely in my pocket.

I picked up the dropped cudgel and threw it at the weasel's head. It connected enough to get his attention. He turned angrily in my direction and took in the tableau: two down and one standing – not in his team's favour. Taken aback by this turn of events, it didn't take him long to decide on the best course of action. A mace is no match for a sword in the hands of an expert. He knew this and ran. I let him get the exercise; he needed it. He's probably running still, back to where shouting 'Chlann Aoidh' is enough to turn a drinking man's knees to jelly.

I picked up Honest Jack and carried the farmer to his bed. He'd live, of that I was sure. The advantage of being semi-conscious before you are brained. I took my tithe from his purse before tucking it back safely in his tunic, friend's rates – his family wouldn't starve this winter and he had learnt a valuable lesson. Agnes's teats would not lose their lustre and her mighty thighs would not diminish through hunger, although Jack might find his wife bending his ear painfully as she bathed his head.

Maybe Honest Jack would even tell the story of his adventures, of the day he went to market and sampled the delights and bright lights of the Big House and only just escaped with his life. Of course, it's possible Jack might go and make a fuss in the morning. Try to get the knights of that fancy Round Table all roiled up, but chances are they'd just say: leave it be Jack, that's Camelot.

2
EMALD

I woke the next morning in a very good frame of mind. Not having to sleep outdoors under a thin cloak can do that for a man. My rush mat had come with fresh straw and, to me at least, had felt almost as soft as the breast of the landlady who had shown it to me late the previous night. I did not partake of the breast, but the smile when she saw the contents of my purse told me its availability would be up for negotiation should I so request.

I had other priorities now, though. Business before pleasure always, because as far as I know nobody ever died from a lack of pleasure, but you can't live off the warmth of a sweetheart's smile, no matter what you may feel at the time.

Somebody who lives by the sword had better take damn good care of his source of income. My financial fountainhead had been neglected of late. Walking, and occasionally riding, across more countries than I could easily name, my sword had not left my side. Except, that is, to prevent any unwanted interruption of the aforementioned walking and occasional riding. Along the way my sword had acquired a collection of dints and notches not expected in the tool of trade of a professional swordsman. And, as I was currently about to go on a job hunt, my credentials needed to be spotless.

I had yet to make the acquaintance of any smiths since my arrival back in Camelot, as I was currently relegated to the transport option that involved two fewer legs than their normal stock-in-trade. I knew I could not afford one of the fancy sword smiths who polished up the pig-stickers and body-splitters of the armoured Lords up in the Big House, so I asked my landlady for the name of somebody more suited to my current situation.

'A good smith you say?'

'A body who is skilled at more than simple horse shoeing at least.'

'Well, that will count Alden the Smith out – with him you're lucky not to find your horse wearing an iron smile.'

'Somebody who at least knows what end of a sword should be sharp would be welcomed.'

'Well, that's not as easy as you might imagine,' she said. The strain of all that thinking was written clearly all over her face, but was erased by a simple trip to my purse.

'You would be wanting Emald! He's on the western outskirts of the Burh. I'll point you the way.'

Her directions seemed simple enough, but now it was I who was forgetting just how large Camelot had become. And, of course, the roads and alleys and occasional street did nothing to help; initial attempts at what the King's advisors had apparently called 'planning' fell through almost before any dwellings could be erected. They did well in the area immediately around the Big House, which allowed easy access for goods and services. It wasn't enough though. As the news of Camelot's wealth began to spread around the poorer villages and hamlets nearby, hovels sprang up all around the walls, as attractive as pustules on a holy woman. Paths joined together these humbler dwellings, creating broken-backed trails, and before long the Castle began to look like a jewel that had somehow fallen down from the heavens and landed, bang slap, in the middle of a cow pat. Which was a bit too close to the truth for many of the people who lived in what was called Greater Camelot, by some, and the Midden, by most.

The place was a maze and as soon as I stepped out of the quarter I was familiar with, I was something not too far away from being lost. This wasn't my first time back in Camelot, although my longest stay by a long chalk. The first time had been mostly about curiosity. I'd had an 'errand' to run for a client living in one of the lands west of the Middle Sea. A delivery to make to this wondrous place he'd been trading with called Camelot. Did I know of it, as I was from the Misty Isles some asked? I made the mistake of mentioning I had some knowledge of Camelot. Therefore I was, of course, the perfect person to deliver, and protect, the parcel in my care.

I hadn't found Camelot that wondrous then, dangerous, yes.

I was impressed by the pace of growth and the sheer scale of the City rising from the land that I had once felt I belonged to, but I wasn't comfortable being there now. I didn't stay that long – just long enough to get the measure of the place and give the parcel to the intended recipient. Which, thinking about it, was far longer than I had originally intended. Then I left at some speed on a good horse. My heart had still been in thrall to the sun and smells, and the women, of hotter and more exotic climes. I'd never had the itch that was responsible for my current visit. The itch I wanted so desperately to scratch – if only I could identify its location.

I smelt the smithy before I saw it. And what a relief that was! How I love the smell of a busy smithy. Worked metal, charcoal and honest sweat, the scents of the flowers of industry. This building was far from a hovel. It was solid outside and well organised inside. I guess it must have had another use before – perhaps a storehouse for produce on their way to the Big House? It inspired confidence in the owner and, accordingly, his work.

This smith was not the sort of monster you often find in his trade – he was a lot bigger than that. Taller than me by a good foot and wider by the same, he did not carry a pinch of spare fat; he was all muscle, glowering in the shadows of his smithy's forge. It was as if he, along with his metal, had been tempered in the heat of his furnace. His eyes, almost glowing in the light of the forge's fire, as he worked a shoe, had a hint of something I had not seen for many years and a lot more miles. It was a look that hinted of the savage or the feral perhaps? This was a man with history.

'Emald the Smith?' I asked politely, because that is always the best first approach when talking to giants with large hammers in their hands.

He nodded, not interrupting his work, or the regular rhythm of his blows.

I looked at his forge. You can tell a lot about a metalworker by his forge, especially the construction of his bellows and the flow of air. This was as good as I'd seen in many a year.

'A nice forge you have here.'

'Know something about them, do you?'

'Enough to know that it's consistency of heating that you require if you don't want work that varies in quality – too soft to hold an edge or hard but too brittle. Good bellows make good swords.'

'I mostly shoe horses.'

'I am told you have some skill at working a blade as well?'

'That is what people say,' he replied, now working his bellows again and sending sparks flying like the shortest-lived of mayflies.

'And what do you yourself say?'

'I've not seen better.'

I took out my sword with exaggerated care. He glanced at it and then looked again, stopping his work by plunging the finished shoe in a water barrel. He then put his tools down and wiped his hands carefully on a rag. I knew he must be doing OK at his work, as most of Camelot wore their rags.

I handed him my sword. It is a rather special and remarkable thing, my sword. Lighter than the common two-handed longsword or claymore, and longer, its deceptive strength still makes it possible to parry an attack with those weapons, while permitting another swordsman's defence to be breached by those fleet of foot. Single-edged, but what an edge, the sharpness of the tip can find a gap through any but the very best of chain mail. The guard is of a type I have never seen anywhere else, and I have travelled some. Such a guard will not only prevent an opponent's blade from sliding down and cutting your hand in two, but it can even shatter an inferior blade thanks to a collar of metal even harder than the blade.

Emald gave my sword a thorough inspection. As well it might be, by anybody with more than a passing interest in weaponry. He held it in his hands for a long time. Finally he spoke:

'This was not made here.' A statement not a question.

I admitted as much with a nod.

'Not from anywhere near here, either.'

'No, some hussy having a bath gave it to me.' This response earned a raised eyebrow. Perhaps jokes at the expense of the Great King were not the done thing in Camelot.

Emald next looked down the length of my sword, before commenting with some disdain:

'Some damage here.'

'Look, just tell me if you can restore it please. I've got some gold in my purse. You need gold to buy things in Camelot now, or so I'm told, therefore I'll give you some of my gold in return for your labour. It's a good system and seems to be working. How about we give it a go?'

The smith nodded:

'Perhaps.'

He swung my sword a few times – enough to show that he was familiar with more than just the makings of such a fine weapon, then examined it even closer — scratching at his beard. I could feel mine growing as I waited. I wanted to leave before I tripped over it.

'This is a sword that has a history and I don't just mean the dints you've made,' he concluded. 'The iron sand is heated together with coal for three days they say, to make such a sword and blades may be folded up to 20 times. Such skills are rare, if ever to be found in this land.'

'Fine,' I said, putting out my hand. 'I'll find myself a boat.'

'Steady there,' Emald said, holding back a smile. 'I said they are rare, but not unknown. I can see to your sword, but it will not be easy and it will take time.'

'I see,' I said, still irked, 'and how is it that a smith then of such quality as you profess to be, is not up in the Big House polishing the pins of the noble lords, but down here putting iron on nags and dobbins?'

'A good question,' he said, still eyeing up the sword. 'Probably the same sort of reason why the owner of such a sword is not living in the Big House, but has worn his boot leather out and is very much in need of a bath.'

I had to laugh at that. 'Good hit, Smith!' My boots were indeed in need of as much attention as my sword. 'Good hit indeed.'

'Call me Emald,' he said casually. The smith was far more engrossed with my weapon than my word play.

'So, Emald, what will this cost me and how long will the work take?'

'It'll cost what it costs and take as long as it takes. I will not cheat you, if that's what you're afraid of.'

'I didn't say that, Emald.'

'Good.'

'I wouldn't dream of suggesting such a thing.'

'Then if it's walking around feeling undressed that is the bother, help yourself to a blade from the store.' He indicated a table, covered with an oiled cloth, by a nod of his head. 'It does not pay to be too bold about all aspects of my trade. The Big House has big eyes too.'

16

I walked over, lifted the cloth and was surprised to see half a dozen good blades hidden beneath. All were in excellent condition and sharp enough to shave with. I tried them for weight and balance until I found one that felt natural.

The double-edged blade was smooth and sharp with a shallow fuller. There was not much taper and the tip, although very sharp, was quite rounded. I cut some air with it; not bad at all. In some ways it wasn't very different from the sword of the Old Empire: the spatha. It was just a lot bigger, much heavier and – at least as worked by Emald – sharper.

Not bad at all. I felt better dressed already.

'A good choice,' Emald said with approval. 'Now, go find the bathhouse.'

'Don't you want to know where to find me?'

'You won't be leaving this in Camelot will you?' He lifted my sword with considerable reverence. 'And when you have found lodgings I'll know.'

I raised an eyebrow at this.

'Camelot is not that large a place that news of import doesn't travel quickly if the right ears are listening, swordsman.'

I acknowledged the wisdom of this.

'Well, Chaucere is my name; rhymes with walker, as they say it hereabouts,' I told him.

'It does indeed. Good morning, Chaucere rhymes with walker.'

'Good morning Emald, rhymes with nothing much I can think of.'

The giant smith gave a short laugh: 'Go get your bath.'

I left for some admittedly much-needed attention to my own well being. Long time no bath.

3
STEAM

The bathhouse was exactly where it has always been, at least since the Old Empire finished its construction all those years ago. Within its walls the hot springs bubbled up from deep under the ground into a number of different rooms all put to different uses. Apart from bathing, you could get your clothes washed, your hair cut, and have a shit and a shave to boot. Everything that is, in my humble opinion, great about what a lot of people are now calling civilisation. Definitely amongst the most positive aspects of city life, the negatives are too many to list.

One room in the bathhouse has rocks heated by hidden fires, and they then splash the rocks with water to fill the space with steam. They say that it improves the breathing and stops the collection of bad humours, bringing about a rejuvenation of mind and spirit. There might even be something in that as it took ten years off me, in both age and accumulated filth.

I had paid up front for the full set – and anything else that they might think up while I was there as well. This was all my birthdays in one and I was going for it like I could even remember when my birthday was.

'Your sword please, Sir,' said the boy on the tally desk. He looked in need of a good bath himself, which is perhaps not the best way of promoting your service.

'By orders of the King,' he added, to pre-empt any arguments. I wasn't actually about to argue. In bathhouses it made sense to have all sharp weapons well out of the way, what with so much of the time being spent with your modesty only covered by a small sheet.

The bathhouse was exactly where it has always been, at least since the Old Empire finished its construction all those years ago. Within its walls the hot springs bubbled up from deep under the ground into a number of different rooms all put to different uses. Apart from bathing, you could get your clothes washed, your hair cut, and have a shit and a shave to boot. Everything that is, in my humble opinion, great about what a lot of people are now calling civilisation. Definitely amongst the most positive aspects of city life, the negatives are too many to list.

One room in the bathhouse has rocks heated by hidden fires, and they then splash the rocks with water to fill the space with steam. They say that it improves the breathing and stops the collection of bad humours, bringing about a rejuvenation of mind and spirit. There might even be something in that as it took ten years off me, in both age and accumulated filth.

I had paid up front for the full set – and anything else that they might think up while I was there as well. This was all my birthdays in one and I was going for it like I could even remember when my birthday was.

'Your sword please, Sir,' said the boy on the tally desk. He looked in need of a good bath himself, which is perhaps not the best way of promoting your service.

'By orders of the King,' he added, to pre-empt any arguments. I wasn't actually about to argue. In bathhouses it made sense to have all sharp weapons well out of the way, what with so much of the time being spent with your modesty only covered by a small sheet.

There was generally a good standard of behaviour here, I knew. Nobody wants to be barred from the bathhouse, not if they desired to smell better than the rest of the Midden. The Lords and Ladies of the Big House also visited the bathhouse, though not at the same time as the rest of us of course – they probably polished the water first. And it wouldn't do for us mortals to see our betters so displayed, even with their sheets. We might start thinking that they weren't so different and what might that lead to?

I received a tally disc on a leather tie for my sword from the boy. I then stripped in a nearby chamber and received another disc for the clothes I had sent away to be cleaned. They even had a cobbler here now and so my boots were sent for some repair work as well. From there I went straight into the wash pool where I applied sand soap to my body with enthusiasm. Something that smelled suspiciously of seaweed did wonders for my hair and from there I slipped into the warmth of the bubbling spring water. I have to admit it felt good to be clean. It's not something that worries me unduly when I am working or on the road, but I could get used to this.

Are you getting soft Chaucere, I wondered?

So what if I was? I wasn't going anywhere – for the present at least. Next then I had my hair chopped to shoulder length, which I had noticed seemed to be the style in Camelot. I can't say that I am a slave to such fashions, but it is good to blend in if you don't want to be marked as a stranger. Clean-shaven seemed to be the order of the day too, so I had a young lad, with the fair looks of one of the overseas tribes, attend to this. He was much more attractive than the boy on the tally desk, but my tastes have never run that way. I am glad he had a steady hand because the blade he was using was impressive in the keenness of its edge.

The boy, whose name was Alcott, wiped clean a brass mirror and handed it to me. It was interesting to see the face now looking back at me in the polished metal. I recognised the straight nose, narrow nostrils and blue eyes, the small, slightly pursed mouth, but I had no idea where all the lines had come from. Had the soap sand revealed them lurking like bandits beneath the ample undergrowth of beard? Some looked like the furrows on a field that had long gone fallow. Maybe I should have left the hair.

'What do you think, Alcott?' I asked. 'Is this the face of a man you would trust?'

'Most certainly, Sir,' he replied. I knew he was only hoping for a good gratuity but I was going to make him work for it.

'And what especially about the face would you say inspired such confidence, young Alcott?'

He considered for a moment before answering. 'Your eyes, Sir. They reveal that you have seen many places and have faced many a hardship, but never have you flinched in pursuing what you saw to be the honest and honourable path.'

I had another look in the mirror. The youth of Camelot had gained a lot of wisdom in my time away!

'And you can see all that from one look at my face?'

'Not just the look, Sir. Remember I have had a sharp razor to your face and you can tell a lot from how a man reacts to that!'

I considered this.

'Yes, I imagine so.'

'Just as I could tell that these paths, although honest and honourable, were not necessarily what others might call lawful.'

He smiled a broad smile:

'Will there be anything else, Sir'

I thought not. He had surely earnt his gratuity and too much insight from your barber is not necessarily good for one's piece of mind.

Later, I was sat, sheet on lap, in the steam room, pleasantly at peace with the world and only dimly aware that the place was empty apart from two men deep in conversation at the other end of the room. One man I noticed vaguely was large, but none of it fat: strong-looking, fair-haired, with moustaches growing in the northern style. The other was sallow-skinned, all lean muscle like the racing hounds they use for hare coursing. An interesting enough pair, but I wasn't interested.

21

At some point I think I heard the debate becoming heated, argumentative words drifted over, but they didn't worry me either. Sleeping in the pleasant steam was much more to my liking.

I awoke with a knife tip at my throat.

'What did you hear?' breathed the man with the moustaches and unmistakable menace now in his hoarse, gruff voice.

Well, so much for that 'exceptional standard of behaviour' and so much for the 'no weapons' policy as well. I looked up at him and felt the hair on my arms rise. There was something about this man…

'*Backpfeifengesicht*,' I blurted out quickly. I would like to say this was the result of quick thinking on my part, but it wasn't. It's simply that travelling as I have, I pick up all sorts of useful languages and phrases and this is one that had stuck in my mind and happened to find my tongue. It sort of means wanting to give somebody a slap in the face, with a chair.

The man with the moustaches grinned and let the pressure off his knife.

'Foreign, eh?' he said.

I looked suitably blank.

'Foreign!' he shouted again.

I nodded, very, very carefully.

'Good,' he said. 'We need more foreign workers. Build Camelot, great and mighty! One day we will rule the world!' He smiled and hid his knife away in his sheet before rejoining his companion.

I was really sweating now, but I felt sure that I needed to know more about what the moustachioed man had been discussing. Some inexplicable inner feeling told me it was very much connected to what had drawn me back to the walls of the city I had vowed to never see again: back to Camelot.

They left a short time after, but my enjoyment of the steam room had waned somewhat. I went and jumped into the cold bath, to punish myself for daring to relax. Of my two companions from the steam room there was no sign. This was good as I didn't want them to realise that I could have understood every word they said, had I been listening properly, which I hadn't. I'd only heard a couple of choice words when the argument had become heated and why a shepherd's hut should be of importance I had no idea. Yet I couldn't help but feel that this large moustached man was of importance, to me, and whatever strange augury it was that had brought me back here. I shivered, from what I had no idea.

The cold bath was large and I swam around a bit to get the circulation going and clear my mind. I had learnt to swim in the Middle Sea, which was a lot warmer than the seas of our island home. It was a skill I was quite proud of because most people I had known had never mastered it. It had come in useful a number of times and had saved my life on one memorable occasion. And as I swam I began to think of a plan. A little while later I collected my belongings. The same boy was on the tally desk and he still needed a wash.

I took my clean and mostly dry clothes and put them on. Unasked, they had put some dubbin on my boots and with new heels I felt like a new man, or at least a taller one. As I buckled on my sword I casually remarked how not everybody seemed to abide by the no-weapons rule.

'The Big House doesn't have to abide by the rules the Big House makes,' the tally boy said, as if addressing an idiot. Which in some senses he was. I had been away a long time after all – a lot can change.

'So, the man with the fine moustaches, he was from the Big House?'

'I surely couldn't say, Sir. Each man's business is his own. It does not do for any working here to answer questions concerning our guests.'

I took out the coin I was about to give the tally boy for a gratuity. I placed it on the desk and then added another to it, and then a third.

'We are especially respectful of those who sit at the King's Round Table,' he said and picked up his coins. I thanked him for his help and departed, wondering about the calibre of men the King had collected around him in The Big House.

4
AN OLD CAREER IN A NEW CITY

L ooking and feeling much better, and with the autumn sun on my back, I went in search of some employment. It just might have looked like I was wandering back to talk with the flame-haired Celtic alewife, but I had that plan I was looking to enact now. Talking to her was a bonus.

It was quiet in the alehouse and the alewife wasn't busy.

I asked for her name and she said Mistress Aila. I asked Mistress Aila to pull up a stool. She considered this, looked around and finally consented.

'I've seen you here before, haven't I?' said Aila.

'I'm new to Camelot.' I replied, not exactly lying.

'Come to make your fortune have you?'

'Perhaps,' I replied, supping heartily. 'You know, this is really very good ale!'

'That would be my secret ingredients.'

'Which are?'

'A secret,' we said in unison, before laughing.

'What's your name then, fortune seeker?' Aila asked.

'Chaucere,' I told her. 'Rhymes with Walker.'

'And where are you from, Chaucere rhymes with walker?'

'All over the place, Mistress Aila.'

'A sword-for-hire?'

'Sometimes,' I admitted. 'Other times I just …sort things out and maybe fix matters for people.'

'What sort of matters, Master Chaucere?'

'Ones that need fixing, Mistress Aila.' I looked around the alehouse. 'Do you get a lot of trouble in here, for example?'

'Not especially; well, sometimes, market days are the worst. Why do you ask?'

'I was wondering if you might have need of a man who was good with his fists and a sword, but even better at knowing when not to use them? A man who could help you keep the drinkers drinking, and not fighting, and keep the fighters fighting somewhere else.'

'I see,' she laughed. 'And what would such a man cost me?'

'No coin or gold or silver. Simply a mat in your nice warm brewhouse, where I can also guard your most precious of goods.'

'And drink me out of a living?'

'Mistress Aila, do I have the face of a drunkard?'

She looked at me closely before deciding. I didn't shy away from her scrutiny. Hers was a face that rewarded closer observation as well. Some women knock you out at first sight; others creep up on you when you're not actually looking. Others make you want to start writing ballads in their praise. Aila, with her flaming hair and inviting honey-coloured eyes, just made you want to keep on looking.

She pulled away first.

'No. I see all sorts of things in there, but drinking to excess isn't one of your weaknesses.'

'Thank you. I won't ask what weaknesses you do see there. ' I smiled, exercising little used muscles.

'Can't you smile better than that? I don't want to scare my customers away!'

I laughed this time – without it being forced at all.

'That's better!' she said, smiling herself. 'You should do it more often, who knows what might happen.'

'There hasn't been a lot of reason in recent years, Mistress. I am out of practice.'

'It suits you well. With the shave some might even call you handsome. In a poor light of course.'

'So, are you in favour of my proposal?'

'I might be, Chaucere, rhymes with walker,' she considered.

'What have you got to lose?'

'My business, my reputation, my standing in the city, my recipes…'

'I take your point!' I interrupted. 'But apart from your very life and livelihood? I should add, I am also handy at fixing things, broken utensils – some metalwork even.'

'You don't look like a tinker!'

'I'm most certainly not, by trade, but you pick things up along the way.'

'We'll give it a try,' she said finally, standing up. 'This next market day will be busy and I could do with somebody to help fill the horns.

'Excellent, Mistress!'

'And, Chaucere,' she dropped her voice, 'if you do have need to exercise your sword arm against those who require it, see if you can arrange for them to take the long fall off the cliff into the river.' She leant over and whispered quietly: 'Not leave them about the streets where they might frighten the children – as I believe you did to those two last night.'

'Mistress?' I was all wounded innocence.

'Not saying they didn't deserve it. From what I have heard of their behaviour in the past, that outcome was long overdue. Camelot will be none the worse for them not taking up valuable space.'

'Space does seem to be lacking.'

Just remember Chaucere, I never forget a face.' She bent over and whispered, 'even if it is now light six months of beard.' She straightened up and smoothed the apron she wore when serving.

'The point is well made, Mistress Aila. Who would want to frighten the children — or the horses?'

'The horses have seen it all before, Chaucere. The children still have a lot to learn, but best they don't learn it all at once.'

She poured me a drink. 'This one is to seal the bargain. The rest you pay for, understood?'

I nodded and thanked her.

We did indeed give it a try and very well it seemed to work out for the both of us. Aila's alehouse turned out to be a very comfortable place to work, rest my head and take stock. The brew-room was also very comfortable. Mistress Aila provided clean blankets, a comfortable pallet and dried rushes and herbs to lie on. The herbs were interesting as she had many of them drying around the room where I made my bed. Some she used for cooking, others, including what I recognised as wild hops, I surmised were the secret ingredients that she added to her ale. It gave the room a most wholesome air and did no harm to the ale either. In fact I noticed that Aila's ale kept particularly well and didn't spoil in the manner of inferior brews.

All in all this seemed a good place to see the winter through and I did not abuse the privilege. I took care of troublemakers, firmly, but without recourse to bloodshed. I always helped out with the serving and horn and pot collecting as well, but made sure that all her customers knew what my primary role was.

The alehouse of Mistress Aila was soon full every night. A man knew he could come here and have a quiet drink or three without getting beaten or robbed. I also made it clear that we would not abide people taking advantage of our more well-refreshed customers when they were on their way back to their homes. We didn't exactly carry them ourselves, but we didn't just throw them out into the gutter either. They got home safely and therefore came back again. Business was so good that Aila hired a young girl, Gwen, to help out as well. Apparently my charms are not enough to keep all the customers happy. This was hurtful to learn, but I coped somehow. The help Aila had hired was bright, attractive and even sang beautifully. Life is tough some times.

Most days at Aila's flew by and I had even learnt a thing or two about ale making, not being one to turn his nose up about something just because it is considered women's work. In some countries I have passed through, it is actually the men who work with the ale and pass down the secrets to their sons, not the other way round. I didn't mind, as long as the ale gets made. I am fond of an ale, but as Aila summarised, I am not a drunkard.

The sallow-skinned man I had seen in the baths was an occasional visitor, but he did not seem to recognise me. He was never with the same group of men twice and never with the blond man with the moustaches. Although none of them had the looks or behaviour of scholars or holy men, they were well behaved at Aila's. One evening I asked her about him after she had been over to top up their horns.

'The party you have just served, Aila – do you know the name of the skinny individual in need of some sunshine?'

'I believe they call him Cecilio,' Aila said. 'He has friends in high places.'

I pointed up the hill and asked:

'That sort of high place?'

Aila nodded.

I had been hearing this a lot recently. Friends and influence in high places meant you had access to the Big House and that was what counted to everybody in modern Camelot. People could, and did, live well on the pickings that came down from on high.

Aila smiled broadly as if suddenly aware of Cecilio's attention. 'Personally, I do not trust him further than I could shit him – although I could not tell you why. However, we are always pleasant to him, are we not?'

'Oh, yes. Always be pleasant to Cecilio,' I smiled, equally affable, but I knew trouble when I smelt it and he was stinking the place out. Some people are like that, trouble clings to them like daglock on a sheep's arse.

'Stew for the party near the door,' said Gwen, in her beautiful singsong voice, bringing food from the cookhouse. That was Cecilio and friends. I fixed my affable smile firmly on and went to fetch their food.

I had fallen into the habit of visiting Emald during the winter and not just because his forge was the warmest place I knew of in Camelot. He was good company, both in the alehouse and outside it. Unmarried, he took his drinking seriously, but did not let it interfere with his true profession, unlike many of his sex and age. I had a similar outlook and there were many periods of life when neither ale nor wine was obtainable, and I survived, hardly giving it a second thought. When it was available, that was a different matter.

Often Emald and I would spar with wooden swords to keep my hand and eye in. Emald was no slouch and I had to be on my toes, What he lacked in style he made up for in strength and enthusiasm, making him the perfect opponent for me. I would often come back to Aila's with more bruises than I had arrived with. I don't think Emald could bruise.

On every visit I would ask Emald:

'How goes my sword?' And he would answer:

'Well enough. Well enough.'

That winter was a long drawn out affair, not particularly hard, and the snows, when they came, did not cause too much distress.

By and large farmers were able to feed their stock with the fodder they had put by and I was sure Honest Jack would manage with no problems. The winter didn't know when to stop though and it had already outstayed its welcome by many weeks. Farmers needed to get planting and put their cows and sheep out on new grass.

With the lengthening days I began to feel restless again. I was not taking wages from Aila and although I had food provided (and drink now I had proven my worth) my own reserves of coin were getting low. I decided to ask Aila if she could put around a kind word for me – a recommendation as it were – for anybody who might need a strong sword arm, with discretion guaranteed.

It was not that I was anything other than happy with my current position, this was purely additional income. I like to have 'falling-back' money, so I needed to broach the subject with Aila. I was helping her make a fresh brew at the time. She produced a different, though equally tasty, winter ale, darker and stronger than her normal beer; it used some special ingredients that could be safely stored over the cold season. Her 'winter warmer' was very popular. This was a new batch though: lighter and fresher for the, hopefully, upcoming spring.

By now Aila and I had established an excellent working relationship. We were easy in each other's company. In many ways we were like an old married couple who had long ago knocked off, or agreed to ignore, any awkward corners the other had. It was a relationship uncomplicated by sex because we both realised that any such entanglement, though undoubtedly of interest to us both, in the long term, was only going to cause more trouble than it was worth.

'You thinking of moving on then?' Aila asked, adding more barley to the mash.

'Not at all, Aila,' I replied, pouring in water. 'I have grown to like Camelot. However, we have your place practically running itself now. On some shifts I am hardly needed, so well behaved are your clients. It would be good to keep myself busy. You know what they say about idle hands.'

Aila gave me a long thoughtful look. 'You don't need to stay you know. I am grateful for your help, but I am surprised you have stayed this long. I never took you for somebody wanting to put down roots.'

'What do you take me for?' I had to ask.

'Somebody with a mission. One he doesn't necessarily want to talk about.'

That was a little too close to the truth – certainly with regard to not wanting to talk about motives. I'm not sure I could explain it sensibly anyway.

'It's just a way of trying to get some coin, Aila,' I said in the end, convincingly enough.

Aila said she would ask around, which she did, and to my surprise I had a very quick response. It was a quiet evening a week later, and winter still had its hold on Camelot. Would the weather ever relent?

I recognised him, when he walked into Aila's alehouse, as one of the people who lived to the east of the warm sea that some call the Middle Sea. Not an old man, but certainly not young any more, he had long dark hair that curled as it hung down and the top of his head covered with the small cap that many in those lands wear.

I had ventured many times to that part of the world on my travels and had found it to be both an enthralling and infuriating place. The people who lived in that baked and blessed land had histories that were more complicated than any our wet and grey isles had to offer. And with such histories, of course, there came the possibility for disputes and accusations and much worse. I had made a good living there, until I grew weary with their religious cant, which too often to me sounded like the bickering of men arguing over who should wield the bucket when the ship they are all sailing in is already taking on water.

To which tribe the stranger belonged I could not say, but there is no doubt that he was a very long way from home. The man took a seat in a corner, where there was a free stool next to the fire. This was a man who did not ask for fanfares on his arrival. Aila went to talk with him and poured a small horn of ale, which he handled nervously. After a short while she motioned me over and introduced us:

'Chaucere, this is Master Abram. Master Abram, this is Chaucere.' We nodded a greeting.

'He is to be trusted,' she said, a comment apparently applicable to us both.

Then she poured me a larger horn of ale and left the two of us to our own devices. After some stilted observations about the weather and anticipation of the coming spring, we got down to business.

'How might I help you, Master Abram?' I asked.

He played nervously with his horn. 'Do you know my occupation, Chaucere?' he asked quietly.

'I imagine that you are a money lender?'

He looked at me levelly before speaking:

'Does that worry you Chaucere?'

'Worry, me?' I laughed. 'Why should it worry me? I thankfully am not in need of a loan at the moment, and even if I was, I have very little I could offer by way of a pledge.'

He looked slightly embarrassed, like a guest at a wedding who has just farted as the host begins his speech. 'I am sorry,' he continued. 'It is just that many people now seem to resent my people for the occupation that is often forced upon us because of the religious sensibilities of the people of the land where we are currently living. They think it says something about our propensities.'

'Master Abram, you must excuse me. I didn't mean to give offence by laughing. It's just that I've been to your part of the world…'

His eyes widened at the news.

'…and, surprise, surprise, I found it to be full of rogues and saints in the same measure as every other place I have lived or visited.'

TERRY
NEWMAN

He nodded his head in agreement and smiled. 'It is ever thus
– whatever the religious texts may say, it seems too often that
man's worst nature will out.'

'But sometimes his better nature does win through as well.'

'Sometimes I wonder which is better, and which is the
worse?' Abram added thoughtfully. 'When so much ill is done in
the name of making the world better.'

'I for one cannot say,' I admitted. 'At the end of the day, I
think it is all just nature. And that I could discuss all day, but as
it is getting late and I have work to do, let me just ask again: how
may I help you?'

Master Abram cleared his throat. 'I have kin in Camelot and
some have the same occupation as myself. They have been
attacked as they carried out their collections in the hamlets and
villages around Camelot. I myself should have made my first
round of the year by now, and if it was not for a chill of the
chest I would have done so. I fear I might have been, and still
might be, robbed.'

Abram looked around. He was clearly very concerned and
now said it directly:

'I am worried – very worried, for myself and for my kinfolk,
who fortunately although robbed were at least not injured – this
time. I require somebody I can trust to accompany me. A sword
arm if you will, as I make my collections.'

I sat back and considered. 'This sounds like a problem that
our King and his knights should be assisting you with – not
saying I won't help, but their intervention would save you gold.'

Abram licked his lips nervously. 'I have made representation
to the Round Table, but they say they cannot be guarding
against every random attack.'

'A fair point.'

'But I do not think these attacks are random – we cannot all
be so unlucky.'

'You think there is organisation at work?'

'I do, Chaucere. I do indeed – the coincidence is too much.'

'Perhaps,' I granted.

'Mistress Aila I know to be a good woman and if she says you are to be trusted, then I will trust you as well. If you will help me – help us.'

'I will help you Master Abram, but honestly, I do not think one extra sword will be enough,' I was obliged to inform him.

'We need more men?' Abram said, looking concerned. 'That might ruin my business as surely as bandits of the highway would.'

'No, Master Abram, I mean we need to see just how organised this threat is and then we need to hunt down its source and kill it at the roots. Only then will you be free.'

Master Abram liked this idea and said as much:

'But how do we carry this out, Chaucere?'

I thought more about this. 'One thing at a time, Master Abram. First though, please tell me where your horse is stabled?'

'My horse?' he said surprised. 'I keep it with the same ostler as the rest of my kinsmen, as it happens. Why should that matter?'

'We shall see, Master Abram. Trust me, as Mistress Aila suggested.'

He laughed. 'I will trust you, Chaucere. Although many say that in Camelot these days trust is harder to find than an untarnished knight.'

Now that was an interesting observation and gave me food for thought long after we had concluded our preparations and the alehouse torches were out and the candles snuffed.

I lay on my pallet, coddled by the comforting smell of barley undergoing its magical transformation. What did Abram's observation say about Camelot now? Where was the dream that was supposed to build and sustain this brave new Kingdom?

Although I hadn't been around much to see it, I could tell that the arrival of the new King and the building of Camelot had indeed brought about a change in this land. People were safer, there was less strife between different folk and a real sense of a community seemed to be building. This is why people flocked here.

Yes, many were still bloody-minded, they still swore and ate and drank too much. But the minor wars that had plagued the land since the dissolution of the Old Empire had been stopped and most people were now sleeping easier in their beds. There was even something like a sense of optimism. People were beginning to believe that their children might not have to struggle and toil as hard as they had done.

This Arthurian Britain people spoke about might be more than a dream, but from what Abram was saying, could it really be that the Camelot era was doomed, almost before it had begun?

As I lay there I realised I didn't want this to be the case. I thought I had divorced myself from this land, but it seemed that some links still remained. I wanted Camelot to succeed and if there was anything I could do to help I would. Perhaps this is what had drawn me back here after all these years? I drifted off to sleep with a new vision forming in my mind.

5
GIPP

I found the stable of Abram's horse easily enough. Aila had confirmed that the ostler, Ilbert, was an Honest Jack and well liked locally. As Aila seemed to know everybody, and their business, I took this on trust. But, of course, the ostler was not the only person working in the Inn.

I wore my worst clothes, dirtied myself up a bit, and spilt some ale down my front. I soon looked suitably down-at-my-heels – it was depressing how easy this was to achieve. I found a nearby wall that looked like it could take my weight and settled in the warm spring sunshine that had finally appeared, to sleep off the drinking session I had just not had.

Abram arrived to tell Ilbert that he would need his horse at dawn early on Thor's day, and they talked good-naturedly for a short while. Abram left and Ilbert gave orders to one of his stable boys. There were three working there: one was hefty and had an ill-favoured look, the second, clearly the youngest and keen to please – like a new hound – was pockmarked and had hair like straw. The last was straight-backed and brown eyed and had a happy winning smile. I had a little wager with myself and put my gold on 'straight-backed and happy smiling' thinking the other two were too obvious. Some time later, after the horse shit had all been shovelled and horses brushed, it was hefty and ill-favoured who asked if he might go visit his mother briefly. This shows you that sometimes you can judge by appearance and also explains why I do not play dice to make money.

Ilbert, being a good man, agreed and 'hefty and ill-favoured', who I now learnt was called Ham, wandered off. He did not even attempt to clean himself up. I am sure his mother would have been very disappointed in him. His mother seemed to live in a particularly nasty alehouse, so perhaps she would not have been disappointed at all. She also had a bad scar down one cheek and wore filthy breeks, had a filthier beard and was called Gipp. I learnt all that in the time it took for me to try begging a drink off the alewife and getting thrown out by the alewife's husband. I concluded, reasonably, that Gipp was, in fact, not Ham's mother, but another piece of filth in Camelot's ever-growing underclass of good-for-nothings.

The floor of the, thankfully still frozen but understandably filthy passageway opposite the equally filthy alehouse, was the perfect place to see Gipp leave, closely followed by Ham, who then lit off in the opposite direction back to Ilbert's. I shadowed Gipp. He looked familiar, but I could not place where from. Gipp led me to a better class of alehouse, where he bought a large horn and a plate of something that looked very tasty. He was obviously going to be here for some time and I needed to report back to Abram.

Abram worked from his house in one of the better streets. You could tell that by the absence of beggars, coin girls and trulls, that filled the poor areas – like the Midden – of the sprawling monster that was Camelot.

Abram's house was one of a number of dwellings constructed at the same time as the castle, in order to house the builders and masons themselves. One of their signs was still visible over the door. Masons did not scrimp on themselves when it comes to comfort. This was a solid, well-built and secure house, with more than one room and a fine thatched roof to keep the chill out. It had a solid oak door with a very impressive lock and the shutters were made to stay shut when required. Abram's was the home of a well-heeled man, who also valued his privacy. It might even have been the home of the master builder himself. Almost against my will, I was impressed. Almost more than I was by Camelot itself! To build a castle for a King, with an army of workmen at your disposal, was one thing. I had once met a traveller who told me about giant pyramids built in the lands south of the Middle Sea, and I had no reason to disbelieve him. Such things, and much more, were possible when you were an absolute monarch. To be able to construct houses like the one Abram owned, to be lived in by ordinary men and women, not Lords and Ladies, seemed somehow a much greater and nobler endeavour.

The speed of construction of the castle of Camelot had been remarkable though, by any measure. A testament to what can be accomplished with enough will and a large amount of existing cut stone. It is surprising that so many houses of the Old Empire's great and good escaped the ravages of the locals for so long after they ran off back to their warmer climes and better wine. And then they built Camelot.

I am sure something of a superstition has hung over these islands of ours since the men and women of the Old Empire departed. People seem to be too afraid to live in their houses or even use their roads, as if half expecting them to come marching back over the hills at any moment with their golden eagles and sharp swords, demanding back what was theirs. Many people would even prefer to make new muddy tracks rather than walk down the Empire's marvellous paved streets – sometimes I do despair of the folk on this island – and most of the newcomers are no better!

And then came Camelot.

No holding back there, no listening to old wives' tales about the Old Empire for the folk in the Big House. The new King's new castle quickly rose high above everybody and everything – the symbol of a new start, new confidence and a new way of doing things. Even if it was built from the stones of the Old Empire, it still looked built to last, as did the handsome young King with his bright new sword.

'I do not charge high interest rates you know, Chaucere?' said Abram who was busy at his writing when I entered his attractive, well-made home – as if we had just been speaking a moment ago.

'It's not my business to ask,' I said levelly.

'But nonetheless I think you should know the type of man you will be working for.' He shuffled his scrolls around and then put them away in a safe-box that locked with a key. He obviously liked his locks.

'I keep my rates low,' he continued, 'to help the people who come to me. I make it simple to explain so that even the most common of men might understand. I have helped many pay their rent and taxes after a bad harvest.'

'Honestly, Abram…'

'I make this point because I want you to know who else would profit if I were not here, if my kinsman and I were not around.'

I paused for a moment before speaking: 'I'm listening.'

'The fancy lords in the High Castle that is who.'

'The Knights?'

'Oh yes,' he nodded grimly. 'The Knights, as landowners, can make loans. And they do not charge two or three percent – they charge twenty or thirty.'

'So much?'

'Yes. It is well documented. And in this manner the honest farmers are pushed into more and more debt, until it becomes too much for them, and they are evicted and homeless, and the Knights gain more land and are able to offer more loans.'

I felt bile in my mouth.

'Is it really that bad?'

'It is, and could get worse, especially if me and my kin were to leave, or be banished.'

'Surely that is not possible?'

'Many of my kin already talk of leaving – who wants to try to make their living, bring their children up, when those lives are in danger, or they face having their goods stolen? And as for banishment ... who can say? It has happened before elsewhere, it will happen again, so I fear – perhaps here.'

'Well, let us see to the undoing of these bandits and rogues,' I said with real determination. I had seen enough of how the strong and powerful could abuse their position to the disadvantage of those they should be helping. A chief may own land and he protects this land, including the people living on it, but they are not his slaves. People should be allowed to barter as they might and work their own land still. I have been to countries and fiefdoms where the crumbling of the Old Empire has led to the emergence of powerful Lords who grab the land and employ rascals to enforce their will. One companion I fought with for many years had run away from such a place, where the 'politics of land', as he called it, was causing great inequality. I mean, nobody expects life to be completely fair, but there are limits.

And I did not expect this from Camelot and said as much.

'Let us hope you are right, Chaucere,' replied Abram. 'You should know, though, for many Camelot is not turning out to be the Promised Land we had hoped for.'

I had this very much in my mind as I went through what I had learnt and how the plan would work out.

'It is as I suspected – there is a squealer at the stables. He has been betraying the trust of his master, who I hold blameless. He tells his criminal connection the day you are to go about your business and they simply have to wait for you to make your return trip, with full moneybags.'

'Of course,' Abram nodded vigorously. 'That would explain why my friends and kinsmen have been robbed so easily. And I have told the stable I will be doing my first collection of the spring three days hence!'

'Which is why I have hired us two horses for first light tomorrow from another ostler that Emald the smith assures me is completely trustworthy because his own sons work with him. We will be out and back before they even know you have changed your day.'

'Excellent, but then what?'

'Then,' I said grimly, 'we shall see how the dice fall.'

6
CAT AND MOUSE

I had a message from Emald waiting for me at Aila's. My sword was ready to collect. Not a moment too soon. It was becoming dark by the time I made it to the smithy. The fire was still lit and Emald, as ever, was working hard. I spoke without thinking, making him jump and miss his stroke and send sparks flying.

'My apologies, Emald.'

'You move quietly, Chaucere,' he replied, through clenched teeth.

'Old habits, I'm afraid. Here, are you hurt?'

Emald held up his arm to show what looked like a painful burn on top of old scars:

'A smith's trade marks.'

'Next time I'll ring a bell.'

'Better not. I don't like to make much of my sideline.' He stopped to lift an oiled sheet to reveal my sword. It shone like precious stones in the forge light.

I lifted it eagerly. It felt good in my hand, the balance even better somehow. The groove that helped make the sword so light, without sacrificing strength, seemed to undulate in the flickering flame with leaf-like markings. The blade itself shone as if some part of the celestial firmament had descended to join us. The grip was new but holding it was like greeting an old friend. To move the sword through the air brought a smile to my face. Even the guard and pommel seemed revitalised.

'Have you ever named the sword?' Emald asked, watching me with some amusement.

'Now, why would I do that?' I replied with a laugh of my own. 'It is a tool – the tool of my trade. Do you name your hammers or your tongs?'

43

'Many do.'

'Would it improve my sword arm or put extra spring in my step?'

'Who knows? People have become Kings simply because their sword had a name.'

'How right you are and if my sword was called Excalibur, or I had pulled it from a stone, would you have followed me?'

Emald took my question seriously and gave it some consideration before finally answering:

'Probably not Chaucere, but mostly because I do not think you would thank me if I did.'

I held my sword upright in mock salute. 'And for that, Emald,' I said, 'I do thank you with all my heart. Who would want their future decided by job allocation based on the ability to free fighting steel from stonework?'

Emald had no answer to that and neither do I.

Abram and I made good time the next day. The horses were amiable and well used to different riders. Abram did not have the best of seats but he knew better than to try to impose his will on the animal, and let it go at its own pace, and so we started our rounds in good time. A useful early mist soon cleared and we reached the first small hamlet in bright sunshine. Abram's customers did not seem feared to see him, and as the winter had been mild after a good harvest the previous year, they were all capable of paying what was owed. The sight of an accompanying swordsman gave some disquiet, but as soon as Abram assured them it was for his protection, rather than debt collection, they were reassured, because they had stories of their own to share.

We were told of travellers being waylaid on the road by gangs of bandits. Honest farmers being threatened in their homes and their livestock run off while they cowered behind locked doors. Not just the odd occurrence either, but systematic, organised even. This was something the Round Table Knights should be

44

addressing. Why weren't they? And why was there not more of a fuss being made throughout Camelot? Was the news being deliberately suppressed in some fashion?

'I don't like this,' said Abram. 'I don't like this at all.'

I had to agree with him.

'I had heard rumours towards the end of last year, but this is much worse than they had suggested. Where is the King?'

I did not know. After consideration, I realised that news of the exploits of the King and his Knights had been very thin on the ground in recent months.

I shared this observation with Abram.

'You are right, Chaucere,' he said, stroking his rather straggly beard. 'It's unusual.'

'There are usually proclamations aplenty letting his loyal subjects rejoice in his every successful bowel movement, but this year nothing.'

Abram tried not to laugh too loudly:

'Perhaps the King is constipated?'

'They say that the Merlin has a potion for everything. I'm sure he must have an answer to such a simple problem.'

'Syrup of figs worked well for me when I was younger,' Abram observed.

'I never saw a fig until I was well into manhood and living under a very different sun.'

Abram shivered, although the day was not cold. 'I do miss that sun sometimes, I cannot lie.' He gathered his cloak around him and we rode on to our next destination, where we were received with large smiles and a welcome cup of ale.

Finally though we came across one farmhouse that had been abandoned completely. Abram was particularly upset. 'I knew this family well, a comely wife and an industrious husband with two young children. They were all hardworking, but did not have much luck – pestilence and rot seemed to haunt their endeavours.

I hoped the money I lent them would see them through until their luck changed, as surely it should have done.'

'It does not appear to be the case,' I observed, picking up a small toy sheep that a loving father must surely have carved for his child.

We walked through the small farmhouse. There were still many other useful items – a crib, a wooden bowl, a stone pestle – and any such family would have treasured each and every one.

'I think that perhaps they left in a hurry,' Abram concluded.

'But why? That is the question.'

It was a dispiriting experience and we left none the wiser and with Abram well out of pocket.

I took us the long way back and we entered Camelot from a different direction and trouble we saw none. Then again, I doubted it was looking for us on this particular day.

Thor's day came soon and it found me in rags begging outside Ilbert's stable yard. Abram's customary horse, a quiet-looking grey gelding, was saddled-up, as we had supposedly arranged, and ready for his rider, when the messenger from Abram arrived. The apology was delivered: 'Master Abram had taken ill with a head cold and would not be requiring his horse after all today.'

Ilbert thanked the messenger and then told Ham to untack the grey. Ham did as asked and then suddenly remembered an urgent errand, and asked for permission to leave, but Ilbert would hear nothing of it. This was hardly surprising considering what Abram and I had told him the previous night. Ilbert had been furious and wanted to confront the boy at once, but we convince him to hold back. Ilbert did not give Ham a moment to himself all day. Only as night was falling was he allowed to go home.

Ham set off from the stable at a run; I could hardly keep up. Fortunately his destination was the same as the last time I had shadowed him. He did not go in, but stood outside anxiously wringing his cap in his hands. He really did, just like worried souls are supposed to do. Eventually Gipp and his filthy breeks arrived and Ham gave him the news and he was not a happy bandit. He let Ham know this via the back of his hand. Ham fell to the floor. Good job Gipp had not used his fist or Ham might have been down still. Instead he grovelled; he really did honestly and truly grovel. First the cap wringing and now the grovelling, Ham really had the whole lower order act down to perfection. I'd almost felt sorry for Ham – if he hadn't been responsible for half a dozen good men being robbed. Still, I did wince when the kicking began. Eventually Gipp let him up and Ham limped off like a whipped hound – or a well-kicked stable boy.

I followed Gipp.

Gipp made his way to a private house, which was not helpful. I could not get close enough to overhear anything being said inside. It was getting cold and I was beginning to wish I had worn something warmer, but sadly beggars rarely do dress for the weather.

When the group of men came out I was almost taken by surprise at their speed. I was about to try my begging routine on the first of the fellows, a black-haired, wild-eyed man, when the last of their party closed the door behind him. I knew him immediately: Cecilio of the sallow skin, who I had first cast eyes on in the bathhouse talking with the arrogant moustachioed man I was now convinced was a Lord from the Big House.

I ducked down behind a pig bin just in time. I think my disguise would have fooled him, but I wasn't going to take the chance. The men made their goodbyes quietly, in the manner of accomplices and went in different directions. Cecilio left with a stocky, muscular individual, who, like me, I took to be a native of this part of the world. I followed carefully behind until they disappeared into an alehouse. I left it a short while and then chanced a look inside. They had not been joined by anyone else and were busy eating and drinking. This seemed a good idea and so I left them to their repast and made my way to Aila's where I changed into cleaner and better clothes. Thanks to my extra income I actually had better clothes.

Aila's was full that evening and even with Gwen's help we were all kept busy. I was hungry by the time the last customers had been shown the road and I got to share the last of the rabbit stew with Aila. I liked rabbit, another thing to thank the Empire for. Many now ran wild in this part of the Kingdom and, what was once a rich man's meal, proved a valuable source of meat for the poor in hard times. As we ate I recounted my day's investigative activities with Aila. She was always a good sounding board and often contributed valuable insights based on her knowledge of Camelot and human nature. She was also extremely irked by the activities of these rogues, personally because she was a decent person who disliked injustice, and professionally because many of the people affected were her customers. People who, in better times, would be coming into the City to spend extra coin on what Aila's house offered – good ale, good food and companionship.

'Can these scum not just be introduced to the sharp end of a fence post?' said the ever-practical Aila.

'Don't imagine the thought hasn't occurred to me,' I admitted. 'The problem, I fear, is that there is now more scum in Camelot than there are fence posts! Put one of these rogues underground and there will be another two ready and waiting to earn some coin by whatever means necessary.'

'And what is the King's Round Table doing?'

I shrugged. 'I have no idea. Whatever it is, it isn't working!' Having demolished my stew in quick order, I pushed my trencher away.

'Whether this is through incompetence or something more sinister I do not know.'

Aila considered this: 'Is there not somebody we can approach about this?'

'I have never heard that the King or his Knights welcomed such input from their loyal subjects,' I commented.

Aila speared a tasty portion of coney and chewed thoughtfully before she spoke: 'Then you need to find the head of this band of arsewipes and cut it off!'

'I'm sharpening my axe every day, Aila.'

'Good! You have your employer's permission to miss the occasional shift.'

I bowed my head with only a modicum of mockery. Not having to worry overmuch about my job, and the roof over my head at Aila's, would help considerably. Yes, I was still in Abram's employ as well, but working at Aila's gave me unaccustomed security that I was frankly now enjoying.

And thus began a game of cat and mouse between me, as the representative of Abram and his kinfolk, and the Sallow Men, as we named the group of robbers and their spies in Camelot. The robbers I believed to be led by Cecilio, or perhaps even a Lord from the Big House. I reckoned that only a Lord had recourse to the information needed to know the activities of so many farmers and traders and to avoid the patrols of the King's Knights. It was a sobering thought that the mighty Round Table might have been so compromised, but in my heart I was sure it was true.

By keeping a string of horses, in a number of different ostlers – who only employed boys they really trusted – and then varying collection days and routes, we frustrated the efforts of the robbers to waylay us on our travels, much to Abram and his kinfolk's relief. We had found out their secret and disrupted their scheming. That made sleeping at night all that much sweeter.

I accompanied Abram and as many of his kin as I could on their collection trips, whenever I could, while still not taking too much advantage of Aila's goodwill. I found Abram's people to be good company, modest and unassuming, but not without humour. They worked hard and had a great sense of family and community, while believing in the ideals Camelot purported to encompass but was failing to uphold at the moment. Abram's people became pleasant additions to my life in Camelot, and all would have been well, if the news from the surrounding countryside had not been so unrelentingly grim. We had cut down directly on the attacks on Abram's people by the Sallow Men and by spreading the word on how best to counter their threat, to other tradespeople and travellers too.

In the rest of the countryside all was not so well.

Farmers complained of high rents and low prices, which farmers always have done of course. However now there was a genuine sense of grievance on the back of the attacks on the farmers' homes, as if the requirements of Camelot were over-riding the needs of the people the King had sworn to protect. And that protection, which had in those early years achieved so much and made the simple folk so full of praise for Arthur and his Round Table, was beginning to be considered to be done more in name than to achieve actual results.

Yes, the Knights patrolled as normal it seemed, so people reported, and looked impressive with their mail armour and fine horses, but attacks were becoming more frequent on isolated homesteads and even small villages, with robbers ghosting in and out before there was time to alert the fancy Round Table. And, worse, the bandits could not be tracked down. I had no doubt this was the Sallow Men at work. Where they holed up and were finding daily refuge was not known, but surely I was not the only one with my suspicions as to exactly where that place might be: in plain sight in fact.

Until I could find the proof I needed, I kept my eyes open and began buying drinks in the right sorts of places, cultivating the people who could tell me things; things I wanted very much to know. When I did find what I needed to know the people responsible for messing with Camelot would discover that in the game of cat and mouse, this mouse had grown some very sharp teeth indeed.

But as to the main grievance of why the King seemed to be doing so little, and was not to be seen, that question I had no answer to. So I went looking for an answer to another question that had been preying on my mind.

7
WELLAN

There is a village half a day's ride from where Camelot now sits on its hill. There is nothing much to say about the village. It is like many in the Kingdom – neither rich nor poor – people pay their taxes, try their best to get on with their lives and, in days gone by, hoped that the next lord would be no worse than the present one. It does have a natural spring of good clean water though, which explains its name: Wellan. It does not look like the sort of place where a King would be made, but it was.

A league or so outside the cluster of small houses that make up the centre of Wellan there is a farm called Spring Farm, although the spring is not on the farm. There is however, a standing stone, a menhir. This stone does not stand though. It lies on its side and, perhaps for that reason. It is known locally as the Sleeping Man.

The word is that this was the very stone that the young Arthur pulled the sword out of, thus announcing to the world his destiny and right to be King. Of course many a village and town now proudly claims that whatever lump of rock they have lying around was the original sheath for this most portentous of weapons. Many villages make a tidy living from those with the time and money to come looking for where the King first made himself known to his people. The others are all wrong, though. Wellan was indeed the place where the sword was pulled from the stone and a new King was revealed.

I approached Wellan as dusk closed in, as was my intention. The farmers had returned home and their small flocks were safely penned or housed. The lands were not yet so safe that valuable sheep or cattle could be left unattended at night. The Sleeping

Man slumbered on exactly where he always had, or at least since he had decided that the standing game was not for him and, thoroughly exhausted, he needed to catch up with some shut eye.

The Sleeping Man lay in a small dell at the edge of the land of Spring Farm that had been the last to be won back from the forest, not the most obvious of places to mark your territory or to perform some unpleasant act of sacrifice. Perhaps the stone had been left there by one of the giants who reputedly walked the land long before the Deluge. More worryingly perhaps it was one of the very same giants, still awaiting the time when they might awaken again and take back their land from these weak and puny creatures that now called themselves the masters.

I had no idea, but the place has a feel, the like of which I have only ever felt in one other place, and that is far away in a brown land under a baking sun. There is no indication where the Sleeping Man might have retained that sword for all the years before the King released it, but I knew it was once placed through the sleeping figure's heart.

I tied up my horse on a long lead so that he could eat his fill. I wrapped myself in a thick blanket and sat down with my back to a tree at the forest edge where I had a good view of the stone.

I sat and I waited. The moon was waxing full but was in no hurry to rise. Around me in the dark I could hear the small noises of small animals, as they went about their business, hoping that nothing larger and hungrier than them was about to ruin that business. Sitting there by the stone first erected by a people now forgotten, at the behest of gods who may or may not be taking our current indifference to their absence very well, I could sympathise with those woodland creatures. The nearby bark of a hound fox did not bode well for all the scurrying brethren.

I had brought myself some strong ale to keep the chill out and some bread and cheese. It seemed wise to share them, so I left a little food on the stone and poured some ale next to it, before continuing my vigil. This did nothing to help encourage anything that might be considered a portent or sign though, unless you count the dormouse that ran over my foot sometime after midnight by my reckoning. Yet still I waited, hoping beyond hope, for some indication of what it was that had so filled me with the need to return to this country, the land of my birth. No such illumination arrived and it didn't arrive very slowly.

An hour or so before dawn I shook the dew off my blanket and led my horse quietly away to let the Sleeping Man continue his slumber. He had provided no answer to the questions in my mind, the questions that had brought me back to the place I had once vowed never to set foot in again. At Spring Farm lights of flickering candles were visible behind the shutters. People would be stirring now to start their duties. The place looked completely unchanged. It was homely, it was modest and it was all a thousand years ago.

At the end of the lane I mounted my horse and rode back to Camelot, my mind no clearer as to its intent and the mystery of why I had felt the compulsion to return. I was near half way home, dawn slipping in around me, when I passed a small cleared hill. On the top, happily breaking their fast, was a drove of hares. Like everybody else brought up with one foot in the Old Ways I had a great respect for hares. They are sacred beasts, and a sign of prosperity, abundance and good fortune. Ēostre, the goddess of the spring, holds the hare in a special place in her heart it is said. I found it a shame that many cleaving to the new religion had little respect for these elegant and joyful animals.

It was not uncommon to find droves of hares on hills or fields in the spring, going about their boxing matches, which many who do not know the countryside believe happens between rival Jacks, when actually it is the Jills who see off their overattentive suitors in this fashion. Which is perfectly understandable. I have no time for men who would try to force themselves on women. Some believe that all that live by the sword consider such behaviour an acceptable benefit of the job. I do not share the company of such men.

These hares were not boxing, in fact they were doing very little – apart from looking at me, or so it seemed. One large Jack was sitting back on his hindquarters and his expression was of someone who seemed to be asking me to follow him.

I dismounted and the hares scattered, but not Jack. He still looked at me with the same expression, his eyes saying 'follow me, follow me.'

So I did.

There was a track up to the top of the hill and it wasn't until I had almost reached its modest summit that the hare bounded off. He did not go far, but stopped some distance away and sat up and waited. I followed him again and he repeated his behaviour. This went on for some time and I had to make sure that I remembered where I had tied my horse. Soon the sun was up fully, and I was getting a little tired of the game, when he led me along a track running through a small thicket.

I moved slowly now for I could sense that I was not alone.

It was a simple snare trap. Fortunately it was designed simply to incapacitate not kill, for the Jill that was caught in it, by her right hind leg, was surely as pretty as a hare could ever hope to be. The brown of her coat was deep and lush and her amber eyes were like burnished gold. The rope that held her was strong, and made by an expert, as it was so tough you could see that she could make no dent in it with her teeth.

She was very scared, I could see, and I drew my knife very slowly, hoping she would know I meant her no harm. It would be easy to cut the main rope attached to the tealer, but that would leave her with the pulled loop around her leg. That might get caught on undergrowth or wear against her fur. I needed to hold her against me to do the job properly.

I took off my cloak and wrapped it carefully around her. Only then did I cut the main rope, as I held her gently to my chest. I was conscious of her faint, almost feminine smell, her warmth and the fast rhythm of her beating heart as I held her tight. Only then was I able to get my knife in under the loop and cut the offending rope away.

I looked down at her trusting, warm brown eyes, and held her just a moment longer, pleased to have such communication with a wild animal. Then I felt her begin to struggle and I quickly placed her down. She shrugged her leg, making sure there was no damage. Fortunately all seemed well. She bounded out of the thicket and I saw her running away across the field, soon to be joined by the dutiful Jack. They ran into woodland and were gone.

I felt a pang of something almost like jealousy. To be so free, to be so alive and to have no concerns about the ways of Kings and thieves! That was a thing!

'You were right gentle with her.'

The playful woman's voice, with its rich local accent, made me jump. I turned. It was a beautiful young maid, dressed simply but prettily, and with flowers in her hair as if she was going to a wedding. Her eyes were so bright the sky looked dull besides them.

'You held her like a lover would,' she continued.

'And what would a slip of a girl like you know of such things?' I replied, suddenly feeling my age.

'I am not so young,' she teased, her lush lips puckering into a pout.

'Then you should beware. There are worse traps laid by men than those made of rope.' I held up the remains of the snare that was still in my hand.

'And I know all about the traps of men,' she continued. 'And how best to avoid them – mostly.'

I laughed, not unkindly, at her supposed worldliness. 'Hadn't you be getting on?'

'What? Are you tired of me?'

'Not at all. I simply mean that it looks like you have a wedding or some festival to be getting to.'

'No. No festival, except the one that is with me everywhere I go.'

I laughed again. She was a strange young thing, but truly a breath of fresh air. I wondered for a moment if she was a little simple and where she might live.

'You envy them, I think?' she continued.

'Who?'

'The Jack and his Jill, running free across hill and dale. Outrunning fox and hound and answering to no Lord or Lady.'

'Who wouldn't envy such freedom?'

'Then do it!' she cried. Her amber eyes flashed brighter still with flecks of gold like small gems catching the morning light. 'Come run with me and we will have such a time and run so far that minstrels will write songs about us!'

'I think not, pretty maid.'

'Why not?'

'Because, as you will learn when you get older, with age comes responsibilities and I have a responsibility, a task I must attend to, before I can consider running off anywhere.'

She considered this. 'Then that is sad and I am glad that I have decided to never grow up – not permanently at least.'

'Age does have some compensation,' I felt obliged to add. 'You might find yourself a sweetheart and that is a fine thing to have.'

'Then where is your sweetheart, he who can be so gentle yet carries a sharp blade by his side?' She cocked her head, as inquisitive as a robin watching for worms while you dig.

'That is a very good question, young lady, but I don't think you would be able to understand the answer.'

'Really!' she exclaimed. 'I think it more likely that you do not know the answer yourself!'

She turned around before I had a chance to reply and was soon skipping away across the field.'

'Wait!' I cried. 'I will see you safely home.'

She turned back and shouted:

'There is no need. You have helped enough, thank you.'

And almost before I knew it she was gone. It was only later, when I was back in the saddle that a thought occurred to me. How did she know I had freed the Jill when what I did was hidden in the middle of a thicket? And when I thought further about it, wasn't the young woman favouring her right leg as she skipped?

Could the Sleeping Man have been sending me a message after all, but I was not quick enough to understand?

8
THE KING'S RETURN

The rumour went round Camelot quickly: the King was coming back. I didn't know that he had been away, but then again he didn't keep me updated with his itinerary. Mind you, I hadn't asked, I'd been too busy. Maybe you can get somebody to do all that for you now in bright shiny Camelot. If he had mentioned it then the reason why so many raids were taking place so successfully in the lands around the Big House would have been obvious. What strength he had left behind, those patrols that were so prominent, were actually insufficient to protect the people hereabouts. Definitely an effort that was more for show, just in case a serious challenge on Camelot itself was actually being considered by somebody somewhere.

Look, we've got lots of Knights, best keep away from Camelot!

The word, as I discovered from an exhaustive search of the taverns and Inns frequented by Camelot staff, a tiresome task that I somehow manage to pull off on a regular basis, was that there was serious trouble in one of the more far-flung parts of King Arthur's growing realm. Whether this was down to raiding from overseas, or something of a more serious internal nature, was not really known.

Whatever the reason, it seems the King had departed in secret, with the strength of his Round Table in their riding clothes, quietly in the dead of night, at pace, shortly after the winter solstice. A tactic adopted to prevent unwelcome eyes from gleaning too much intelligence on His Majesty's activities – especially the size of the remaining troops at home in Camelot.

Somebody had known, though, and somebody and their Sallow Men had used this to their advantage. And one of these somebodies was Cecilio. Of that I was sure. But now, presumably successful, the King was back and Camelot knew all about it, and had come out in their droves to cheer him home. Any excuse for a party in Camelot, and the opportunity to sell a few baked goods, if the appetising smells were anything to go by.

My reasons for my being there? Curiosity maybe or just a chance to see what all the fuss was about. You can't be over-prepared or over-familiar. Fate favours the well-informed. Well, that's what I have always told myself to disguise the fact that I am just outright nosy. There was certainly a festive atmosphere to the gathering, with a lively, smiling, crowd assembled at the outer gates and downhill from there on both sides of the Great Eastern Road and away through the homesteads and farmlands that feed the Big House's voracious appetite. Spring was finally here and the air was fresh, even if the people of Camelot were not. Not everybody can afford the baths.

So great were the numbers of onlookers that one couldn't properly glimpse the Royal Company as it approached. The first we, at the outer gates, knew about their arrival was the silence that proceeded like a wave before them. It wasn't until I got a sight of the outriders that I saw the reason why. This was not the triumphant homecoming of an all-conquering inviolable monarch. This was the return of a group of men who had just completed a very hard day's work in the harness. Mail was no longer shiny. It was covered in mud and blood. The source of a least some of the blood was made clear by the number of wounds and bandages that the horsemen displayed. The horses steamed in the spring air, as hard-worked as their riders. There were also two handfuls of horses with no riders at all – and a handful more with blanket-wrapped bodies folded over them. If this was victory, the fate of the defeated must have been truly grim.

The King, although as weary and mud-splattered as his men, was nothing less than regal. He looked a lot older than I remembered, of course, but hadn't that brass mirror told me a similar story recently. His long wavy hair was still untouched by grey, as was the beard he wore in spite of fashion. His back was straight and he still carried himself as only a king chosen by the Old Powers themselves would be expected to do. What this new God would make of it all I had no idea, but his head was held high and the quietened crowd all bowed as he passed. I tipped my head too. It was something you felt compelled to do. He had that effect.

The crowd thinned quickly after his depleted force entered Camelot. The sight of their King as almost akin to a normal mortal man must have been sobering to most of the population who were still believers in the Fairy Tale of Camelot. I wasn't sobered, I was actually thinking about finding a drink, and something to eat as well, when I heard a man call my name. Training – and a naturally suspicious nature – meant I did not turn immediately. To do so under normal circumstances is to welcome a thrust of a dagger from a hired killer unsure of his target.

'Chaucere, hold on there!' the man shouted again. He was persistent – best to get it over with. I turned and was faced with the sight of a man of middle age and very ordinary garb. He held his cap in his hands as he ran towards me, allowing a coxcomb of hair to flap on his prematurely balding head.

I took my hand from my sword hilt, but left it near the dagger on my belt.

'Yes?' I said.

'Ah good,' he said pulling up. 'I thought I might lose you there!'

'Do I know you, Goodman?'

'Know would be a rather strong term for our acquaintance, Master Chaucere. I met you in Aila's Alehouse.'

'Oh yes. I remember now,' I replied – having met a large number of people at Aila's it was entirely possible.

'You said that you were available, for "errands" of the sort that required a trustworthy man, not afraid to travel if needs be. Is that still the case?'

Ah, a potential customer! I had indeed pitched my case to many at Aila's without any response so far – today was looking up.

'Of course,' I smiled. 'Come, let us find a more comfortable place for such a discussion.'

The more comfortable place was, of course, an alehouse. Not as comfortable as Aila's, but ale is ale and he was paying.

The job that my new drinking companion, whose name was Eduard the Baker, went on to tell me about sounded simple enough. He had an older brother, Nash, who farmed just over a day's ride south of Camelot. Eduard needed a package of important family papers taken to him. How important the papers of a baker and farmer might be, it was not my place to ask, but the demands of helping supply Camelot's incessant need for bread meant he was not in a position to deliver said papers.

We haggled for a bit, but I don't think his heart was in it and we soon agreed on a reasonable price. He assured me his brother would welcome me and provide a meal and shelter for the next night as well. The weather looked to be set quite fair, for the time of year, and I had no other work on – Aila could spare me for a day or two, I had the regulars sorted out by now and she had Gwen to help. It looked to be a pleasant break, so why did I have this nagging worry?

I asked Emald this question later.

'Your problem, Chaucere, is that you have a suspicious nature.' he told me, in between enormous blows to his metal work. 'You can't accept that your life is now full of ordinary events, like getting a job to do, doing the job, and getting paid for the job – all without having to wave your, admittedly very handsome, sword about. This circumstance doesn't sit well on your shoulders. It's not your nature.'

'That's not true, Emald. Once upon a time perhaps, but now I am only after a quiet life.'

Emald gave a mighty snort that I swear blew embers up from his forge. 'Oh yes – of course, Chaucere! The quite life, and soon you'll be a house holder, sitting with his feet up and a hound laid out by the fire.'

'All right, Emald!' I replied, just a little testy. 'No need to take matters to ridiculous extremes! There is just something about this that makes me uneasy. And it is listening to these warning voices that has enabled me to live long enough to become so suspicious.'

Emald put down his forge hammer and wiped his brow with a rag that had probably had a previous duty as a sail on a medium sized barge.

'If you're at all worried about being waylaid on the road, why not see if there is a King's Messenger heading south tomorrow?'

I brightened up immediately: 'Emald – you are wasted as a blacksmith! You should be one of the King's top advisers.'

'I would Chaucere, but, to be honest, I fear I could not take the heat.'

Emald had made a joke, whatever next? Perhaps he would end up with a goodwife and a faithful hound sitting by his hearth. In the meantime, I gave him a restrained round of applause and my thanks and he went back to smashing the guts out of the unidentifiable piece of metalwork on his anvil.

The King's Messengers were another of Camelot's innovations. Less showy than a large round table, but equally effective at making the country manageable. In essence they were just a way for the King to keep in contact with his, and his knights', local administrators and sheriffs on their home turf. Just a young man on a horse wearing the King's livery. However, it was made very clear early on in the King's reign that if anybody interfered with said messenger, or failed to give him aid when it was required, they were buying themselves a whole ocean of grief. It has only happened once to my knowledge. A messenger was robbed and killed and his horse sold on. The miscreants thought they had got away with it. There was no possible way that the ill doers could be traced. No one knew, or suspected, their identity – except maybe the horse purchaser, and he wouldn't be stupid enough to mention a word. The lawbreakers had not considered that the King did not arrive to his throne through the picking of straws. The King had powerful allies and one in particular who was something more than just an ally. This attack, as Emald recounted to me over an ale at Aila's, had happened only months after the Messengers had become a fixture of the King's court. They had killed and robbed the messenger – hid the body where they must have thought nobody would find it, and took the trouble to sell the horse a considerable distance away. They had forgotten that the King does not rely on the same means of investigation as ordinary men.

To most he is called Merlin, or the Merlin sometimes – like a rank or a court position. He has been with the King since before he was the King. Advisor, magician or the architect of his whole adventure, nobody is sure of his role, and those with any criticisms generally have the sense to not share their opinions. All the good folk of Camelot ever found out was that the two men who had killed the King's Messenger were found within two days, which coincidentally was exactly how long their screams could be heard ringing around the Big House. Nobody has touched a King's Messenger since then.

The King's Messengers leave early in the morning, with first light. This was no hardship for me; Camelot had not given me any new bad habits, well not as yet. And there was a rider, not only heading south, but also passing close by to my destination, which is known as Bleakers Farm. As chance would also have it, I vaguely recognised the Captain of the Messengers – a solid, rather taciturn sort called Dramon, who drank occasionally in Aila's alehouse. As the Captain, part of his job was to check over anybody requiring the company of one of the King's Messengers. This was not an uncommon practise, but today I was the only candidate. After a few words concerning my business and destination, he gave me the nod, introduced me to the Messenger, and we set off as dawn began to put colour back into the world. It was looking to be a particularly fine day as well, full of greens and blues. Just like the world should be in spring.

The King's Messenger was a young man with a winning disposition and the energy of two young men. Tall, with the blue eyes and the blond hair typical of the more recent tribes from across the Narrow Sea, the earnestness typical of many of the King's younger servants was offset by a remaining boyish enthusiasm. It was customary for the Messengers to not introduce themselves – as far as the populace was concerned, the King's Messengers were the instruments of his Royal Majesty, extensions of his Grace, and to be acknowledged by an actual name was demeaning to this role. It was this that also gave them and their families such immunity to molestation.

We were barely out of the shadow of the Big House before the messenger had informed me that his name was Dale. As he pointed out, this was not that he didn't respect his position but, as he was also quick to point out, we were travelling together for a day and a bit – at least – and it would be rather tiresome for me to have to keep calling him 'King's Messenger'. He was right. 'Dale' was much simpler.

Dale and I fell easily into the sort of comradely chatter that riders usually share on a long journey. This, after all, was one of the reasons why messengers don't object to the company; plus, an extra pair of eyes never hurts.

We passed quickly through the well-cultivated and cleared land around the castle. The roads were not yet busy and I could easily see that we were not being followed. My diligence was not lost on my companion.

'Expecting company?' he asked.

'I sincerely hope not,' I replied, sounding as casual as I was able. 'I have heard stories of organised gangs waylaying travellers, especially those on business trips.

Dale's young face crumbled in distaste. 'It's true,' he admitted, 'while the King was away seeing to the troubles in the East, I was often on the patrols sent out to try to apprehend the rogues! There were just too few of us to be effective and they always seemed to be one step ahead. Curse them!'

The young man was much put out. It was good to see such concern in one of the people's protectors; maybe there still was hope.

'Where did they get their intelligence?' I asked, hoping that I might gain more insight into the problem. Dale shook his head: 'we never found out, but it seems that they were paying close attention to the comings and goings at City ostlers. Some astute body in the outer town worked this out and let us know – more power to his sword arm I say!'

I agreed. My sword arm can always do with more power. Passing my suspicions up the line to the appropriate people wasn't easy mind.

'But as to how the rogues evaded our patrols – our sergeants and captains have never worked that one out.'

This astute body could have provided some insight into that as well, but at this moment he doubted that he would be believed.

I checked behind me again and then had to laugh as Dale noticed:

'Old habits die hard,' I explained.

'You have the look of a well-travelled man, Chaucere.'

'And there was me thinking I had washed the dirt from my face.'

This earned me a smile and to my relief Dale did not press me any further for details. Not that there is anything that I am ashamed of in my past, it's just that there is now rather more past than I care to remember, or tell other people. This did not worry Dale. Like many young men he was very fond of his own voice and only required an audience to be kept happy. Fortunately he had an apparently bottomless collection of tales and yarns that he told well, with enthusiasm and style.

'And so the alewife replied that it wasn't her daughter anyway, but the local blacksmith's and he wouldn't care if my friend was the Lord of Westham's youngest son, he would still expect him to pay for the wheel to be put back on the cart!'

I laughed at the appropriate spot, although I had heard the story before a half dozen times before with the names of different people involved, of course.

I will give the lad his due, all the time he spoke his eyes were busy, checking every copse and ditch for potential ambushers. I know, because my eyes were looking in exactly the same places.

'There are still too many thieves on these roads for my liking,' he said finally.

'I have to agree,' I responded, although I continued to make a good income from the problem it didn't please me to earn coin in this manner.

'The King thinks the same,' he said, as if the King's opinions were something he was privy to on a daily basis.

'Has he said what he intends to do about it?' I found myself asking, 'now that he has returned from his adventure?'

Dale corrected himself, as if realising that he had perhaps misspoken. 'The King does not give me his counsel,' he laughed, 'but I can say that patrols are now more frequent, but less regular, in case notes are being taken. It does not hurt for people to know their King is thinking of them.'

'No, it doesn't,' I agreed.

However, diminished the attacks may be, people were still being stopped and robbed, so what was the answer? Probably, as with so many things these days, a little more thought was required. If patrols were not doing the job, then perhaps consider why not?

The land we passed through was now ideal for outlaws: a steep-sided valley with dense unmanaged woodland and a number of meandering streams that joined together into something more like a river. The road was little more than a muddy track and I wondered how the farmers got their goods to market. A small bridge – nothing more than a collection of rough planks – indicated that some attention was being paid to the problem. I was glad to be out of there and into somewhere a little more cheerful, where the hazel coppice showed that there were at least some foresters around.

We stopped before midday in a natural glade to give the horses a rest, and for a piss and a drink and something to eat – in that order. We shared our provisions, as men on the road will do, and I was pleased to see that the Big House treats its messengers well. Not that there was anything shabby about Aila's pork pie. This was a pie that a man could really survive on, with a proper thickness of crisp pastry and a good cut of meat with just the right amount of fat. Dale appreciated it too and I for my part was glad to taste one of the last of autumn's apples: a bit wrinkled but still sweet at heart.

Just like you Chaucere, I thought to myself.

Before we set off Dale checked his horse's feet, like a good rider and I followed suit. His mount an attractive bay gelding and apparently his favourite from the King's stable. It was one of those horses that could ride all day and then still break into a sprint before nightfall to outrun any pursuers. My mount was a solid grey mare that was never going to win any races, but she was sweet tempered and not given to spooking. That's all I look for in a horse, I fight better with my feet firmly planted.

As we remounted, it began to cloud over. We had made good time in the morning and broken the back of the journey. Dale, who knew this road well, suggested we look for shelter for the night. He could not remember any hamlets or farmhouses nearby as we were currently riding through poor heathland with patchy wood cover and gorse, but he did remember a shepherd's hut. One of the many that dotted the landscape for the use of herdsmen and the occasional traveller. As the sky continued to darken we upped our pace, neither of us fancying a soaking before mealtime.

We found the shepherd's hut just as the skies opened. It was only a rough shelter, four walls and a hole for the door, but the roof was watertight and the wind didn't blow in through the entrance space. There was also an overhang outside to provide some cover for horses, so – given their evening nosebag – I knew they would be quite content.

I returned from feeding the horses to find that Dale had already started a fire. That was impressive skill with a flint and I was also pleased that I hadn't needed to touch the tinder box that I kept tightly wrapped in an oiled cloth in the inside pocket of my jerkin.

'Somebody has left us a good supply of firewood,' said Dale, pointing to the stack in the corner furthest from the door.

'I wish we could repay the favour,' I said ruefully, warming my hands, which had begun to feel the chill. 'But if it continues to rain like this there won't be a dry twig this side of Avalon.'

As if to underscore my statement lightning rent the air to be followed soon after by a crash of thunder and an invigorating downpour. Dale winced noticeably before he continued: 'So, Chaucere, do you believe there is a Blessed Isle then? Where the land is so fertile men need never even till the earth?'

'And where the King's sword Excalibur was forged?' I asked.

'Yes, so it is said.'

I shrugged. 'I am not sure about that, but beyond the mountains of the West where the Celti tribes still thrive, there is an island that is sacred to the people of the Old Religion and certainly there are many groves full of fruit there.'

'Really?' said Dale, doubt obvious in his tone.

'Oh, yes! Haven't I eaten from them?'

'You have been to Avalon?!' Dale blurted out.

'I didn't say that,' I said with a laugh. 'To the locals it is called the Dark Isle in their own language. As to whether it is our Avalon, well there are certainly tombs and Standing Stones aplenty. The Old Empire did their best to conquer the island, for it also had abundant metals but I never think they fully succeeded in conquering its people.

'Was this Avalon? I think on balance probably not. I'll let you know it I ever do find my way to the real place.'

'Bring me back an apple, please. I am told they are wondrously sweet.'

'I'll try,' I promised.

Dale gave me a considering look across the fire glow. 'You have indeed travelled far, Chaucere. I too wish to see distant lands, witness amazing sights and have adventures.'

I smiled in what I hoped was not too patronising a fashion.

'Well, there are sights to marvel at, that's for sure. Palaces and temples that would make the Big House look dowdy, but as for adventure, I'll say this.' I placed a few more faggots of wood on the fire, before continuing.

'Wherever I have been I have found that people remain pretty much the same. There is good and bad in similar proportions in all places, fortunately favouring the good. It goes to say then that your chances of having an adventure are also similar wherever you go! Who knows, we might be in the middle of an adventure even as we speak!'

Dale looked sourly out at the pouring rain: 'It doesn't feel very much like an adventure at the moment, I have to admit to that.'

I laughed at this. 'The thing about adventures, King's Messenger, is that they seldom feel like adventures when you are in the middle of them. Believe me! Most of the time they feel like uncomfortable interludes full of alternating periods of risk and boredom.'

Certainly the rest of the night felt nothing like an adventure. It continued to rain and only some clever construction on the part of the builders of the shepherd's hut prevented the floor from being awash. We sat, wrapped in our cloaks, and dozed by the fire, grateful for the heat it put out. The rain stopped just before dawn and soon the sun was starting the long hard job of drying out the sodden world. Good luck there.

'It shouldn't be far now,' said Dale, as we rode through freshly cleared pastureland where a few of the large, horned cattle that the region favoured grazed contentedly. 'I would have expected there to be a herdsman – or a boy at least – to be at hand, as rustlers are by no means uncommon hereabouts.'

I took his point.

After attending to what all men must in the morning, we had broken our fast on hard bread and cheese and pressed on. Dale left a King's Messenger token in the hut. This was another Camelot innovation. Not as good as gold or coin but these tokens could often be bartered for goods or services in Camelot.

Soon we were out of the woody wasteland and into a cultivated landscape with proper strips and fields. Every indication was that it had been busy thereabouts, but now it wasn't. I also shared Dale's sense of unease and this feeling grew stronger as we saw a crude sign that indicated Bleakers Farm at the end of a well-used cart track.

'I think,' said Dale quietly, 'that I will accompany you to see this Bleakers Farm.'

'And I will thank you for your company.'

We rode quietly together towards a small collection of buildings just visible over the hedge-line.

A farm is never quiet. This farm was no exception, but – somehow – it was the wrong sort of not quiet. There were geese going about their business, pigs enjoying the mud in a sty and hens chatting amongst themselves. What was missing was the contribution the farmer and his people should have been making.

We got off our horses and tied them to a post.

I unsheathed my sword. Dale did the same. 'I'll look in the main house. You check the animal shed,' I said quietly. He nodded and we split up.

It was a tidy collection of buildings. This was no smallholding or a serf's hovel, where most of the labour was done on behalf of the Local lord. This was one of the farms that the new King's laws had allowed to spring up, where common Freemen were now permitted to make a decent living for themselves and their families.

I did not hear the man standing behind me draw his bow. I was too busy looking at the body of the man lying by the kitchen hearth, his blood pooled on the compacted earth floor from the slash across his stomach that had also released his innards.

I did hear Dale's loud voice:

'Put down your bow, friend. I am a Messenger of the King and the sword that he has armed me with is now pointing at your back.'

Fortunately the archer heard him too. I turned to see the man, his arrow now unnotched, looking at Dale in some confusion, as he spluttered:

'I just walked in and there he was! This man has struck down the farmer Goodman Nash Bleaker. Look, there on the floor! I saw it.'

'No you didn't,' I said to him. 'Or you would have known that my sword has no trace of blood on it.'

'I was only protecting myself in case he turned on me as I came in!' The archer tried harder to convince Dale.

'Unlikely,' I said. 'If you had just come in you would have seen that the King's Messenger and myself arrived together.'

'I was only trying to do my duty!' he insisted, in a final appeal to Dale. He received scant reward.

'No, I don't think you were,' I said evenly. 'I think you killed this innocent man and waited for me to arrive, not realising I would have company. Your sole intention was to make it look like you had indeed acted as you have just said.'

You could see in his eyes that he was considering trying to make a run for it. There was only one entrance though and Dale was standing in it. He thought about stringing his bow again, but with one swipe of my sword it was just so much kindling.

'No!' he cried, now desperate. 'I am an innocent man!'

'I think you are anything but innocent,' said Dale. 'There is some conspiracy at work here. You will be coming with us and we will return to Camelot to get to the body of it.'

Which is just what we did. There was indeed a conspiracy and they might have got away with it as well. If I had not enjoyed the company of a King's Messenger it could have been my body that was now hanging outside the outer gate of Camelot and not Eduard the Baker's. The younger Bleaker had conspired with the archer, name of Darnard, to have his brother murdered, so that he could inherit the farm and have, for free, all the grain he would ever require for his bread making. As he had arranged to have this happen when his brother's attractive young wife was away visiting an ailing mother, it seemed likely that he expected to get her too.

All Eduard needed was somebody to take the fall for him. He chose me, which I found slightly insulting. Did I really look so gullible? Some ridiculous story about 'papers' – they must have thought they were home and dry. They weren't, which is why Darnard the Archer now hung with Eduard the Baker. They had not departed easily, they twitched a good while, but they did not deserve otherwise.

The whole episode had been a little too close a shave for my liking, mind. I needed to up my game again. Perhaps Camelot was making me soft.

9
THE HARDENING

I am not fond of exercise. I have nothing against physical labour, I can chop wood until the cows come home and they are safely tucked up and snoring. I can, and have, marched without rest for days – until I dropped in fact. Dropped somewhere safely that is! A dozen armed men on your trail is a remarkable incentive.

What I do not enjoy is exertion for its own sake. I like to have a reason or, even better, a mission. So, lacking such a goal, I volunteered to work for Emald.

'I can't afford to pay you,' he said.

'Good job too, you couldn't afford my wages.'

All that safely established, I moved into the smithy for a few days.

I am no stranger to working some metal, but smith work is of a different order and a different skill. So, Emald had me work the bellows and that did indeed show, as I had suspected, just how soft I had become. Who would have thought operating a pair of bellows could be so tiring? It was useful work though and I was delighted to learn from Emald just how much fresher he felt at the end of day, even though I could barely stay awake long enough to drink a beer with him.

'You'll get used to it,' Emald explained.

'I know and I like the fact that I will get used to it. It's just the getting there that's the problem. So for a fourteen night I worked bellows by day and served ale by night. Then, sensing my growing frustration, Emald let me hit things. That I enjoyed. Of course I wasn't allowed to hit expensive things or important things, but after a while I became pretty good at hitting other things and felt better for it too. Some of the soft edges were certainly hardening up again and Emald and I would have the occasional tussle and mock sword fight. He would usually win the tussles, of course, being both larger and stronger, unless I cheated. I cheated a lot, as I felt obliged to keep him on his toes.

'You are one sneaky son-of-a-malkin, Chaucere,' he said one day as we faced off, stripped to the waist, out back of the forge ready to wrestle. 'But I do believe I have exhausted your bag of tricks now.'

'I don't know about that, Emald. The thing is, when you are fighting against somebody who is both larger and stronger than you are, you have to use the thing you have more of.'

'And what would that be, Chaucere?'

'Why brains, of course!'

As if spurred on by my comment Emald leapt at me, hoping to catch me in a large bear hug that would squeeze the air from my body. It might well have done too if I hadn't slathered goose fat all over my skin. As it was, I slipped from his grasp faster than butter drips from hot cakes. Once behind him I tripped him over and had my knee in his back and his arm ready to dislocate if it had been required. It wasn't.

'Goose fat,' he said. 'Is that really goose fat?'

'Yes,' I replied, giving his arm a friendly tweak.

'I should have smelled it.'

'Too late now.'

'That is going to take you forever to remove.'

'I know,' I said. 'Nobody said victory came easily.'

Our sword fights were much more evenly matched at least with wooden swords. He knew better than to try to fight me with the real thing.

It was all very enjoyable and after a while Emald even let me look after the forge while he went for a wazz or a longer stay. I enjoyed this as well, although I was under no illusions as to my ability and was fully prepared to ask potential customers to wait or come back later.

Then, one late afternoon, as I was busy hitting a piece of metal, a man rode up. He was wearing a worn travel cloak over much finer clothes and I could see that his horse was not the sort a man of means would normally ride either. It was a sure-footed mount with plenty of stamina, better for a long distance trek than for transporting a Knight of the Round table about Camelot.

'Hey, you! My horse needs shoeing!'

I recognised his voice immediately. It was the blond-haired man with the fine moustaches and very unpleasant manner.

'Don't just stand there gawking. I said I was in a hurry! Didn't you hear?'

I recognised him but he didn't recognise me, which was not surprising as my beard had now regrown and my face was covered in soot.

'Get a move on! I was told that Emald made the best shoes in this stinking part of the midden. Do not disappoint me.'

So I pulled my neckerchief up higher to protect my mouth from smuts and recognition and went about making a horseshoe. I could make a reasonable horseshoe by now, so I took my time. Eventually I held up the fruits of my labour.

'Finished,' I said, my voice full of pride, as my tongs grasped the misshapen lump of metal more suited for braining sheep before butchering. I was pleased to see my work had the desired effect as his eyes did actually bulge.

'I was told Emald was the best!' he spluttered furiously.

'He is,' I replied. 'But I am not Emald.'

I swear he thought about hitting me, but then he saw the hammer in my hand and thought better of it.

He managed a sort of strangled curse before getting back onto his horse.

'Hey!' I shouted after him, waving the shoe. 'Don't you want me to put it on your horse?'

It was then that Emald returned and saw the rider disappearing down the street.

'Was that a customer?' he asked me.

'A potential customer,' I replied.

'I don't know if you are aware of this, Chaucere, but the object of being in business is not to turn away custom.'

'You wouldn't have liked him,' I said by way of explanation. 'He wasn't good enough for one of your shoes.'

Emald considered pursuing this but realised it would probably be futile, so he continued his work and I went back to the bellows. This activity did not fully occupy my mind, so I thought at greater length about my dissatisfied customer. I knew from Emald that the Big House had its own smithy. They also had many horses finer than the one that had thrown a shoe that afternoon. So why had the loud-mouthed oaf come looking for Emald?

I couldn't say for sure what it was, but there was something beyond his loud mouth and ignorant behaviour that really worried me about that man.

I usually sleep like a log on my pallet on the brewhouse floor after a day working at Emald's and a night serving ale, but that night I was restless. That night I dreamt, for the first time, but not the last, of the Round Table. I had never seen it, not that many had despite its fame.

In my dream the table seated twenty-four. King Arthur was sat there of course – not that I knew what he looked like not covered in mud and blood; but the crown was a give-away. Around him sat his Lords and knights all shimmering with other-worldly goodness. But in one seat to the King's right there was a large fat rat. The rat was sleek and well-groomed and instead of whiskers had fine blonde moustaches. Nobody seemed to notice as they went about their knightly business.

What was more disturbing was that behind the rat there lurked something darker and even more worrying. I couldn't work out what this was, despite the interesting fact that I was actually seated at the table too. I tried to tell everybody sat there, of the danger in their midst, but nobody listened to me.

The rat looked at me though, its mean eyes full of hatred. I thought it might leap at my throat and take a chunk out. It didn't, as by then I was awake, wide-eyed and sweating in the brewhouse. It had been a close thing though, and I rubbed my neck as if to check it was still intact and bite free. I didn't return to sleep that night for many hours and I awoke to a new realisation that did little to bring me cheer.

IO
DEPARTURE

A bram was leaving Camelot.

He didn't tell me he was leaving of course. I suppose a lifetime of being on the move, watching your back carefully – and your fellow man more carefully still – had instilled certain habits in him that he found hard to break. I knew he was leaving though and I was sad about it.

Working for Abram and his kin gave me a good introduction to a side of Camelot life I would not otherwise have become aware of; the world of decent people trying to make a living and raise their children in the midst of all this hurly-burly. They were good people and I liked them. Although we had sorted out a way to stay clear of the bandits that had plagued Abram and his friends in their rounds, I knew that other merchants and traders were still being waylaid. I also knew that Abram's kin still suffered at the hands of the ignorant and stupid. I did what I could of course, but I was only one man.

Abram was a man with certain sensibilities and a keen survival instinct. He had a good nose and his nose was telling him something that the rest of us were not aware of. He could smell change and it wasn't the sort of change that he favoured.

'I need to take a large parcel of goods to the port Chaucere,' Abram said one day. 'In a fourteen nights. Important goods so I need more than the normal protection. I know we have successfuly foiled the rogues, but more organised bandits are still attacking caravans.'

It was true, the bandits did indeed seem to have become more organised and looked for larger targets.

'Leave it to me,' I told him.

'We'll need a pack animal.'

'Easily sorted, my friend.'

I know it is very easy to use phrases such as 'my friend' in everyday speech, but it wasn't until that moment that I realised that I did think of Abram as a friend. For somebody who had only had comrades-in-arms for a very long time, to have a friend like Abram was something of a pleasant novelty. I would miss his quick wit, astute observations and great, unshowy, generosity. However, if he did not want to make a song-and-dance about leaving, then who was I to gainsay him?

The pack animal was simple to sort out – a type of pony from the west country renowned for their stamina and hill climbing, if not their speed. It was the best part of a day's journey to the inland port that marked the highest navigable point on the river. There was a longer flatter route and a shorter hillier route that wound closer to the steep riverbanks. We took the latter way, hence the pony and our own sure-footed steeds. I was betting that any outlaws would be inclined to look for speed in their rides and not be so confident on hillsides.

I was right – outlaws can be very predictable. They hit us on a narrow level path through a thickly forested track that allowed us little escape on either side. Five of them, bristling with weapons, but steeds built for open country.

'Leave the pony,' I shouted to Abram.

'No – my goods! Don't lose me my goods!'

'They're no use to you dead,' I said and hit his horse on its rump.

We took off at a good speed, the heavily-laden pony had no chance to stay with us. Two outlaws tried to keep up with us but the path sloped steeply down to a ford and they soon gave up. The going was treacherous, as I knew it would be – that's why I had picked a particularly wet day.

'Are you alright?' I asked Abram, after we were safely across the river and up the other side.

'Yes, just a little winded,' the older man replied. 'I don't get excitement like that much these days.'

'Long may that be the case, Abram.'

'Thank you.'

'And excellent mumming. I had no idea you had such a talent.'

'Thank you. I suppose none of us know what we are capable of until pushed.'

I kicked the support out on the log pile I had prepared and stacked up at the top of the other side of the river valley as a way of discouraging pursuit. It wasn't necessary, the outlaws had truly given up – but I'd gone to the trouble and wasn't being put off by the robbers' lack of determination. Even now I guessed they were looking at the strong boxes and wishing they could smash them open right there and then. It would take more than a casual blow to break these locks though and I don't think their master would be well pleased with them. No, they would take them back to somewhere much safer, leaving us with plenty enough time to get to Portside.

The rain had stopped by the time Abram found the boat he was looking for. The Captain was one of his own folk, or so I surmised. We took the saddlebags off our horses carefully; after all they contained a small fortune in jewels and gold coin. Whereas the strongboxes contained nothing but rocks – very nice rocks that rattled around almost as if they had been something of worth, but at the end of the day just rocks. Oh, and a couple of turnips for the pony – hopefully they wouldn't take it out on him.

'You always knew I wasn't going back?' said Abram, as he stood awkwardly by the boat which his sea-faring friend now waited to push off.

'You didn't manage to hide your intentions very well.'

'Yet you never said anything?'

'It's your business, Abram.'

He smiled at me kindly. 'And Chaucere, you have never had any mind to comment on my business.'

'It has always been carried out fairly and without favour as far as I have seen.'

'Thank you, Chaucere, that means a lot.' He looked around, searching for the right words. 'I wasn't going to just walk out without an explanation.'

'You don't owe me one.'

'No. It's just that … I feel Camelot is changing and I'm not sure it's for the best. The King has nothing but the best of intentions, of that I am sure. However, I am not convinced the same can be said about some of the people that he now surrounds himself with. I think some look for nothing but their own wealth and advancement. Thus they care little for the ordinary person, whose lives they are responsible for and who the King, on taking the throne, said he would best protect.'

'Were you there that day? The day of the coronation?'

'I was, Chaucere. And it was as glorious as the balladeer's now sing. The sun shone brighter, the people looked happier and healthier and there was such an air of hope. We all had hope.'

'And now you have none?'

He smiled again. 'I wouldn't say that exactly, but it is going to take more good people to sort things out. The King cannot do it by himself. He needs people, people like you Chaucere.'

I laughed unwittingly. 'What good could I do? A simple soldier?'

'A soldier, yes. Simple? Hardly. Which is why you need this'

He took a key from his pocket and held it out. I recognised it; the key to his house and to his business.

'I don't understand.'

'It's yours. Take it. I have had the deeds written over to you.

'But I could not be a money lender?'

Abram laughed:

'No, I don't think you could be Chaucere! But a man is not a man of consequence in Camelot unless he owns land and property. You now have both!' He thrust the key at me again.

Eventually I took it from him. Not sure what else to do with it.

'The only thing is I ask of you is that you take care of Timothy.'

I nodded; momentarily over-come by long unexercised emotions, unsure whether to trust myself to speak.

Abram was away quickly after that. There was a tide to be caught. He stood at the stern of the boat and waved to me from it until both man and boat disappeared around a bend in the river on their long journey to the sea. I looked down at the key in my hand as if it was an object that had fallen unannounced from the sky.

I had a house and it had a door with a lock. I had never had a house with a door with a lock before. I'd never even had a door – not that there was really much need for one without the house to go with it. I went to look for a bed for the night and feed for the horse. Consideration of my new standing could wait until tomorrow.

I found bed and a stable with ease; Portside was bustling but there was plenty of accommodation. This was obviously the coming thing! One day a soul might cross this land from sea to sea and rest their head on a soft pillow every night if he had the coin. What a thing that would be. I was soon taken back in my mind to another road, one I had trodden as a much younger man. A lot younger and a lot wetter behind the ears – and not just because of the weather. My experiences from that adventure had been one of the main reasons behind my decision to cross the Narrow Sea and try my luck in the warmer, and much drier, climes of the South. Probably the best move I had ever made.

It was a toss of one of my sparse collection of coins that had initially sent me west. I didn't have much of a clue to be honest, about anything. I vaguely knew that in the East there were new tribes speaking strange new languages and many mighty handy with an axe. Whereas in the West there were several old tribes speaking strange old languages, and mighty handy with an axe. A coin toss was as good a way of deciding the direction as any – or so I had assumed.

I thought it a good choice because I knew there was a well travelled road that led in that direction, built by the Old Empire. I didn't know it was a bad choice because at the end of that well travelled road there were the warring kingdoms the Old Empire had called the Celti. More exactly, the mountainous, wooded impenetrable land was inhabited by four tribes: the Ordovices and Deceangli in the North and the Demetae and Silures in the South. I learnt all of this later, and I was very lucky there was a later. For the moment, I was strong, healthy and full of the optimism of youth. I was also tall for my age, easily as tall as my older half-brothers were, and although not as broad, all those years working on the farm had not produced a weakling. I could pass for older, until I opened my mouth and displayed my incredible ignorance. Usually I kept my mouth closed. Thanks to my brothers I also knew how to wield a short staff. Not being bruised and battered is a very good incentive to get good with a short staff.

One of the first things I did on the road was to find myself a good sturdy staff that would serve for this function. That was my first bit of good luck. I had found an ash coppice, in need of some good management it must be said. The winter gales had brought down an old oak tree and that had fallen directly onto a coppiced trunk, breaking several poles just after the curve where they grow out from the stool. I had my choice of staffs and chose one the width of my thumb. This was heavier than I was used to but I would 'grow into it' as my old man was fond of saying. The length of a short staff should be around the height of its user, plus one hand set upright on your head, or so my father had also told me. Certainly no longer than eight to nine feet or what you gain in reach you lose in versatility.

Long poles – over nine feet – are great if you want to prod at men with swords on horseback, but that's a fool's game for a start! If you see a man heading towards you on a horse, especially if he has a sword in his hand, then I advise getting up a tree very quickly. If you are obliged to make a stand then just make sure your pole has a good metal spear point at the end and plant it well.

A short staff is not a glamorous weapon. It is not a noble's two-handed sword for example – although it is very good training for the use of such arms. I knew this, as everybody did, but I did not know anybody with a sword. We were not that wealthy! That hadn't stopped us playing 'swords', when young, as children always do and probably will for another age or two! I had no horse either, such riches were also well beyond me, but I could walk – oh, how I could walk! I was an excellent walker. I needed to be.

The first few days were no real effort. It was good to be away from the tedium of farm life, of mucking and raking and carrying and digging. The break of routine was exciting for a young man and I had enough food with me and could forage as I went along as well. I was young enough to wake up in the morning after a night sleeping on the ground and not feel like I had taken a thrashing. The worse thing was the rain and the further west I went the worse that became, especially as I had not brought any tools for fire making. I did not even have a flint or kindling. So I slept under whatever shelter I could find but never felt properly dry. And that was why one day about a fourteen-night after I had left home, when I saw flames flickering invitingly to one side of the road, I decided to investigate.

I saw a shape sitting by the fire. Just the one – neither tall nor short nor fat nor thin. This looked promising. I moved as quietly as I could and was sure that nobody could hear me. Such is the folly of youth.

'If you're thinking of thievery, I have nothing to thieve. If you are just after warming your bones, please come and join me,' said the neither-tall-nor-short-nor-fat-nor-thin man sitting by the fire.

So that is what I did and my life was never the same again. His name was Beryan and he was a tinker. He came from the West – not the land of the Ordovices and Deceangli, and the Demetae but the Far West, where the land runs out; the place that the Empire called Dunmonii. Beryan called it Kernow and had little time for the Old Empire or any other of them 'recent' newcomers.

Beryan worked the tin. As a boy, as he was to go on and tell me at length over many of our journeys, he even dug the tin from the ground of the land he obviously loved so much. I never found out why he left Kernow, but isn't it often the way with men, that they leave the thing they love the best? I suspected a broken heart, but, as I may have mentioned, I was young and romance was a world I knew nothing about. It scared me nearly as much as what had set me out on this adventure.

Travelling with Beryan I always felt safe. Tinkers at that time were much respected and honoured. Metal was not so plentiful that common folk, or their betters, could afford to throw anything away. Yes, he carried valuable tools like his iron, but what was most valuable was the knowledge in his head. That could not be easily extracted, as it was a lifetime of learning and experience. However, as we travelled and I assisted where I could, he showed me the secrets of his trade. They stood me in good stead in many a difficult situation, especially before the sword became my new mistress.

As Beryan told me it is impossible to say who first discovered how to stick metal to metal. He swore that goldsmiths of ancient Egypt knew how to join gold to gold before men on these islands had scarce left their caves! And then came tin – now that was a thing – and the origins of that discovery are hidden even to one such as Beryan. The word of its usage spread, that much is known and it was the Old Empire that saw it taken to perfection – as with so many things – and they produced pipes of lead with soldered seams that ran for many miles! Or so Beryan swore and I have no reason to doubt him. The Old Empire also heard about the tin that came from the ground of Kernow. Some say that tin was the reason why they came to these islands in the first place! Beryan doubted this as it seems they had good tin in other places they had conquered, but it would not have dissuaded them.

As we progressed on our journey I gleaned many important things from Beryan. Matters like the best clay for making a tinker's dam; the wall built up around a hole in a metal pan or pot so that the hot solder can be poured in to plug it before it is rasped and smoothed. Above all, he shared with me the secret of charcoal flux and the mix of tin and lead that makes the best solder, one that melts at the magic point only. This is one of the tinker's great secrets. I felt honoured to share it and I was sworn not to tell others.

And as we travelled further I met the Celti: the Ordovices and Deceangli in the North and the Demetae and Silures in the South. I found them to be just like any other people – fierce but not unfriendly when you got to know them. Much given to bouts of drinking and singing, and to periods of melancholy when the rains that washed these lands so often, fell in great torrents. Their language was to remain a secret to me! Too many noises in too short a time and while often lyrical at other points it was so much throat clearing to my ears.

There were many Kings there and as Kings will they made war, and passed judgements, in consultation with their tribal elders, but few others. They had camps but many tended to ride around in armoured warbands of closely-related friends and families that they called 'teulu'. I picked that word up at least! So we found work and shelter where we could find it and I was ever grateful for a roof over my head and some sun on my face.

There was one exception. One day, as we traverse the Kingdom of Powys, we come across an impressive fortified encampment, high on a hill with smoke rising from the dwellings built within. It was as large as any we had seen on our journey.

'That looks like a likely place to find work. Master, ' I said to Beryan.

He shook his head: 'Never go near that place boy.'

'Why not, Master?'

'That is the home of Morgen an Spyrys. Keep away!'

I knew enough of his native Kernow tongue by then, which was close to the language the Celti spoke, to know he spoke of an enchantress. This was strange, for by then I also knew that Beryan was not one to believe in magic and such tomfoolery. He was a man who worked metal and was practical with it.

'But Master, you have always said…'

'Let it be boy. There are many sorts of enchantment in this life and some are best avoided and never questioned.' Beryan's tone did not brook any discussion.

I stared harder at the house of Morgen the Enchantress. From this distance it was not exactly inviting! It resembled a number of hill forts we had seen on the road, which had been rebuilt and reoccupied since the Old Empire had left, sometimes after lying unused for hundreds of years. Some of these seemed much more about displaying status and power, rather than providing defence – but not so this one! The earth works were high, with three rings of fences and deep ditches. Morgen was not welcoming visitors, that much was sure. So we moved on, although the weather was getting chill and the rain falling – yet again.

And so our travels might have continued for many more years, wandering where we wanted to and making enough coin to keep body and soul together – just. Beryan was a good master, and an excellent teacher and no mean swordsman either. Many an evening we would spar before supper – at first with sticks like children – then later he bartered work for a sword of my very own. It was a sorry thing really, but I loved it and as he pointed out: 'You can't really do yourself or anybody else any damage with a sword like this at the moment!'

It was not a bad life. My skill level improved and if it hadn't been for the weather I might have been content. Then, just as the weather was brightening at last and winter was finally loosening its grip, Beryan spoke seriously to me as we sat before the campfire.

'I think it's time you were moving on son.'

I was shocked: 'But, Master! What have I done wrong? How have I displeased you?'

He smiled: 'You have done nothing wrong! It is simply that time. Look inside yourself and you will see. Whatever is in store for you, it is not a tinker's life.'

I went quiet, because I knew what he said was correct. I needed to be moving on. I needed to be seeing some clear skies and some sun. I needed to be heading south. There was a world waiting for me out there, I knew it in my bones and so did he.

I said my farewells to Beryan in a port called Caerdydd, on the south coast overlooking the estuary of the mighty river they call Hafren in these parts, but on the other side of the water they call the Severn. Beryan, of course, knew may of the local captains and he found one who would let me work my passage to somewhere he called Neustria. To my delight Beryan had prepared a small gift of my very own materials to carry, taken from his own stock. I was speechless, as I knew that these tools were all hard come by.

'You'll have to find some way to earn your supper whiles you make your fortune at whatever it is you turn your hand to eventually.'

'How can I thank you, Beryan?' I was moved more than I could say. I hugged the man as I had never hugged my 'father', for I knew I felt more for him than I had ever for the man under whose roof I was brought up.

'Perhaps when you're a rich man,' Beryan continued, 'with your own house – perhaps in this Camelot the new King is building – you'll be able to put some work the way of an old tinker.'

Beryan waved to me from the shore, just as I had waved to Abram. And now thanks to Abram, here I was, a man with his own house. I had never heard a word of Beryan in all my travels since and I can still fix my own pans. Perhaps I should look for him now, I owed him so much.

It was only as I finally found myself dropping off to sleep, the key clutched tightly to my chest, that it occurred to me to ask myself the question: who on this earth was Timothy?

11
TIMOTHY

I sat in my house wondering what exactly a house owner was supposed to do when he was in his house. Generally when I am indoors I am eating or drinking – usually both together – or else sleeping. If I was lucky I might not be doing them all by myself. If I was really lucky there might be another activity included on this short list that definitely requires company. But that hadn't been on the list for a long time and, actually, it had been outdoors then now I came to think about it. In much warmer climes I should add. So, here I was, sitting in my house rather unsure about the whole idea. It also occurred to me that, now being a house owner, I was also a Freeman of Camelot. Never once, since I had picked up the sword, having considered myself anything but a freeman, I didn't think this was going to change my life much.

The journey back from Portside had been uneventful. I'd attached myself to a group of traders heading for the Big House to sell some fabulous new commodity that they were very excited about. I never actually got to find out what they were selling, mostly because I could hardly understand one word in three. Plus the other two words were in a language I had no knowledge of at all. They were clearly from somewhere that saw more sun than we did though! They had arrived expecting to make their fortunes – maybe they would – certainly there was an appetite for luxury.

I left the horses (my 'horses' now it seemed!) with the ostler and made my way to Abram's house, which was now my house. It didn't look any different. It was in the same street – one of those built at the same time as the Big House to help serve functionaries that didn't warrant a bed in the castle. It had the same walls made from the same timbers and the same lath and the same thatch, but now it was totally different – it was my house.

I took the key and put it in the keyhole, (my keyhole) noticing for the first time how cleverly the door and frame had been reinforced to prevent unlawful access. The key turned very well, I was pleased to notice. I opened the door and just looked inside for a moment. Then, for want of anything better to do, I went in.

I pulled back a chair from the table. The same one I had sat on many times during my conversations with Abram, I wasn't yet actually up to sitting on Abram's chair – and then I sat. And sat some more.

My musing was interrupted by a knock on the door (my door!) and just as I remembered that this normally required a response from me, the door opened. I had left it too late – I had missed my chance to either welcome or refuse my first visitor! What a novice I was at the whole door and house business.

The woman that came in had a large bust, a large nose and a large woollen hat. All that rather passed me by because she was also carrying a large woven basket, from which came the most appetising of smells.

'You'll be Chaucere then,' she said – definitely more of a statement than a question, and not spoken altogether approvingly.

I nodded, not wanting to do anything that might antagonise the owner of the fine-smelling contents of the basket.

'Master Abram has paid me up until the end of the week. After that we need to make our own agreement.'

'For what exactly, Mistress?' I was obliged to add.

'For a hot evening meal with bread and cheese enough for breakfast. What did you think?' she eyed me suspiciously, daring me to suggest something else. 'Did Master Abram not mention me – Gunnhild?'

'No, sorry,' I had to admit.

'Well,' said Gunnhild, generously. 'I suppose he had other things on his mind.'

'And what price had you agreed with Master Abram?'

She named a price. I suggested half and felt I had still probably not made the best deal when she agreed immediately. I didn't mind too much, as by this time I was very hungry.

'Leave your dish by the front door and I will pick it up in the morning. If you are not here I will leave the basket by the back door.'

I didn't know I had a back door too! And to my surprise it now turned out that I was the owner of the basket's contents. Better and better!

She placed a cloth-wrapped parcel, from the basket, onto the table. I easily unknotted it. What was inside looked as appetising as it smelt.

'Mutton! Mistress Gunnhild! A dish of mutton, this is very, very agreeable indeed.'

'Good!'

'The quantity might even challenge my appetite mind'

'Don't forget,' she said disappearing through my open door, 'Timothy has a large appetite as well.'

If I hadn't already fed my face with a very large cut of very hot mutton, I would have asked who exactly this Timothy was and where I might find him inorder to honour Abram's last request. But as I had, I didn't.

The mutton really was excellent, roasted with herbs but still dripping with juices. The bread was very fine too. Fresh and moist and accompanied by a wedge of good, strong cheese. One thing I had missed on my adventures was a good strong hard cheese.

I was so preoccupied I didn't notice the scratching at first. It was a persistent scratch though, and coming from the other room, which with a flash of insight, I realised was the only location for a back entrance.

The backdoor was double-bolted. I not only had a lock, I had two bolts as well – three if you counted the monster on the front door, which I did of course. Good bolts make good neighbours. I unbolted my two smaller bolts and opened my back door. To my great surprise on the other side I found the largest hound I had ever encountered. I had seen otter hounds, deerhounds and wolfhounds before. I had never seen a bear hound before, but this grey shaggy monster could easily have fitted the bill.

The hound walked through into the main room as if he owned the place. I bolted the door, just because I could, and followed him. He stood by the fireplace and kicked a bowl that I had failed to notice before. This, I belatedly worked out, was Timothy – the hound, not the bowl.

I decided to take my new responsibility seriously and scraped some mutton into the dish. Timothy gave it another kick and I scraped some more into it. Timothy ate his mutton, rather grudgingly I thought, and then – after turning a couple of times – collapsed in a heap in front of the unlit fire. The state of the fire, judging by his mournful looks, was of some concern to him.

I finished my meal in a thoughtful frame of mind. I mean, locks and bolts were one thing, but I had never considered owning a hound before. And it was sharing my food! Not having much knowledge of such animals, I didn't realise at this juncture that, in fact, you did not own hounds like Timothy, you lived alongside them – and if lucky you were tolerated.

Of course, not all were tolerated to the same extent.

We quickly established a sort of routine. Timothy would return most evenings around the same time, eat his supper, sleep, and in the morning scratch the door again to be let out. What he did with himself while I was seeing to putting food on the table for the both of us I did not know. I didn't begrudge him, not considering this was Abram's last request. It was hardly onerous. However, when you have had no responsibilities at all – beyond keeping yourself alive that is – any chore can be a challenge.

I'm not sure if it was my unfamiliarity with door locking, but one evening – about a fourteen nights after Timothy and I first met – I woke up in my bed (my bed!). I was startled, struck by the knowledge that somebody else was now in the house with me; somebody with two less than Timothy's four feet.

I reached very slowly for my knife, my ears straining to identify what they could now hear: heavy panting and ragged breathing I concluded, as I crept through to the main room. There in the moonlight I was greeted by a scene that, for a full minute, I didn't quite comprehend. On the floor, a little away from his normal spot, was Timothy. And in his mouth he held the throat of a man, his neck at a strange angle with his body collapsed under him very awkwardly. One of the man's hands I could see very clearly in the cracks of moonlight breaking through the shuttered window, because it was still reaching out for the knife he had dropped when Timothy had downed him. The hand never made it to the knife and the ragged breathing now stopped. Timothy still held onto the man's neck – just in case.

Timothy had earned all his suppers from then on and if ever he wanted the fire lighting, he got it lit – even if it was the middle of summer.

There was something familiar about the dead man that I couldn't quite place. Of course all dead men look alike to some degree; the slug-like eyes, the slack slit of a mouth and the distinct lack of animation. Yet...

Nothing I found about his person was any help. In fact there was really nothing about his person – not even a snot rag! Perhaps he was just a chancer, who had heard about Abram's wealth and didn't know about the change of ownership, or his live-in guard? Perhaps.

I found a barrow and wheeled my would-be attacker through the moonlit streets to the drop-off point that Aila had told me about. If this carried on I would have to get my own barrow.

12

AIDAN THE CARTER

Perhaps it was my new found status as a homeowner and the automatic respectability that comes from being a Freeman, but I suddenly found myself with offers of work coming in from all directions. First though, I needed to make my peace with Aila. She had been good to me and she was a true friend. I had neglected her, and I felt bad about that. I needn't have worried, Gwen was not only proving herself time and again, but she now had an admirer, Gryf, who was only too happy to assist for the occasional horn of ale. I began to worry about my regular work, but Aila wasn't at all concerned. She was pleased to see me though and after all was finished and cleared away, the four of us chatted amiably until I made my way back to my bed, in my house with my hound; well as much as Timothy belonged to anybody but himself.

Still, all things considered, I am not sure then why I took the job of work from Aidan the Carter. Perhaps I just felt sorry for him – never the best reason for doing anything. He did look a sorry little man, with a sad face that even a mother might have struggled to love. Not that it was mean or unpleasant, there was just nothing particularly loveable about Aidan the Carter, neither in looks or personality. He was stocky and strong and carried a large wooden mallet, hanging from his belt. He would use it for changing a cartwheel, but it could make a nasty weapon as well.

As a carter his work often took him away from home, a small-holding outside of Camelot, and he would be obliged to stay overnight. And therein lay his problem, or so he thought. He suspected that his goodwife, Gurta, was taking the opportunity of his absence to provide hospitality, on a regular basis, to a neighbour, Calend, who was a widower of some means. Or, perhaps anybody else who happened to be passing, such was her desirability and her availability, according to Aidan at least. He had no actual evidence for this, of course. Apart from reckoning that she always seemed to be tired when he got back from his travels.

I have come across men like Aidan before. Many believe that their wives must be automatically irresistible to all men, just because they found them worthy of their beds. Mostly these woman were grey, prematurely aged matrons, worn out by the continued suspicions of their husbands. By proving the extent of her virtue, I would probably give her a few months of rest before Aidan the Carter's doubts started up again. That is the way such men are.

I found myself a small copse to hide in, some way from the lane but with a good view of Aidan's insignificant dwelling and some fine oaks to provide good shelter. His cart was loaded and a large draft horse hitched up between the shafts. It was a full load but the horse did not look particularly bothered.

Aiden came out of the farmhouse followed by the woman who had to be his wife Gurta, as I knew he had no children. There was a sharp intake of breath. It was from me. Gurta was absolutely ravishing. Hair of spun gold, fresh cream skin, lips as ripe as cherries. The sort of woman you hear balladeers sing about. The sort of woman you always wish you could dream about. The sort of woman who might make any husband anxious, let alone sad suspicious Aidan the Carter.

I wondered how he had come by this prize. I know that daughters are still something akin to a currency in this part of the world, frequently used to pay off a debt or even as a gift between friends. In my travels I have seen how women are treated in many different lands. From venerated leaders to mere chattels. I am sad to say that my own native land was not amongst the most enlightened of the places I have visited. And from the fondness of their farewells I did not think this was a love-match either. Spring and autumn had not found a special pairing.

I watched as the cart rolled slowly down the lane away from Aidan's lowly dwelling. Whilst not wishing to doubt the chastity of Gurta Carter, based solely on her surfeit of beauty, the chances of her straying from her wifely duties had just increased considerably. I made myself comfortable and waited to see.

I had to wait until dusk had fallen to have my question answered. He came down the lane at no great pace. A travel cloak hid most of his clothes and the hood allowed only a few wisps of long blond hair to be seen. He could not disguise the quality of his ride though. This was no widower's elderly nag – no matter how great his means. Nor was it a casual traveller or rover's steed. This was quality. You could tell it in the sheen of the animal's coat and the spring in its stride – and the workmanship of its tackle!

I did not know who this visitor might be, but he had the Big House written all over him. Aidan the Carter, you had a serious problem here.

Gurta's guest left early next morning. I tracked him from a distance. I didn't need to be close as I was sure of his direction. I was right. Casually, without a care in the world, he rode through the main gate of Camelot. I wasn't close enough to hear any of his conversation with the King's Guards, but I could tell that respect was offered and accepted as a due.

My job had not been to identify any admirer, simply to ascertain Gurta's faithfulness and whether the widowed neighbour had been availing himself of her hospitality. One out of two was not going to be much consolation to Aiden. I was sure of that.

I met him in Aila's alehouse as we had previously arranged. He looked tired from his journey and had obviously not yet been home. I had ale waiting for him. He could tell immediately from my disposition what news it was I had to impart.

'It was Calend, wasn't it?' he said too loudly, his ale untouched. 'I knew it. I just knew it. The way he looked at her whenever we were in the market. Nasty piggy eyes he has, well I'm going to have them. See if I don't!'

I put a hand on his arm as he rose to go enact violence. 'Sit down, Aiden! Before you make a fool of yourself and find a rope around your neck.'

'Then tell me she has been chaste! Tell me that and make my world whole again.'

'Sadly I cannot, Aiden,' I said. 'I wish I could. But your problem is not with Calend.'

'Then who?'

'The man who has done you harm is not your neighbour. He lives in much grander accommodation,' I said quietly, my eyes flickering towards the castle that loomed over all our lives.

It took the carter a moment to realise his predicament and then his head slumped.

'Oh no.'

'I'm sorry, Aiden.'

'Really, what really? You're sure?' He looked at me with desperation in his eyes. He knew there could be no easy answer to his predicament. Not when the Big House was involved.

'I'm sorry, there is no doubt. I followed him all the way back to the castle. From the attitude of the guards and the quality of his mount he was no churl. I did not get a name or even a good look at him, but his position is not in any doubt.'

'Stupid woman!' he said, his voice a mixture of anger and distress and I realised that, whatever else, Aiden the Carter truly loved his wife. 'What did she expect, that he would deliver her to a life of silks and comfort? More fool her.'

I shrugged. 'I honestly do not know. Hopefully you can still salvage something of the vows you made to each other.'

'Perhaps,' he said, placing a small purse on the table and pushing it across to me.

'No, I don't want payment for this. I hoped to ease your worries, not add to them.'

'You must take it!' said Aiden, in a voice that would brook no argument. 'I shall still be a man that pays his debts, even if I cannot be a man who can hold onto his wife. '

I took the money, but later gave it to Emald. He said he knew of a Healer who helped the poor and destitute of Camelot that came to him seeking medicines for their ailments. This coin would assist many who deserved it more than me. I wanted none of this restitution and that night I vowed to never take on work of that ilk again.

Two weeks later I heard that Aiden the Carter had killed his wife Gurta with a single blow from his mallet. He then hung himself from an oak tree in the very copse I had sheltered in. I hoped that the knight in the Big House had also heard and was losing sleep over it. I very much doubted it.

13
THE ERRAND

I had been left in a pensive mood and sat dwelling on how my return to Camelot was turning out to be very different from what I had expected. Not at all in line with what I had desired after my last visit and the errand I had been undertaking then. These musings took me back to that eye-opening adventure in the city I now called home.

It had been a long trip back, after all it was a considerable distance, but it was much more comfortable than my outward journey had been. I now had coin to ease the way and buy me passage on boats and ships. When I had left the Misty Isles that first time I had tried making my way as a tinker, but there was a lot of competition and so I often fell to doing whatever work was available; basically the jobs nobody else wanted to do. This was a very different journey; I was pleased to say.

I found a ship to Tarraco, but then decided to go across land with a trading party and reacquaint myself with the court of King Ruderic. This turned out to be a little more adventurous than I expected as the land was in considerable turmoil. I headed to the coast once again and got board up the coast to Burdigala. There I picked up a trading ship heading to Hamwic, which many still called by the Old Empire name of Clausentum. Wanting to find my land legs again, I bought a good horse and headed north with a group of Frankish masons that I had met on the ship who happened to be heading for Camelot. They were full of excitement about this great adventure and the coin they hoped to make. I was excited to see what the fuss was all about. I spoke their language well and we soon became good friends, as men on the road do. Their expertise was certainly much needed. The post-Empire superstition that had sent most of my fellow islander's back to their mud-huts had meant that stone dressing had become a lost art. They were a good healthy bunch of lads and each had at least one very handy-looking hammer at his side: we would not see any trouble on our way to Camelot. We were all excited for our first sight of the city that was already something like a legend.

It was impressive, this huge city growing on the cliff overlooking the mighty river Hafren flowing speedily on its way down to join the Mor Hafren and the Celtic Sea. Every Old Empire dwelling must have plundered for miles around for the local creamy white stone they quarried hereabouts and every building almost glowed in the summer sun, especially the magnificent Fortress that rose above everything like the palaces I had seen around the Middle Sea.

My Frankish friends were impressed and so was I.

'Now that,' said Bertger, the unofficial leader of the troop of stonemasons, looking on in admiration as we rode closer, 'is a pretty sight. If I had known you were capable of building something of that grandeur, I would have been kinder about you blue-faced, shit-eating, cow fuckers!'

The Franks did not have a high opinion of the different peoples of the Misty Isles, as it was still often called, and any such comment was sure to get a cheer from the band.

'Hush!' I said to Bertger, pretending to whisper. 'Don't tell everybody or all you Franks will come over and try to grab the prettiest cows!'

That caused even more laughter and when ever a cow was sighted from then on there would be an appreciative 'moo' from the spotter. I decided to work with my new friends. Of course I had no skill in stone dressing, but it is surprising how much lifting and carrying is required on a building site when everybody is busy. I had already shaved my head in their style and spoke nothing but Frankish in their presence, unless other translation was required. This was not because I needed the coin, or the exercise. It was because I realised that there were people looking for me.

This was obvious, even in Hamwic. There always seemed to be a couple of hearty fellows around, buying ales and asking questions; always asking many questions. Had we seen a man travelling by himself? A mighty warrior perhaps, well armed, with plenty of coin?

I liked the 'mighty warrior' bit.

I had been forewarned about this; that there would be other parties interested in what I carried. And forewarned is forearmed, at least for this 'mighty warrior'. It was one of the reasons I had joined the Frankish stonemasons in the first place. It made you wonder what was so important in the small parcel I carried. I had been told not to open it, of course, and I was not one to go against a client's instructions.

That didn't stop me feeling the package.

I knew exactly what was inside this parcel of oilcloth that had been sent across hundreds of miles in the care of this 'mighty warrior'. It held two nails. That was all, just two nails.

Now, I am no expert when it comes to this new religion or the old gods and magic for that matter, but even I had an inkling why nails might be considered of importance to many people today. As to whether they could carry any special properties, I had no idea.

They did hum, though.

It wasn't a noise you could hear but I swear you could feel it even through the oilcloth. And this was why I wore it next to my person at all times, as part of a belt that also held my coin and a variety of trading items that had been given to me by my client.

My client had a reputation as a sorcerer. He didn't advertise himself as such, of course. The fact that inside his home was painted with mystical signs and runes didn't exactly hide the fact, but I thought it rather over the top. Surely a real sorcerer would be more discreet? His name was Ansaldo and apart from his house he was also renowned for his garden. It was a marvel and contained plants and flowers of every variety, many undoubtedly grown for their so-called magical properties, but others, it seemed, purely for their beauty. I am not a man who is moved easily by such displays, but neither do I have a heart of stone. And that is what you would need to not be enamoured by the sight and smells of the garden of Ansaldo. I do believe that it is mostly on the fecundity of his garden that his reputation as a sorcerer is based.

We sat under a vine-covered arbour as he explained my mission, should I agree to carry it out.

'I am told your are a man who helps people, Chaucere.'

'I can and have,' I replied.

'And you are reliable and not easily intimidated?'

'Such is the reputation I have earned, but you know this as you would have checked me out very thoroughly before inviting me to this meet. Lovely as it is,' I said, looking around his wonderful garden.

Ansaldo laughed. He was not a young man but he still had all his own teeth and his eyes were two dark spheres of polished walnut, remarkably distinct against the whites. In his long azure robe, with hair and beard braided, he was every inch the wizard he was renowned to be.

'The thing is, Chaucere,' he continued, 'I like to get the measure of a man by finding out first how he sees himself.'

'I have never been one for self-examination to be honest, Ansaldo. I have never had the time. But, now you come to mention it, I am a man who has seen death, murder, and other transgressions, carried out every day. Yet I am still willing to believe in the essential goodness of people and the rights of those who have nobody fighting their corner to none-the-less lead the best of lives.'

'And you will fight their corner?'

'If given the opportunity and enough coin to keep body and soul together.'

'I think, under the tough exterior, that perhaps you are something of an idealist,' Ansaldo observed.

'I would like to think so. But I worry that under the tough exterior there is simply a tougher interior, that might even smell even worse.'

'And you know Camelot?' he said, changing track.

'I know the country and the people. I was born there.'

'Then I believe you are the man for me.' He handed me a small parcel wrapped in oilcloth and noted how I jumped as I held it. Most parcels don't hum.

'Yes,' he observed. 'You are the right man.'

I left the garden, already making plans for my journey. I had mounted my horse and was half way home before I realised that I had never actually said I would accept the job, or even asked the price he was paying. Now that, for me, was very strange

Ansaldo had not told me who to deliver the parcel to, simply that I would be contacted when the time was right. When I asked how the contact was to find me, Ansaldo simply smiled and said it would not be a problem. He would know me and I would know him. I could feel the parcel now, humming tight against my skin, behind my belt, as I worked, shifting stone for those more skilled in dressing stone than I was.

I had been working on the building site a fourteen nights and there had been no sign of my contact. There were plenty of other people lurking around asking questions about strangers. I was concerned about one who called himself Adalman, who had attached himself to our work gang. He said he was Frankish and my new friends did not argue with that, but even I could tell his accent was subtly different. I kept my eye on him and was conscious that he did the same in return.

One evening, after finishing on the seemingly never-ending task of building the City Wall, we were drinking in one of the many alehouses that were springing up outside the walls we were still busy constructing.

Bertger, as normal, was complaining about the wine:

'It tastes like piss,' he moaned. 'And not even good piss.'

'I wouldn't know what good piss tastes like,' I replied. 'But, as this is an alehouse, try drinking ale! It is both better than the wine and cheaper too.'

'I don't like ale, it is a drink for old men and women.'

'Adalman drinks it,' I said. He did, I had noticed.

'Adalman is not a Frank.'

'He says he is.'

'He says he is many things and he asks about even more.'

This gave me pause for thought.

'Such as?'

'"Where you come from, Chaucere?" "Where we met you?" That sort of thing.'

'And what do you think about that?'

'We think your business is your own Chaucere. You work hard, you buy your share of lousy wine and ale, that is good enough for us.'

'Thank you, Bertger. I appreciate that.'

'And we think Adalman should have an accident.'

I nearly spilled my beer on hearing this.

'Building sites are dangerous places, Chaucere. You know that! It is easy for a stone to fall and split somebody's head open.'

'It's true, Bertger and do not think I don't appreciate the thought but if there is an accident to happen I can certainly arrange it myself.'

Bertger shrugged and poured his dregs of wine onto the rushes before answering:

'All right! Buy me the least worse ale then anyway!'

I did and he enjoyed it and he drunk far too many and was close to having an accident himself the next day.

Over the next week I got to know the ways of Camelot better, although I didn't venture far outside into the surrounding countryside. I knew that already. Although the weather was remarkably fine, I couldn't say the place felt anything like home. Maybe I needed the rain and cold for that, but I wasn't looking forward to either.

And then after another week everything happened at once.

The moon was full and we had all worked late. We were building a difficult section: where the wall finished by the drop into the river ravine. The wall itself turned a right angle, so that one section would have been floating in the air, if it had not been for extensive underpinning and lime mortaring.

As usual I was humping stone – stick to what you are good at, I say! I was handing material through to Bertger and the rest of the band who were climbing the rock face like so many goats, when I was aware of danger. The nails hummed louder and I threw myself backwards as a stone hurtled down from the top of the wall.

It missed me, but I nearly lost my balance and fell down into the ravine.

It was Bertger who pulled me back and stopped me.

'See,' he said, 'accidents happen.' We looked for Adalman but we couldn't find him. He was not at work the next day either. Somebody else was waiting for me though, when I broke for lunch. He beckoned me to one side. As Ansaldo had promised I had known him straight away. The nails had told me.

He did not introduce himself and he was well covered, with a hood over his face, despite the heat, but I knew who this must be. There was only one such man in Camelot.

'You have been hard to find,' he said in Frankish, without preamble.

'I was told it would be no problem for you,' I replied, slightly aggrieved.

'It wasn't until yesterday that the parcel spoke to me,' he continued unabashed, as if it had all been my fault.

'It helped save me from danger,' I explained, but he wasn't listening. I took the parcel from its hiding place and handed it across to the mysterious stranger. He took the parcel and for a moment we both held it and he spoke something in a language I should not have known but while we both held the nails in our hands, I understood clearly to be:

'And now the sword shall be complete.'

He was far too preoccupied to notice this strange thing happening. I wasn't.

'You have something for me in return I believe?' I asked him.

He nodded and reached into his voluminous cloak and pulled out an even smaller package.

He stared at me for the first time, with eyes of an intimidating blue:

'Tell him to plant them well. Their like will never be seen growing outside the Blessed Lands again.'

I swallowed hard. What had I got myself involved with here? I needed to stick to hitting people that needed hitting in future. Speaking of which:

'The danger I was placed in □ those people are still around.'

He nodded, as if this was of no consequence.

'They may be interested in this package too,' I continued.

'That is true,' he said finally.

'Well, we both need to be careful,' I insisted.

He laughed briefly at the idea.

'I am not laughing,' I said, a little tersely. Even he noticed that.

'Yes, you are right. You need to leave immediately. There is a horse in the stable opposite.' He pointed to a new building close by. 'There are clothes in the saddlebags. Put them on, you will not be stopped. Do not wait to make your goodbyes. Travel to Hamwic. A ship will be waiting for you.'

'How will I..?'

'They will know you by your clothes. Keep the package close.'

And with that he got up and almost in the blink of an eye was away.

I did what I was told. In the bags I found the clothes of a Lord, nothing like anything I had ever worn before, and there was a fine sword too and good boots.

I dressed myself and became another man. I found the boat and, again, was treated like a Lord. They even called me Lord Chaucere! We sailed the entire way, with me as the only passenger. I wondered if I could ever get used to living like this? I didn't think I could. It didn't come naturally and rubbed against the grain, but for a few weeks I managed.

Ansaldo was delighted with his package and I was delighted by my pay and so finished my adventure with sorcerers and what might be called magic by some. I vowed to have nothing to do with either again.

And how had that worked out, Chaucere?

It seemed that my destiny was always to be linked to that of this island realm and its King, no matter how hard I had tried to free myself from any such involvement. Perhaps that was the itch that had forced me back again? How then was I to scratch it?

It seemed, judging from past experience, that I did not need to do anything. The Fates, as ever, would put the path before my legs. I just needed to walk it. And with that concluded, I finished my drink and went to sleep in my own bed, on my own mattress. I could get used to that.

14
SIR DACE

I woke up in a better frame of mind and was enjoying the novelty of sitting in my own chair and putting my feet up on my own table, when the man who was to change everything in my life knocked on my door and walked into my house.

He was neither tall nor short, broad nor slim and was handsome in that way that many women seem to like. His hair was well trimmed, as was his beard and his face seemed to glow with health and well-being. He was, overall, neat with tidy looks and tidy manners. He had thrown what he obviously considered to be an old travel cloak over his finery, but even with this there was something bright and shiny about him and I immediately christened him Sir Dace, after the small fish that dart through the streams in these parts.

'Do I have the pleasure of addressing, Master Chaucere?' he asked, stressing the soft 'c' in a voice that gave very little clue as to his origins – unless you can count 'wealthy' as a location now. Perhaps you can, I have been away a while.

'It's Chaucere, rhymes with walker,' I corrected, 'and just plain Chaucere at that. Titles can slow a conversation down.'

'Excellent Chaucere, and may I take a seat?' He took a finely made leather glove off and indicated the only other chair.

'Of course, please excuse my manners. I never did finish the full manners lesson, I got stuck at fore-lock tugging.'

He laughed as he sat adding:

'I am quite sure you did.'

'And how should I address you?' I enquired.

'Call me...' he began before stopping to consider how much he should give away.

'Sir Dace has a nice ring to it,' I finished for him.

He found this amusing too. I had a feeling Sir Dace found a lot of things amusing. A good tune on the lute he would find amusing, an expensive foreign wine would be very amusing, but most of all I think he would find resting his head on the ample bosom of a young woman very amusing.

'Sir Dace! I like it! But I thought titles slowed a conversation down?'

'Dace is a very short word,' I conceded, which he acknowledged with a slight bow.

'And how might I be of help to you, Sir Dace? As we are getting on so well.'

'I have heard,' he said in his beautiful tones, 'from a Messenger of the King, that you are a man who knows what is what, and what's more, is a man to be trusted. And that once that trust is bought it stays bought and is not won over by a higher bid.'

'You have heard correctly, Sir Dace. That is the very definition of trust I believe. The other instance you describe is faithlessness and not worthy of any man.'

'Quite so, Chaucere. So… I have a delicate matter to attend to – for a friend.'

'Would this be a friend of the female gender?'

'My, you are as quick as the Messenger says. It is a lady … of some reputation, shall we say. A certain token of hers has fallen into the wrong hands and the current "owners" require gold before they will see it safely returned to her.'

'And you want me to do this?'

'No, no. I will do that chore – the token must be authenticated. But the exchange is to be carried out in public – in an alehouse – and I would like somebody to "watch my back" as one might say.'

'Somebody less noticeable than one of your friends from the Big House, like Dale?'

'Quite so and ... oh, I see what you have done! Very sly, Chaucere.'

'Not at all, Sir Dace. If I am going to put my neck on the block for someone, I generally like to know exactly what I am getting into.'

'I am afraid I can tell you no more.'

'Then that will have to do. Although a date, a place and time would be helpful too.'

'That much is easy.'

'Let us hope the rest is.'

I had five days, but I made a point of assessing the alehouse in question that very evening. It was not a place I knew well, although I had been there – as I had been most places – when I first arrived back in Camelot. I wore a woollen hat that I could tuck my hair into so its blackness was well hid. I put on a smock that I had seen charcoal makers wear, and to complete the impression, I smeared charcoal across my face. Charcoal was in great demand in the Burh and many burners could be seen selling their goods around the town. I hoped they would think me just another.

I sat and had two ales and a plate of indifferent food that I ate as if hungry – simply a busy working man having his evening meal.

By the third day I was getting a nod of the head from the alewife and I noticed my helping had increased. I hoped she just liked to encourage regulars.

So it was that nobody really even bothered to look up as I entered on Sater's day afternoon. I found my usual empty table. It was further from the fire, but provided a good view of the entrance door and the rest of the room. The alewife offered me ale and I took it gratefully, but said I would wait to eat. No point in wasting good food, I might be in a hurry. I sat with the hood of my cloak pulled down low as if catching up on forty winks, but I didn't miss a thing.

The alehouse was already full, but there was a steady turnover. The all-night professional drinkers weren't in yet to stake their claim on insensibility. Three likely lads entered. All three looked like the Western Celts I had known from my youth with the curly black hair and the full beards of their race. They might have been brothers. The seemed to know another two equally Celtic types who came in shortly afterwards but did not sit with them, despite there being enough stools. They took a place near the door. And one of those men I recognised thanks to his red hair. He had come out of the private house along with Gipp and Cecilio. I love that sort of coincidence; I am told that's how the gods arrange things. But we are also supposed to worship the one God now and I'm not sure what his position is on such chance occurrences. Not in favour of, is my thinking.

I tried not to stare too hard when Sir Dace came in – well, no more than anybody else did. He had on the older cloak that I had lent him, but he still had that poise and swagger that comes with a seat in the Big House. The three likely lads waved him over, smiling. I didn't like the smiles. I also didn't like the smiles that their two friends were trying to cover up. A horn was put in front of him, but he didn't drink from it.

I moved and stretched a bit. My sword was now a lot easier to reach. I ordered another ale and slopped this one about a bit, making some noise – obviously the drink was getting the better of me tonight. Sir Dace was in deep discussion with the leader of the three Western Celts. A lady's handkerchief was briefly shown, embroidered with family colours and a special symbol stitched, but I could not tell its meaning. It was obviously the work of a lady of some significance.

Sir Dace was getting angry. Not a good sign. I had the feeling there had been a price increase and the sellers were even willing to walk away from the deal. I think they were enjoying themselves. Sir Dace slammed his horn down on the table before speaking:

'We agreed the amount. I do not have more coin on me.'

'Then you'll have to get it,' said the leader of the Celts, with a nasty, nasal, tone.

I got up too quickly, bumping into the alewife and apologising profusely while stumbling backwards into Sir Dace's table. Mouthing further apologies, I turned proclaiming my need for the piss-house. Insults in the singsong language of the Western Celts were levelled at me and one of their number stood to reach for his sword, but I was quicker and behind the leader with my knife at his throat before they'd even finished cursing.

'Now, everybody sit down again,' I said politely. 'Sir Dace, please mind your back and keep an eye on those two by the door.'

Sir Dace drew a long knife:

'I most certainly will, thank you.'

'Good,' I continued, and pressed my knife against the leader's windpipe. 'You, my friend, will please pass the kerchief to this gentleman and he will in turn give you the agreed amount of coin. You will do this without argument and with discretion and I will not ask how you came upon this trinket.'

I gave him another reminder with my knife:

'I said now, please.'

The kerchief was handed across and Sir Dace left a purse with the agreed amount on the table.

We walked my captive out of the door. Before I let him go I left him with something to think about:

'I know you now,' I whispered in his ear. 'But you don't know me, because I am like the wind that never blows two nights the same and you will never find me. If I need to find you I will and that will be the end of you and the only wind you will ever know again will be blowing over your grave.'

I had no idea of what I had just spoken, but it sounded impressive to me and it had the desired effect on my captive as, when I threw him to the floor, he did not move to argue. Sir Dace had the two horses as requested. I jumped on mine in one impressive leap, which was very impressive, and the stubborn mare absolutely refused to move. I pulled on her reins and still she refused to budge an inch. That is the way with horses sometimes I have realised; always a mind of their own and this one did not take kindly to being leapt on by strangers.

'Stop messing around, man,' said Sir Dace, as he, with expert horsemanship, took my horses leathers and led her off – to my embarrassment and mortification. We were soon lost in more of the numerous backstreets and passageways of Camelot. The streets where beggars, trulls and working women seemed to outnumber the lawful folk going about their business.

We returned the horses to the ostler, Ilbert, who had become something of a friend. There I changed into my normal clothes and washed my face free of soot and charcoal from a bucket of water.

'Very clever, Chaucere,' said Sir Dace, looking at me closely in the twilight. 'I did not recognise you at all and for a moment I thought you had abandoned me.'

'As if I would, Sir Knight,' I replied. 'Besides, I think you have another purse for me about your person.'

He laughed and threw me a bag of coin. 'As we agreed, Chaucere. Many thanks from me, and if I can ever be of assistance to you, ask for Lord Petroc at the castle. But with you I will remain, Sir Dace.'

'Thank you, Sir Dace. Now best be getting up the hill. You don't want to be dressed in all that finery at this time of night, in this part of Camelot.'

He looked thoughtfully at me before speaking:

'Has it got so bad then?'

'Was it ever any different?' I replied.

He nodded. 'Yes, I do believe it was – when The Big House was first built. Now though, going through those back streets, I have seen poverty and disorder of a scale that I did not believe existed. I do not think that the King and his advisors are aware of it either.'

'That's the problem when you live in a Big House on the hill. You only look down on people.'

'Is that why you would not live there, Chaucere?'

I had to laugh at this: 'I have never been invited, Sir Dace!'

'Yes, I believe I am right though. You wouldn't live there would you, Chaucere? You would not be comfortable.'

I laughed again and affected as thick an accent as any local farmer or peddler. 'It's not for the likes of me, Master Knight.'

It was Sir Dace's turn to laugh. 'You don't talk like a local any more, Chaucere,'

I tugged my forelock respectfully.

'If the Master says so.'

Lord Petroc's own horse stirred restless in the stable. 'We will talk on this another day, Chaucere. For now, fare-thee-well.' He mounted his horse easily and rode away, back up to the Big House on the Hill.

15
RACHEL

I was not dressed for company. In fact I was hardly dressed at all.

I would be the first to admit that my owning a house has led me into some bad habits. I did get some kecks on before I opened the door at least, but the blushes on the face of the young woma n standing in front of me led me to believe I still needed some practice with the whole door business.

'Yes?' I said, more aggressively than I intended.

This was not me at my best, but then again I was not at my best. The previous evening I had discovered a new alehouse. The alewife had a new beer. It was good and I had drunk my fill. Then I had drunk some more. Finally I had drunk too much.

'I will come back later – at a better time,' the maid said, turning and casting her eyes to the ground.

I remembered my manners, or at least that such things existed and were best used when talking to attractive young women with masses of very dark hair that their coif could barely contain.

'Excuse me, please,' I manage to splutter out. 'Give me a moment and I will be back with you – more suitably attired.'

She didn't look sure. I didn't blame her.

It only took moments to find a tunic and my boots and to let Timothy out of the back door. I think I had frightened the woman enough for one day without introducing her to a hound the size of a pony. Timothy, though, seemed quite interested in meeting my guest, but gentle encouragement of the booted variety convinced him to begin his regular tour of the neighbourhood by departing through the backdoor. Hounds, I believe, are all essentially very male, and like good comrades-in-arms are not likely to take offence at a friendly tap or ill-chosen word. Cats, by

119

comparison, are all like wives and you'd best be on your best behaviour in their presence at all times – not that I have had either wife or cat. So, what do I know?

The woman was still standing where I had left her, looking as if she was unsure whether she should be there, or at home with the cat I am sure she cherished.

'Please, do come in,' I said with more gallantry than I normally generate at that time of the morning. I gestured for her to enter with what I hoped was a welcoming air. She responded as if I was clearing the air after a particularly ripe fart. Eventually she entered, but I swore she took a quick breath first.

'Master Chaucere,' she began as she sat on the seat I kept free for these occasions. I sat on the other.

'Chaucere will suffice, thank you,' I responded. 'I feel as comfortable with "Master" as I do with "Sir" and "Lord", but although I am obliged to use those I can at least refuse the title of Master.'

'Of course. And I am simply Rachel,' she said, with a pleasing twinkle in her eye. 'I have never much cared for Mistress Rachel either.'

'And how might I be of assistance, Simply Rachel?'

' My father is a close friend of Abram. He told us you were a good man. A man to be trusted.'

'That was very kind of Abram. I liked him. I hope he is doing well.'

'As do we.'

'You have heard nothing then?'

'Sadly not,' she answered, shaking what was really a very fine head, in which two beautifully round and very brown eyes sat above a well-formed nose and generous mouth. She had a healthy colour and the whole effect was without artifice or adornment. It was not a look favoured by courtly ladies, but was no less appealing for that, and simply showed that when women were dressing to impress each other they often forgot what men found attractive.

'He did promise to send us word when he was safe and settled,' she added. 'But messages can take forever and are often lost on the journey.'

'As are the travellers,' I added without thinking, but catching the concern that crossed her face, I quickly corrected myself.

'Not that any such fate has happened to Abram, I'm sure. He is far too clever for that!

She smiled rather weakly. Was she contracted to Abram in some way? She seemed rather young but older men have their attraction too, or so our young queen would have us believe.

'Perhaps you should tell me how I can be of assistance to you, Rachel.'

She nodded quickly, as if glad to move on. 'My father Isak is a healer of some renown. I assist when I can, but mostly I help make ends meet with sewing jobs. We are not wealthy, for some reason the sick believe that our religion prevents us from being deserved of a fair return for my father's administrations.

'Also,' here she stopped to smile warmly, 'my father is a good man and would rather go hungry himself than see a poor body suffer if he can do anything to prevent it. But lately he has himself not been well and we have struggled.'

'I am sorry to hear that, of course if I can help in any way – as friends of Abram.'

'That is very kind of you, Chaucere, but that isn't our problem at the moment.' She bit her lip, obviously angry. 'We have a small house where my father helps the sick. Last week a young horseman came to our door. He was shaved and not unwholesome, his clothes looked clean enough and he spoke well as if he'd had an education. He told us that our "business" and those that visited us were in great danger from robbers, but that he and his friends – for what he called a trifling sum – could keep us safe from these bad men who would otherwise, he was sure, do us great harm.'

'He said that, did he? Offered you his protection?'

'So he said. My father told him exactly where he could go with his protection! This stranger said he would be back in a week, with his friends, to show us exactly how easily bad things happened.'

I leapt out of my seat as I exclaimed:

'Protection! What is the world coming to? Before towns the bandits would only just come and burn your house down if you couldn't fight them off. At least you had a chance! Protection, how low is that?!'

I realised I had made the seamstress cower back in her seat.

'My apologies, Rachel. This is a new form of wickedness to me and we must stamp it out before it takes hold.'

'Then you will help us, Chaucere?'

'Oh yes, I will indeed help.'

'We do not have great wealth, but I can perhaps mend clothes that are in need of repair if that would suffice – or even make a new tunic or kecks if you can purchase the cloth?'

I sat down again and put her at her ease.

'Don't concern yourself about such things. This is one sickness I can help stop spreading and that is payment enough.'

'I should tell you that he warned us off trying to get help. He said his friends were not as easy going as he was. I fear they would out-number you.'

I thought for a moment then replied:

'Unless, of course, I was the one outnumbering.' I thought on. Who did I know that would benefit from a healer?

'Tell me Rachel, does your father make a cream or potion for burns?'

'Well, yes, he makes one that is very soothing and healing. Why, if I may ask?'

I smiled with some satisfaction. 'Because that is all we shall need. But we might need a lot of it. Can you put together such a quantity? Say in a week?'

Rachel nodded.

Rachel and Isak's house was lowly, but very comfortable. A lot of work had gone into making it homely and warm. Wall hangings, in bright designs, stopped the drafts and gave everything a very cheery aspect. More hangings divided the one room into sleeping and living quarters with a further area for private discussions with the healer.

Isak was clearly the father of his daughter and had a manner that immediately generated trust and made you feel better. His hair was long and hung in ringlets around his large head on which a small cap was precariously balanced. His beard was full and streaked with grey. Sadly, as his daughter had confided, he was not in the best of health.

'Sometimes I am convinced, Chaucere, that we were not meant to live so close together and in such numbers.' He spoke lightly, but you could tell even this effort tired him.

'I have seen large towns, cities they called them, in other countries that I am sure were larger than Camelot. People live there, raise their children and many do not die before their time,' I felt obliged to point out.

'Perhaps the people grow in harmony with their surroundings and they learn to live together, to reach a balance. Camelot grows too fast – not the castle of course, but everything else – the ramshackle huts and hovels that surround it. The wretches, the dispossessed, those without hope – they all flock here hoping for a better life.' He did not speak as if he thought they were ever likely to find this exalted ideal.

'Isn't that what we have all been promised though, Isak? A better life?'

'Perhaps, but for all now actually living in Camelot? I fear not and certainly not all at once.'

'Yet, you came here, Isak?'

Isak laughed, somewhat wearily and Rachel looked over from where she was stitching by the fire to smile in her turn.

'My people are travellers. Our homeland was taken away from our forefathers many, many generations ago, and since then few of us put down roots easily and often we are forced to move on as we become the brunt for anger and superstition. Yet Chaucere, thank you for pointing out my own hypocrisy!'

'I assure you I didn't mean it to sound like that.'

'No, it's fine, Chaucere.' Isak settled back further into his seat. 'I suppose you could say I displayed opportunism of the most self-interested kind. When a large number of people begin to congregate, so the Nosoi will not be far behind.'

'I don't think I am acquainted with the Nosoi,' I added.

'They are the spirits of plague, sickness and disease. At least according to those whose empire preceded the one that governed these isles for so many years and left us with such a legacy.'

'It seems that there has always been a previous empire?'

'Oh yes, as there will always be a next.'

'And men to profit by them,' I added, hearing a horse arrive outside Rachel and Isak's small hut.

'Come out old man!' the rider called.

Isak and Rachel looked at me nervously, but I smiled to reassure them:

'Let them wait.' I gestured for Isak and Rachel to remain seated.

'Don't make me get off my horse, old man. Remember, this is all for your own protection. Protection is important!'

I got up out of my seat and straightened my tunic, adjusted my sword belt and strolled to the door. I opened it, smiling:

'How right you are,' I said to the young man on the horse. 'Isak has taken heed of what you said and has indeed found some protection. You will not be needed, so just piss off like a good lad. Your mother will be wondering where you are.'

As Rachel had mentioned, the rider looked surprisingly well presented for such a nefarious activity, youthful, well-cut brown hair, cleanly shaven and a clean tunic. He looked familiar as well, perhaps I had known his father. I sighed, you know you are getting on in years when even the toe-rags are looking young. His composure was only momentarily disturbed.

'Oh, found themselves a swordsman have they? Any good with that pig-sticker?'

'That's for you to find out,' I replied, stretching a little.

'Think you can take me?' he sneered.

'Boy,' I replied, to his obvious annoyance. 'I wouldn't need my sword for that, just my belt to give you a good hiding.'

'Let's see what my friends have to say about that, shall we?' He gave a whistle and another three horsemen appeared, not as well groomed but looking more suited to the job. They rode up to pose in line with their cocky leader, whose agitation was now being felt by his horse.

'You've gone rather quiet, pig sticker' he gloated. 'Cat got your tongue?'

'One moment,' I told him, raising my hand.

'What?' he said, becoming irritated.

'I must insist,' I told him.

'Do not...'

'Hush! People are concentrating here!'

He looked around, now much put out, realising something must be wrong. One man should normally be quaking in front of four horsemen.

'Emald!' I shouted. 'Have you all had a good look?'

'Yes, Chaucere,' he replied, stepping out of a nearby hut.

'I recognise two of them,' said a new voice upon leaving another hut.

'Me too,' added a third man.

'I know another,' someone else chipped in.

The horsemen wheeled around as Emald and eight of his fellow smiths appeared, as if by magic, to surround the riders. Each of them was armed with the largest of hammers that they owned and blacksmiths have large hammers.

'Now,' I said, clapping my hands. 'If I can have your attention.' I certainly did have it. 'As you may just be beginning to realise, from now on you are all marked men – you too, handsome!'

The young man bristled noticeably and looked round flapping his soup-hole trying to think of a witty answer. He failed.

'So listen here: do not think of plying your dirty trade in Camelot again, because not only will you never get your horse shod here again, you will all have trouble walking with your kneecaps shattered. The smiths of Camelot are not people you should bother and you have succeeded in annoying nine of them.'

'Ten,' bellowed a new voice, boomed from a redheaded and bearded giant of a man joining us from the main street. 'My apologies for my tardiness.'

'No apology needed, my friend,' I said.

'Glad I could make it in time to catch Joss Winbourne who still owes me for two shoes.'

One of the riders, a surly sort with a pockmarked face, stirred uncomfortably.

'Joss Winbourne, how fortunate for you to have this chance to settle your debt. Please do so before you leave – which you will be doing straight after.'

Winbourne went to look through his purse.

'Best to just throw him the full purse,' I said. 'It'll save time and I know you must be keen to be on your way, as you will need to be out of Camelot by nightfall.' Winbourne complied, as the others similarly shifted uneasily on their horses.

'This is not ended,' Handsome finally managed to spit out.

'Wrong again, you nasty little sard,' I replied. 'It is well and truly over, so piss off. And, everybody with the sard, you can piss off too! So that's communal off pissing starting now. I thank you.'

The blacksmiths opened a gap in their circle for the horsemen to ride though, which they did at some speed, jeers and insults helping them on their way.

'Well,' I said, rubbing my hands in satisfaction. 'I don't know about you men, but I have to say that I rather enjoyed that. Now, who's for beer then?'

The smiths didn't need asking twice. They set off to the nearest alehouse while I said my goodbyes.

Rachel came out of her house, looking ten years younger now that the worry had been lifted.

'We are indebted to you, Chaucere.'

'Not at all, Rachel. That was so enjoyable, I feel I should be paying you!'

'You seem to make a habit out of helping people.'

'Sadly,' I sighed, 'I wish I was more charitable, but my life has been mainly about taking care of myself.'

'I doubt that somehow, Chaucere. After all, did you not give Emald the Smith a purse of money to be spent on medicines for the poor?'

And there I was, Chaucere the Sword-for-hire, Chaucere the Brawler, Chaucere the Hard Man, suddenly blushing in front of a maid nearly half his years, caught in an act of charity with his tongue tied.

I executed a quick bow and hurried to catch up with the drinkers, needing a large pot myself. As I walked, a thought crossed my mind. I remembered where I had seen handsome boy, with Cecilio of course. Now that was interesting, very interesting. I wasn't sure how, but I would certainly think on it.

16
THE BIG HOUSE

I was seeing Sir Dace quite regularly at this time. He always
'just happened to be passing by' and found himself in need of
a drink. He had a big thirst, but never so much that he couldn't
get on his horse to head home. We would talk about not very
much, but the hours soon passed by most pleasurably.
Sometimes we would eat and he was always complementary to
the alewife, especially Mistress Aila when we frequented her
alehouse – as we did often. She took quite a shine to him, and
why not? He was handsome, good company, not married and
not everybody could see the sadness in his eyes that was obvious
to me.

It was in the early spring, when I realised I had not seen him
for a handful of weeks. I had been busy that year seeing to yet
more of the scum threatening our honest tradesmen on their
rounds outside the town. I was becoming hard pressed to think
of more ruses and diversions. I was musing on the subject when
the guard entered my house without knocking on the door.

It's strange, but since gaining a door I have become very
particular about people knocking on same. The acquisition of
such indulgences as a door has brought about changes in my
character I am not altogether sure I approve of. However, as I
am even less taken by sleeping in ditches and eating slops, I
suppose I will just have to live with this alteration.

'You are wanted at The Big House,' the guard said, without
preamble.

I continued to clean my nails with a pocketknife that I had
acquired for this very task. Further evidence of the changes that
were being visited upon my person. Not only would I once not
have used a special knife for this purpose, I would not have even

noticed that my nails were in need of any such attention. Having bought the knife I was keen to make a good job of the task and rude guards who did not know how to treat a man's door could go piss up their own arsehole.

'Did you hear me, cur?' the guard growled, in a fashion he must have learnt from somebody who could do it for real. He needed to work much harder.

'I'm sorry,' I said, as if just suddenly aware of his presence. 'Were you addressing me?'

'I don't see anybody else in here,' he said, attempting the growl again – but still not getting it right.

'That's true enough,' I had to concede. 'But from the way you spoke I just assumed you were talking to the table or chair or that chest, because it is certainly not the way I expect to be addressed. Especially not in my own house.'

I looked at him levelly. He was only young, new to his beard, perhaps the nephew of some minor noble who was hoping to bluster and bluff his way to a seat at the Round Table. He wasn't going to get it this way.

'You should jump at the opportunity to please your betters,' he said, getting really quite worked up now.

'No. Actually I shouldn't. Now, get out of my house and try the whole knocking on door business again and then we'll see how well we get on.'

'How dare you?!' I could see him bristle, his hand hovering over his sword, which would be a very silly thing for him to contemplate doing and I thought I owed it to his parents to let him know this.

'How dare I? Let me consider that for a moment.' I considered away as he fumed. 'First of all I would say that I "dare" this because somebody of importance wants my assistance and will therefore not be pleased if I arrive incapacitated or even not at all. Secondly I dare because you have not given me a good reason why I, a free man, should put myself out to assist you – a mannerless pig. And lastly I dare because you are in my house uninvited and that makes you little better than an intruder and if I was to stick you I think most sensible men would consider me within my rights.'

The hapless guard was obviously not accustomed to anything other than total obedience from the gull he had been told to fetch. He had no idea what to do next.

'Come on then,' I said, taking pity on him, picking up my best coat., and running a hand through my hair. I had a feeling I was not going up the Hill to empty the grates.

This was actually my first time in Camelot proper, the castle that is. Certainly since it was finished. I wasn't exactly welcomed like a visiting nobleman. It was interesting to find that the building now had so many servant corridors and staircases that I was soon quite lost. Eventually we arrived in a corridor that looked in good order, with some rather fine tapestries and wall hangings. The guard knocked on an equally fine door – I am something of an expert on doors now. There was an answer from within and the guard entered. I sauntered behind, giving it my best saunter.

Sir Dace was dressed in what I presumed were his everyday clothes, a number of elaborate under and top shirts and a heavy tied robe that looked ideal for keeping out the chill that filled the room, despite the fire pan he had burning merrily near an open window.

'Chaucere for you, Sir' said the guard, somewhat testily I thought. So as he left, to help him on his way, I gave him one more piece of advice:

'Don't ever call anybody a cur, son. It just sounds vaguely ridiculous, as if you had never been taught to speak normally but had to learn insults from a teacher.'

The guard really did bite his lip as he bowed to the knight and departed.

'Making friends, Chaucere?' asked Sir Dace, very amused.

'Always,' I affirmed.

'I told him to treat you politely, as he would my own self.'

'In that case I can see why you have taken to your bed, less all this politeness knocking around causes too many fights and arguments.'

'My apologies then. Dale offered to go, but was then sent away on the King's duty. Shall I have that fool reprimanded?'

I threw myself down onto a chair that turned out to be more comfortable than it looked.

'It's just a normal day for most in Camelot,' I replied.

'Yes, I have heard rumours of such overwrought behaviour. I don't like it! It's not how these guards are trained to behave. Which is why I think a reprimand is in order.'

I waved my hand in what I hoped was a suitably dismissive manner, leaving it up to him. I needed to work harder on these subtle gestures as I have found a kick in the teeth can often offend.

'So, Sir Dace, you could perhaps tell me why you were not capable of making the journey down the hill. Nice as it is to visit and taste your hospitality,' I added, eyeing his wine.

Lord Petroc laughed and poured a healthy measure into a real silver cup. He handed it to me and I had a careful sip. Then I had a proper drink. It was good, very good – without the heavy spicing that has to be used so often in our northern lands to hide the spoilt taste.

'Now this,' I observed, 'could put me off ale for a lifetime, or maybe a month or two. I am glad the stress and strain of knight-hood has some compensation for what you must endure.'

The young knight laughed. 'It's not all wine and feasting, Chaucere. Whatever you may think.'

'Then I am disappointed. Perhaps I won't bother looking for advancement after all.'

'For example,' he continued, filling up his own cup. 'At the moment I must while away my days drinking … while under arrest, awaiting news of whether I will be tried for treason.'

The wine tasted suddenly sour and I put my cup carefully down to better concentrate on what the man in front of me, whose welfare I suddenly realised I cared more about than I had previously suspected, was about to tell me.

'And I must not leave the castle, by order of the King, less my life is forfeit.'

'When I asked for an explanation, Sir Dace, you didn't have to come up with something quite so dramatic. A head cold would have been ample excuse.'

'I must admit Chaucere, I look forward to a head cold, if it means I still have a head to suffer it.'

I sighed and felt sorely put out. For some reason I remembered an incense tent that I had relaxed in many years ago in a country now so far away, in miles and time, that I could scarce remember its name. Various seeds, herbs and flowers were put into a cup and the cup placed on a fire. The incense created filled the tent and all lying and seated within were filled with a great peace which gave way to a feeling of relaxation I have never known before or since. I wish I had some of that incense to throw on the fire pan now, instead I took another draught of my wine.

'All right, what is to be done to free you from this slur? How can I help?'

Lord Petroc smiled.

'Thank you my friend. Not just for the offer of assistance, but for not questioning my loyalty to my Lord.'

'Sir Dace, I would question my own loyalty long before I would even think to consider yours. I have a feeling that it concerns the business that first brought me to your attention? The lady?'

Lord Petroc nodded shortly. 'It has been dressed up in other clothes, but that is the gist of it, lacking the evidence you helped me retrieve they cannot state an accusation directly.'

'And the trial you mentioned is what?'

'A pretext – it will ensure that the matter comes to public attention and the resulting fuss will condemn me, while the original trial will be soon forgotten.'

'And the answer to this is what then?'

'I can ask you to be my second,' he said with a smile.

'A second? Do you talk about a duel? Are you mad?'

'I do. And no I am not mad.'

I stood up, much agitated. 'The King himself has banned single combat, under penalty of death!'

'Only within the bounds of Camelot. The meeting will take place on the Field of Penitence. The challenge has been made and accepted. I would not ask, but my knightly "brothers" seem suddenly reluctant to tie their colours to my lance.'

'Oh hell man, I am not worried about that! But single combat is not something to take lightly. People die!'

'It is to first blood only.'

'But that first blood can be a sword plunged into your gut!'

'With armour on?'

I paced the room, much put out. 'Who is it that you fight?'

'Lord Hudde.'

'What manner of man is he?'

'He is loud and brash and boasts continuously of his wealth. He has many lands in the North it seems, but I do wonder how they can be so productive as to make him quite so rich, or perhaps his tenants are simply squeezed for their contribution to his well-being.'

'Is he a fighter? Is he practised?'

'He is large and strong and always talks about his skill with the sword.'

'Then you must count on your speed, wear light armour, tire him down, do not try to trade blows with a stronger man. If he is overconfident, then you can beat him – use your brain!'

Lord Petroc clasped my arm: 'Of course, how can I fail? I shall bludgeon him with my brain until I draw blood.'

17

THE FIELD OF PENITENCE

The Field of Penitence is a water meadow, an hour or two's ride from the Castle, where the river begins to broaden out on its journey to the sea. Nice enough on a fine summer's day; on a misty spring morning when winter has still not released it's grip on the land, this 'field of honour' feels exactly like what it is: a boggy piece of poor grazing with a big smelly ditch running down one side.

'I don't think Lord Hudde is coming,' I said cheerfully to the Justice, there to see that the newly created idea of chivalry was upheld. 'If we wrap this up now we can all be back in Camelot for a hearty breakfast.'

'It is not yet late,' the Justice replied. He was a sour-faced individual of middle years with closely cut grey hair, who I imagined had long ago traded his blood for a colder and more unpleasant liquid, such as that which sluggishly flowed along the ditch.

I looked back down the path, along which we had recently ridden. I could see no sign on the man or his second. There was hope yet that we might be spared this show.

It had been a week since Lord Petroc had broken his news and in that time I had tried to teach him the skills that might save his life. As I suspected, he was not a bad swordsman, but he hung on to ideas such as fair play and honour that would surely see him skewered. Unless, that is, Lord Hudde was of similar mind and likely to play by the rules that half-wits had invented in their dotage – in which case they might as well have been fighting with rose briars.

The sound of trumpets woke me from my contemplation. They weren't coming from along the path though. Approaching the Field of Penitence by river, lit by coloured lanterns, and rowed by uniformed oarsmen, came two barges full of people. One barge held only ladies in their courtly attire. It was gay and festooned with banners and bunting. Minstrels entertained the passengers; lutes and harps were being strummed with vigour.

'He's brought bloody minstrels!' I exclaimed, exasperated, in the direction of the Justice, who at least had the decency to look properly embarrassed.

The other barge held Lord Hudde, his helm flung back and his manly locks flowing in the breeze. I recognised him immediately, although the last time I had seen him he was not wearing bright shiny mail, but only a single sheet. The moustached face was still unpleasantly the same. I looked amongst his companions. There was no sign of Cecilio that I could see, however...

'Shit, shit, shit,' I muttered.

'What is it Chaucere?' Lord Petroc sounded genuinely worried for the first time, which considering his situation may just have indicated a distinct lack of imagination.

'Your Lord Hudde, I know him,' I spoke quietly, only for my companion's benefit. 'It was not a happy encounter.'

'No,' said Lord Petroc, looking at the barges with some distaste. 'Hudde does not go out of his way to make friends, because he has no need of friends. He only needs an audience.'

An audience Lord Hudde did indeed have, even if he had brought it himself.

His barge approached a small wooden pier that I now noticed protruding some way into the river. To the strident blast of a new fanfare, Lord Hudde grabbed hold of the tie-up post at the end of the pier and heaved himself from his barge. There he posed for his audience and even elicited a small round of applause. He did look a sight, polished mail now shining quite magnificently in the early morning light. But all that armour would be heavy and, on this surface, tiring.

'Remember,' I hissed, to get Lord Petroc's attention. 'Wear him out. Keep to the boggy ground. Do not get into a trade-off of blows!'

'Yes, I hear,' said Lord Petroc. He heard but did not listen.

The fight did not go well from the start. Despite my protestations, Lord Petroc still wore mail of some weight. Therefore he could not take maximum advantage of his fleetness of foot and better mobility. Also Lord Hudde had a remarkable reach, which did not assist our strategy, and he wielded a mighty ring-sword. It was the largest I had ever seen, perhaps measuring three foot, and he was pleased to introduce it to everybody as 'The Man Cleaver'; news that only reinforced my attitude with regard to the naming of weapons. He also pulled out a bejewelled dagger; rubies and sapphires both from what I could see. That was just made for showing off, but I was certain it was also sharp enough.

'Make the big clod run around, back him into the marsh!' I muttered under my breath, as such advice can attract censure from the Justice. I also didn't like the look of some of Lord Hudde's lackeys. Although there were obviously one or two from the wrong end of the Round Table, some of the men now debarging were much more seriously equipped for mayhem. Cecilio was not amongst them, but I was sure that they were all kindred spirits.

They had no compunction about cheering their champion on.

Lord Hudde did not do much, but what he did do, he did well, relying on his superior strength and his expensive mail and toughened leather. Lord Petroc should have been aggressive and taken the initiative, but he was far too hesitant and patient. Instead of intercepting his opponent's attack or using body leverage he ended up receiving the edge of 'The Man Cleaver' with the edge of his own sword – an elementary mistake. One time he had Lord Hudde on a wet patch of the ground, which caused him to slip and instead of pressing home his advantage, when Hudde raised his hand, Lord Petroc let him get up again.

'No, no, no!' I cursed the decency of the genial, friendly, Sir Dace and wondered what I could do to save his life.

The outcome was inevitable, but it could have been worse. Lord Petroc went to counter strike in the middle of Hudde's attack but his timing was out. He caught a blow on his arm, which slid down the mail and easily cut through the leather near his elbow, down into flesh.

'First blood! First blood' I shouted, racing to where Sir Dace, his sword arm useless, stood. I caught the look in Hudde's eye and for a moment I thought he would strike his defenceless opponent.

'Sheath your sword, Sir!' the Justice added to my cry. 'Honour is satisfied.'

I reached Lord Petroc as he slipped to his knees and immediately tied one of the bandages I had prepared around his upper arm under the mail. Quick thinking like this has saved many a man from bleeding out on the battlefield from what looked at first to be minor wounds.

'Damn, that stings,' cursed Lord Petroc. 'I have been bested it seems.'

'Only because you fought like a fool,' I replied, none too pleased. 'Did you want to die?'

'No. At least I don't think so.'

I looked into the young Knight's eye and for the first time became aware of a deeper malady lurking there that I had not previously been aware of.

'Come on. It's not that deep. You'll live yet. But let us get somebody better qualified than me to see to this and stitch it.'

I stood up and realised that the victor Hudde was busy taking plaudits from his supporters on the barge. He strutted like a cock and for a moment if my sword had been out I could easily have run him through myself. A cough from his second brought me to the Lord's attention. For a minute he seemed taken aback by what he spied written in my face. The cheers though soon restored his swagger and he approached me, sneering:

'I know you! Two times you have come to my attention now. Do not let there be a third or it will be an end to you.'

He stomped off back to his lickspittles and lacy ladies.

'And I know you,' I murmured to myself. 'And I know the company you keep, Sir Knight.'

The contempt in my voice would have given him pause for thought, had he heard it. I considered an appropriate response, but I couldn't afford to stand around posturing while my friend bled out.

With the help of the Justice I sat Sir Dace on his horse. The bleeding seemed to have abated, but I did not like his colour. He was also starting to sweat although the day was still chill.

'I will be fine,' he insisted. 'Just get me back to the castle. All I need is some rest.'

'I don't think so, Sir Dace! We need to discuss that perform-ance of yours in some detail I feel, lest next time you do not fair so well.'

I got onto my own horse as the Justice approached.

'The wound is not deep,' he said, with something approaching derision. 'The Knight will mend.'

'Yes, thank you so much for your augury and your time today.' I pressed the customary purse into his hand. He took it with something like bad grace, before replying:

'Forgive me when I say, I hope I do not get to meet with you again for a very long time.'

'I can assure you Justice, the feeling is reciprocated.'

The Justice grunted something else I missed and returned to his own horse. On the river, Lord Hudde had moved his large bulk back onto the barge and somebody had opened a firkin of ale and everyone was making merry. I hoped they all sunk.

I rode up to the defeated knight, keeping a smile on my face:

'Come Sir Dace, I have a rather attractive lady I would very much like you to meet, if you are of a mind.'

Lord Petroc smiled weakly:

'How could I not be of a mind? An attractive lady? Lead on, Chaucere, lead on.'

I led him, and his horse, back to Camelot.

Rachel had a small corner of her humble house curtained-off for the sick in need of constant attention and despite Lord Petroc's protestations we placed him there. He complained, of course, but I noticed that he was grateful to lie back and drink the hot, sweet, brew that Rachel made from dried fruits and herbs.

Isak pulled the curtain across to examine the knight's wound. I joined Rachel and took a seat by the window.

'Here,' said Rachel, passing me another cup. 'This won't do you any harm either.'

'Thank you Rachel, and your father, for seeing to the knight.'

'As if we would object! Do you think so little of us?'

'Of course not, my apologies. I know you to be good people.' I drank my drink. It was very refreshing.

'Thank you, Chaucere. Your good opinion matters to us both.'

I nodded, slightly embarrassed, before speaking again:

'And, whatever needs to be done – if you require special medicines – anything, just ask.'

Rachel nodded then also sipped her drink. 'You like this knight I think, Chaucere.'

'Like you and your father, Rachel, he is also good people.'

'It is unlike you, I have never yet heard a good word to pass your lips concerning the folk on the hill.'

'That is because I believe too many of them are like Lord Hudde and too few like Sir Dace.'

Rachel knotted her brow:

'And who might Lord Hudde be?'

'My friend's opponent in this foolish game of single combat,' I said, with a sigh loud enough to threaten to do some damage to my frame. 'An unpleasant man, if I am any judge, and one whose choice of acquaintances leaves something to be desired – at the very least. At the worse I think he may not be worthy of any title, let alone Lord and Knight.'

'I see,' said Rachel. She looked at me very seriously before she continued. 'And what Chaucere, are you going to do about it then?'

She had me there. Some part of me wanted to say: 'why me?' But another part of me, the much larger part, knew I would not get any rest unless I did do something.

I was saved from further uncertainty by the return of Isak.

'I have given him a sleeping draught, but he wishes to speak to you before Morpheus claims him,' he said.

'How does he fair?'

Isak looked unsettled for a moment:

'Although it is a large wound it is not deep and I have sewn it up. I would have expected it to stop bleeding by now, but it still weeps. Tell me, was he in good health?'

'Always, as far as I could tell.'

Isak seemed relieved:

'Good. Then I am sure we have nothing to worry about. I have attended men with much worse injuries than his and they made full recoveries as long as the wound is kept clean. Now, hurry before he sleeps – he was most insistent on talking with you.'

I pulled the curtain aside to reveal the bed where Lord Petroc was now laid out, his eyes closed. I didn't know exactly who

Morpheus might be, but I hoped he was only a temporary custodian of the man. I had seen men brought lower from a single sword thrust, but I had seen men look far better as well.

'So Sir Dace! I hope you have no more similar duties on your mind for me to assist you with? I must admit to a certain weariness. I might even need to have a nap myself.'

The knight, usually so full of cheer, could barely open his eyes. I'm not sure what Isak had administered to him, I just hoped it wasn't too much.

'I need you to go to Camelot, Chaucere. A most important favour to ask.'

'Of course.' I replied.

He held up his right hand in which there was grasped a simple token. He thrust it into my hand.

'Take this to the castle. Give it to a guard and you will be taken to the Lady Ansithe. Say her ... honour was ... upheld.' His voice was getting weaker as Isak's draft had its effect.

'Why not wait until you're better and give it to her yourself?' I said, in what I hoped was a light-hearted tone. But by then Lord Petroc had surrendered to what I hoped was simply death's more affable kin.

18
THE LADY

The guard at the wicket gate kept me waiting for a ridiculous amount of time, but it didn't dent my smile one bit. It paid to smile at Camelot guards, not because it speeded matters up one jot, but simply because it got up their noses in a way that they couldn't do anything about. Not even the most brutal of captains would have taken 'smiled in an annoying manner' as a good enough reason for one of his men beating up on a local. Not yet anyway.

A ferrety young man wearing unpleasantly coloured leggings, and a frankly ludicrous cap, turned up in response to Lord Petroc's token. He muttered something that I assumed meant 'follow me', so that's what I did.

I followed him up and then I followed him down and then I followed him up again – a maze of stair wells that served to reinforce just how large the castle of Camelot was; as if the simple sight of that massive pile of stones wasn't enough in itself. I don't think I was being taken the scenic route as there wasn't much to see, but it was nicer than the servants' back ways I had trod before.

Eventually I arrived at a door. It was a very nice door, better than Sir Dace's, but as I had one of my own now, I wasn't as impressed as I might have once been. The boy left with another mutter that didn't say much for castle staff manners. Behind the door there was something much more impressive. Slim and coy with large downcast brown eyes that a forest doe would have envied, she was dressed in a simple gown of linen and her nut-brown hair was discreetly covered with a simple veil held in place by a plain coronet. I judged her to be a handmaiden of the Lady Ansithe and smiled in what I hoped was an appropriate manner for handmaidens. I was still saving up the smile I had been practising for the Lady Ansithe; my stock of smiles for high-bred ladies running somewhat low of late.

'Please, this way,' she said. Her voice was low, rich and unassuming and only sent shivers half way down my back. What it did the rest of the way down was nobody's business but my own.

I followed her into a series of rooms that were not as showy as I was expecting, although it was well decorated with very expensive tapestries. If anything, the rooms reminded me of what I had come to think of as "Rachel's house": colourful and comfortable without being too full of the trappings that many women seem to favour. This is all according to my limited experience of course, experience which does, however, include ladies of royal blood from many other countries and climes. This is not a boast, just a statement of fact with regard to the more colourful parts of the life that I have, on occasion, lived.

One tapestry that stood out was of a hill rising from the shimmering water. At the top of the hill was a tower. I knew this by reputation to be Glestingaburg, which many considered a sacred place although I had never had occasion to visit it myself.

Two finely carved chairs were arranged by a small table at the centre of the room. In one of the chairs there sat a woman who had to be the Lady Ansithe. She was everything I expected of a lady of Camelot. Gorgeously dressed in what I took to be imported brightly coloured silks, perhaps more handsome than beautiful, but none the less attractive for that. She had a strong jaw and deep blue eyes that were brighter than any gems I had ever seen, although they were also just about as warm. She smiled winningly enough though, as she offered me the other chair.

'Please do be seated, Chaucere. I understand you prefer to be addressed in that fashion?'

'Yes, thank you, my lady.' I attempted to offer the chair to the doe-eyed beauty first, but she had stepped back to the wall where she could see us both, presumably to be at her mistress's bidding.

'Some wine?' she asked.

'No thank you, My Lady. I wouldn't want to acquire a taste for fine Castle wine and have to go back to the mouthwash that has barely even been introduced to a grape.'

'We have ale – not just small beer.'

'Perhaps, after I have delivered that which is expected of me.'

The Lady Ansithe placed the token Lord Petroc had given me, and I had given over to the guard at the wicket gate, onto the table.

'Then please do unburden yourself, Chaucere.'

'Sir Dace,' I began, before correcting myself quickly. 'I'm sorry, I mean Lord Petroc, told me to tell you that "honour" is satisfied.' Lady Ansithe let out a sigh of relief, as, interestingly, so did the demure handmaiden lurking in the periphery of my vision.

'And why is Lord Petroc not here to give me this news himself may I ask, Chaucere?'

'He was wounded – not badly,' I added as I heard both women take a sharp breath.

'Where is he then please, Chaucere?'

'Sir Petroc is with a healer that I know of, a very capable man. He says that although the wound is not small, it is fortunately not deep either, and he sees no reason why it should not heal safely.'

'Would he not be better seeing healers here in the castle?' she said, obviously concerned about the younger man.

'Lady Ansithe, if I might be so bold as to offer an opinion?'

She smiled, a little nervously. 'I doubt, Chaucere, that much has ever prevented you from giving your opinion, whether asked for or not.'

'I can personally vouch for this healer, whereas those physics that attend to the rich and powerful may often look the part, but do not necessarily perform so well.'

This prompted a quickly suppressed giggle from the hand-maid.

'Yes, Chaucere. I do believe you are right,' Lady Ansithe continued.

'The healer has a daughter, who is an excellent nurse, and is with Sir Petroc at all times. He will not want for care.'

'That is a relief. And you must let me give you some money for the healer.'

'Thank you, my lady, but I was his second and he is my friend. It won't be necessary.'

'Of course, I understand.' She nodded approvingly.

The handmaiden coughed politely before speaking up. 'Sir Chaucere mentioned a daughter, the nurse, perhaps a gift for her would not be out of place?'

'A good idea,' Lady Ansithe said.

I thought for a moment, trying on my aggrandisement for size, before I continued. It didn't fit. 'I believe that would be appreciated, yes. I do not think they have much money for what some might consider fripperies – though you would have to choose something suitable. And it's just Chaucere, thank you.'

Lady Ansithe smiled at her handmaiden before continuing:

'Of course, we have much more experience in such "fripperies" do we not?'

'Oh yes, Lady Ansithe,' she replied, very seriously. 'Sometimes it seems that life is nothing but fripperies.'

I knew they were having fun at my expense. I thought about apologising for my lack of manners, but decided that I had dug my midden deep enough. Besides I had other matters on my mind.

'Lady Ansithe, may I continue to talk frankly?'

'Of course Chaucere, whatever you say here is in confidence.'

'Please, what more can you tell me about Sir Petroc's opponent, Lord Hudde?'

Lady Ansithe's face took on the look of someone who had just bitten into an apple only to find the worms had got there first. 'He is a loud, unpleasant boastful oaf who is willing to spend his riches on buying friends he cannot make in other ways. Those riches must be great, as he has bought a lot of friends.'

'I didn't think that was the way the new King intended to people his Round Table and rule his Kingdom?'

Lady Ansithe looked uncomfortable, and glanced at her maid-servant for a moment before answering:

'Neither of us are privy to the King's mind of course, but I would judge that attempting to forge the Kingdom you speak off, and bring many squabbling lands together, is no mean task. Lord Hudde has a lot of land, and a lot of influence it seems, and that makes him a useful addition to any Kingdom and should help cement peace over all the disparate lands.'

'And do you know where these lands of Lord Hudde's might be found, Lady Ansithe?'

'To the North I believe. I could find out. Why though?'

'I think I would like to visit these estates that Lord Hudde boasts about. A little excursion, for my health's sake. I have been feeling under the weather lately.'

'Indeed,' Lady Ansithe answered, a small smile playing around her full lips. 'And I think we would both be very interested in hearing about your little jaunt. And we, of course, wish you the very best of health.'

I thanked her.

'When I have discovered exactly where Lord Hudde's many lands are located, where then shall I send the directions regarding this expedition, for your health's sake?'

I told her. The handmaiden then bought us both the promised beer. It was good beer. Lady Ansithe didn't toy about with her mug either. I like a woman with appetites. It brought some cheer to her handsome but otherwise rather grand face. Perhaps I could see something of what had taken Lord Petroc's fancy.

The doe-eyed handmaiden saw me part way out, down yet another set of corridors and stairs. A guard waited at the end, but she stopped mid-way and spoke softly before we got close enough for him to hear:

'I know that the Lady Ansithe would like to give you something for the trouble you have taken.'

'With respect, I told the Lady that I do not need a reward,' I replied, a little peevish.

'Yes, you misunderstand me, Sir,' the handmaiden coloured most delightfully and held out her hand. 'This token should help you if you ever find yourself in need of her assistance. Day or night, help will come.'

I took the proffered gold coin, simply but elegantly wrought with a single symbol I did not recognise.

'If you show it to the guard at the gate where you are going to now, you will have speedy access to her Ladyship in the room where we just met.'

'Thank you,' I replied, with what I hoped was gallantry. I smiled, anticipating some response from those beautiful doe-eyes, but I must be out of practise. She turned and was gone in the time between two heartbeats.

The guard led me to a small side gate opening into an orchard. From there I found my way easily to the main road down from the Big House, which somehow now felt more properly Camelot in a way it never had for me before.

A lot of things occupied my thoughts that evening, but it was the doe-eyed handmaiden who came back to bother my dreams. Sometimes as herself, sometimes her skin was the colour of molasses; her brown eyes were amber and her brown hair now black as night over a dark sea. Yet still it was she each time and I knew this with a certainty I did not question.

I once rested on an island in the Middle Sea, a wild unforgiving land isolated by mountains and water, yet beautiful in its way as islands in that blessed place can be. The Old Empire had occupied the island, but like our own mist-covered lands had never fully claimed it. On this island, which the locals called Corsis, at least to strangers, there lived Mazzeri – mostly women – who were renowned as dream-hunters. I doubted their supposed powers, this ability to hunt, heal, and even kill animals or even men in a particular dream world of their own creation; a death that could foretell the passing of a neighbour or even a friend.

The people of Corsis, a fierce, independent but hospitable people thought highly of the Mazzeri and I never voiced my doubts to them about the supposed ability of these women. I did not have much time for prophecies and scrying. I was a practical man who wielded a sword for his living. Yet that that night I truly felt as if I had been walking in the world where the Mazzeri went to carry out their dream hunts. I woke full of fear and concern for my friend Sir Dace's wellbeing.

19
MERLIN

As a rule, I eat something cold to break my fast, usually whatever is left over from the night before. Hard bread or cheese would do me and I would be grateful, having faced enough breakfasts of wind, water and sand – sometimes without the sand. Today though I felt like something hot, probably the effect of my dreams from the night before. In particular I fancied eggs. That would set me up for the day.

I find eggs to be very undervalued in this country of my birth, more likely to be associated with hedgerow foraging than good husbandry. I, however, believe an egg – chicken, duck or even goose – to be a wholesome start to the day. Yes, I was looking forward to my eggs – and considering how to have them cooked as I walked to Aila's – which is probably why I never saw them and whatever it was they hit me with.

I awoke with a start from my enforced slumber, my head still ringing and my nostrils burning from the smell that had brought me back to sensibility. I coughed and sat up in the bed where I had been placed at some point after the assailant's service to my good person.

A man was walking around the room, which was so full as to appear cluttered. I had never seen so many, and so diverse, a collection of belongings in one place. Not even in the largest of the new churches they were building across the sea. Pots and beakers and even costly glass vessels containing who knows what sorts of unguents. Plus many diverse books and scrolls, the like of which I had also never set eyes on before. Then there were lamps and candles in great profusion and I had never before seen a room without windows so well lit – yet strangely the room's corners still seemed drenched in shadow and full of menace.

Hanging on the wall of this room there was a sword. It didn't look a great sword. It wasn't an Excalibur, a sword able to split a man in two. It wasn't even a fine fighting tool like my own sword that I refused to name. This was an old sword and I tried and tried not to look at it, but my eyes kept getting dragged back. We had history, that sword and I. A history that was nobody's business but our own.

I attempted speech. I made a poor job of it, but enough to attract the man's attention. He turned to look at me. At first sight he looked to be an ordinary man of medium height and advancing years, but with his back still straight, his long straggly white hair still full and his long white beard carefully knotted. Look closer though and you would soon notice that there was much more to him than that. This man was infused with a restless energy more suited to a boy in his first flush of manhood. Catch his eye and then you could sense the power that made him one of the most feared men of these isles. This was the druid Merlin. I knew this for I had first met him, after a fashion, many years previous, perhaps twice – a fact that I hoped he now had no knowledge of at all. I had changed, he had not.

Merlin remained a bearded, mysterious, figure who carried with him the feel of immeasurable age, even though he moved like a man in his prime. He was robed in a gown of darkest blue in which the heavens themselves seemed to have been inlaid in silver.

He sat himself down on a high-backed chair and pressed his hands together before addressing me.

'The guards were over-enthusiastic in their mission, but I have been told you can often be loath to respond to a request.'

'Yes. Apology accepted.'

'I did not apologise,' said Merlin. 'I do not apologise for anything done in the cause of the King and the good of this land.'

'That's all right then,' I replied. 'Because I didn't really accept it anyway. I seldom accept apologies from people who knock me out – intentionally or otherwise – because it hurts. Have you got anything to drink? I have an awful headache.'

'You are an unusual man, Chaucere.'

'Not really. I piss when I want to and shit when I must. Same as any other man.'

'Still, your name has come to my attention several times in recent months, yet I know nothing of you.'

'I wouldn't lose sleep over it, to be honest. Mine is a very ordinary life.'

'That I would dispute,' he said, picking up my sword, which I now noticed on the table next to him. 'You have a sword from the very farthest East. From islands that are only spoken of in the most knowledgeable circles.'

'I own it after winning at dice,' I interrupted. 'I'm lucky like that. Any chance of that drink?'

'Yet in your sleep you mumble and curse in at least five different languages – that I know of for certain.'

'Me and my big mouth, eh? My big dry mouth.'

Merlin finally took the hint, got to his feet, and poured two drinks into valuable glass vessels from a ridiculously expensive flask. I supposed the contents must have been equally costly, as he was not generous with his measure.

'Here, drink this,' he said, passing me the vessel of clear, faintly oily, liquid. 'It will clear your head, but do not drink it all at once.'

'No, I'll try not to' I said in a tone that I hoped wouldn't result in another knock on the head.

I sipped my drink with exaggerated care, and was immediately very pleased I had done so. The spirit, if spirit it was, brought tears to my eyes and stung my lips, but the effect on swallowing it was immediate and not at all unpleasant. Not only did my head feel clearer, I swear I could hear and see with a new facility. It also banished any compulsion for sleep and I would swear that my yard was now four times its length and I might have sard a thousand women. That part I could have done without, given where I was – in the depths of the castle of Camelot, unless I was very much mistaken.

'So, that's how the dead get raised,' I remarked as casually as I could.

Merlin sat and sipped his drink without any apparent side effects. Surely he could not be that old?

'I was told you like to play the fool,' he said finally.

'Play the fool? No, I don't think I play the fool. Surely I am the greatest fool in the land?'

'And why do you say that, Chaucere?'

'Because if I wasn't a fool of that size, I wouldn't be here at the tender mercies of the most powerful man in the land.'

'The most powerful man in the land? That is the King.'

'Who many say does nothing that his chief adviser has not advised.'

'You know me then?'

'I know you, Merlin. Who does not know of the Great Druid Merlin?'

Merlin nodded once before continuing.

'But would that make such an adviser more powerful than the King? When everything the adviser says is to benefit the King, his land and his people?'

'I would not know, I am but a simple fool.' I took another small sip of my drink. I suspected I needed my head to be as clear as possible if I was to walk out of here on my own two feet.

'You are neither simple nor a fool, Chaucere. When tales of your deeds first reached my ears and I thought to send for you, I imagined I would meet a fox of a man, a creature of nature full of sly cunning who rode his luck well.'

'I'll not object to that portrait, if it pleases you.'

'No, Master Chaucere, it does not please me.'

'Plain Chaucere will do for me thank you good Sir, I am no man's master.'

'And no man is your master?'

'I did not say that.'

'But it's what you think, isn't it? In the castle of a King, the greatest King this land will ever see – you think you are without a master?'

'Now, your words confuse me again—

'The sword knows you!' Merlin interrupted my ramblings with a voice as savage as the look that now came into his eyes. He leapt out of his chair like a man of half or a quarter his years, towering above me.

'The sword should not know you, Chaucere!' he continued, mightily perplexed. 'And I think I might know you too.'

I was now walking on quicksand. One wrong step and I would be sucked down, never to be seen again. Or perhaps I would be later taking the long drop to the river. Whatever, I would not return to my house with breath still in my body.

I looked up at him, the bearded, mysterious, robed figure that carried with him every appearance of immeasurable age, yet moved so well. Suddenly I saw, as if from nowhere, a door open, a door the colour of a night sea and behind it there was this man.

And suddenly I saw a woman with amber eyes and hair darker than a raven's wing.

Why do they always say that?

What's wrong with a raven's back or its tail? No, it's always its wing!

Bloody minstrels.

Think Chaucere, think! Get your mind back to the here. Concentrate or die. That was half a world away and more years ago then I cared to count. It was the dream of a different man.

Merlin was already well known as Arthur's magician and he was building Camelot for him then. It couldn't have been him, no matter what my injury-induced delirium was and what my mind had been telling me. I certainly wasn't going to mention here my dreams of poisoned lands, and the pressing need that had brought me back to Camelot.

The world shifted around me, and I was once again not sure where I was or what my role here might be.

'Master Merlin,' I said finally, searching desperately for an explanation that would appease this man, said by many to be begotten by a demon on a princess and brought into this world to challenge the upstart Christ. The man who scared me more than any man I had ever met or fought before.

'I am what you see,' I continued, my mouth desert dry again. 'A soldier who has travelled far, through many lands to ply his trade. I have killed men who wanted to kill me, for coin and gold, but I have never plundered or raped like many in my profession. Sometimes I have been asked to do a little more; to find things, or find things out. It seems I'm good at that too. I have handled many swords; I have, or had, one in my possession that as you mentioned may have come from a land almost beyond legend at the other end of the Earth. But I cannot say that any sword has ever known me. How could a sword do such a thing?'

The man who scared me so looked hard at me again and I fought to stop myself from trembling. He now fixed me with one eye before he spoke again:

'Then why do you so studiously avoid looking at it? An old sword hanging in pride of place on the wall of the demon Merlin? Surely that should raise the curiosity of a soldier and swordsmen?'

'I will not lie to you, Master Merlin,' I choked out. 'I did see the sword and it scared me. It scares me still.'

'How?' Merlin insisted.

'I would not call myself a superstitious man and while I say that no sword has ever known me, I know swords. And that sword, which hangs so innocently on your wall, it has killed, or instigated the deaths of more men, women and children than I can comprehend. Not by its own blade, but it is responsible. And it will be responsible for the same again, of that much I am sure.'

Merlin continued to look at me for some time after that, but I had nothing else to say. I dare not speak in case I betrayed myself.

Eventually he got up again and walked around his room, stopping before the sword on the wall. He walked some more and topped up his glass, not offering me more, as if he knew my limit. When he spoke again it was as if the previous conversation had not taken place.

'I have need of a man of your skills, Chaucere.'

To say I was taken aback would be to understate my reaction considerably. I coughed nervously, because I was very nervous.

'What do you say to that, Chaucere?'

'If I may be honest, Merlin, you have a whole table full of knights to call upon to do your bidding, each of which I'm sure is equal or better than me. And, as you have pointed out, you also have eyes and ears everywhere else in Camelot and I doubt I could help you much there either.'

'Indeed, I do have the Knights of the Round Table to assist me. Whether or not they are your equal, and whether or not you believe this to be the case, is another matter. I somehow doubt that you do not have a very exact awareness of your abilities. Informants I have too, many of which you could not even begin to comprehend.'

Merlin sat down once more and seemed to age as he relaxed.

'However, the knights advertise their presence before they even arrive and are too used to giving orders to be mistaken for anything other than what they are. My "eyes" and "ears" in this country, although useful, are too often keen to tell me what they think I want to see and hear, not what I need to know. I need somebody who can move with impunity, be able to talk with cut-purses and princes and above all be not afraid to tell me what it is he really finds out.'

'This isn't some jest – you want me to work for you?'

'You would be working for your King and your country.'

'And would I have some token of the authority placed in me by the King?' I had to ask, although I was already reasonably sure what the answer would be.

'No, Chaucere. That would defeat the object entirely. I want to hear what they would not say if in front of a King's man or do what they would not do, if in front of a King's man.'

I finished my drink and perhaps was thereby emboldened to ask:

'I'm clear on the King of course, but I am rather more vague on the "country" business – we've had so many different King-doms here, no offence, that I don't quite understand what this "Britain" actually is.'

Merlin got up and moved up close to me. I thought to decide whether or not I was again pretending to play the fool. But actually he approached in order to fix me with his eye again, which wasn't disturbing at all. I could no more have turned away than I could have leapt the river gorge.

'Britain is no mere Kingdom, Chaucere. Britain is this island in its entirety – no mere idea, but a living breathing spirit – and it must be whole, if it and our people are to survive the coming onslaught that my visions have revealed to me.'

Visions eh? I don't know what is worse, a man with a vision or a man with visions. Both can be equally dangerous.

Merlin came closer still.

'This must be one island Kingdom, with the one King and one people, with a government that puts the people first. It will be a new era. People will be able to raise their families in peace, free from hunger and disease. Britain will then build an empire greater than any that has gone before in this world, even the Old Empire that occupied these lands for so many years. And we will take these new freedoms to oppressed people everywhere, take down the warlords and tyrants and herald a Golden Age. This much I have seen; this much I know.'

Merlin continued to approach me until he was at a distance that I was far from comfortable with. As he looked me straight I could feel a much-neglected and barely remembered part of me, that might be called a soul by some, begin to wilt under the attention.

'What we must do,' Merlin continued, 'what we who are alive today must do, is ensure that this Empire happens sooner rather than later. Nothing must stand in its way. It must be founded now and it must happen around Arthur King. We must build our castles now; we must unite all people on these lands together. Only then will all of the people of this island be saved a thousand years of terror and torment, as we herald a new Golden Age: the Arthurian Age.'

'I see,' I said, and after an eternity cleared my throat again. 'Well, if you put it like that I suppose I have no choice!' I tried to effect a light-hearted air. I failed. 'So, I'm working for King and country, but you're still holding the purse strings, eh?'

Merlin laughed and, freeing me from his unbreakable stare, turned away.

'You will receive your reward, Chaucere. Have no fear of that.'

Suddenly I did fear, for my reward seemed something to be very afraid of and not to be hastened at all.

'Your first task, Chaucere,' said Merlin, picking up my sword and examining it with interest, 'is to find out more about Lord Hudde for me.'

So surprised was I that I almost dropped my sword as he threw both weapon and scabbard back to me.

'Lord Hudde?'

'Yes,' said the Merlin. 'He has been asking questions about you.'

'Has he now? The noble Lord Hudde asking questions about one such as me?'

'Is that what you think? That he is noble?'

'Oh yes, and surely the moon is made from fresh cheese!'

'No, it's not made from cheese.'

Merlin spoke with the certainty of one who has been there or at least has very good evidence for his knowledge.

'No. Well – Merlin, I could tell you one or two things about Lord Hudde, I'm sure.'

'I am not interested in hearsay, Chaucere. I want proof.'

'Proof?'

'Proof I can put before the King.'

'Oh, that sort of proof.'

So, the Merlin was interested in Lord Hudde. The Merlin wanted to know, which told me something, although I wasn't sure what exactly.

I later thought of many things I would have liked to ask, should have asked, but at that moment caution got the better of me. I did not want Lady Ansithe brought into our discussion. Not at this point in time and not when I was so unsure of my own position.

Anyway, the meet was over. Guards appeared from nowhere and a hood was put over my head. I was picked up off the bed and then walked a surprising distance, but as far as I could tell I stayed indoors or at least in tunnels. The guards were not talkative. I do not think guards who worked for Merlin could afford to be chatty. I think any chatty guard that did work for

Merlin would not work for Merlin for very long. Finally the hood was taken away and I blinked in the bright daylight.

It transpired that it was now a full day later and I was completely by myself in the middle of a field outside of Camelot. Of the guards there was no sign. A farmer shouted at me, asking what I thought I was doing walking over his fields. When he saw the look on my face, he thought better of it and went hurriedly on his way. I sighed and started the long walk back to the Big House.

I thought long and hard on everything Merlin had said to me. Merlin's dreams of a Kingdom of Britain seemed grandiose to me at first consideration. The land was too large and too diverse, surely? Too many different people and too many different landscapes: the mountains, the heaths, the marshes – how could these be pulled together into one Kingdom? Especially with all the different tribes crossing the Northern Sea to have a piece of this land with its fertile soils, ample supplies of iron and tin and reasonable climate? I say reasonable, as I, for one, much preferred the warmer climes of the Middle Sea. But here I was, back again and living the life that a soothsayer once told me I was obliged to live.

I had assumed that the activities I now suspected Lord Hudde of were purely motivated by greed, to increase his holdings and thus promote his position at court. While it might be considered almost productive, as it placed the Round Table in a constant state of readiness, it undermined the peace, as it also created an atmosphere that was the very opposite of that desired by Merlin for Arthur's Kingdom of Britain, a land of accord and harmony.

What then, if instead of this all being a by-product of Lord Hudde's base deeds, this had been the main intention all along? The undermining of King Arthur's new realm was what was intended and the thieving was simply a rather useful secondary result – and a way to fund the subversion.

Lord Hudde obviously had no fealty to King Arthur, but did he have his own aspirations to majesty or was there another man that he himself was calling Liege? This was an important thought and I knew that. I should think on it further. I would need to, as I was now the wretched instrument of the (second) most powerful man in the Kingdom of Britain. I may once have considered myself to be my own man, but I was now Merlin's cat's paw.

And, somehow, I still hadn't had breakfast. That, at least I could remedy, the rest would have to wait for another day.

20
THE WORD FROM THE FORGE

I went to find Emald as he is a man who can generally be relied upon to eat a meal, regardless of the time of day. He was busy making horseshoes, for which there is a continuous demand. I sat by his bench as he worked. He spoke between blows to the metal.

'Timothy came to visit last night.'

'Did he now?' I managed to reply, without feeling too guilty.

'He was hungry.'

'Oh.' Now I did feel guilty.

'Again.'

'Sorry.'

'Don't apologise to me. Apologise to Timothy.'

'I will.'

'You didn't make it home then?'

'No.'

'And I imagine you weren't out whoring and drinking.'

'Not at all.'

'Sometimes you disappoint me, Chaucere.'

'I often disappoint myself.'

'Perhaps better if you had been.'

'Perhaps.'

Emald plunged the shoe into cold water, where it hissed satisfactorily, and then threw it onto a pile with some fellows.

'I have some news that may interest you, Emald.'

Emald sighed before saying:

'Or it may not.' He took off his apron. 'Come along then. Let's get some ale. Alia's new batch is ready.'

The new batch was indeed ready and Emald drank a huge draft of it before he sat back and looked at me, slowly shaking his head.

'The Merlin you say? You surely do know how to land your-self in some of the deepest shit in Camelot, Chaucere.'

'It's not as it I ask for it, Emald.'

He shrugged. 'Do the mountains ask for rain? They get it anyway.'

'Very sharp, Emald. If Merlin ever departs you should try for the position of Camelot Wise Man.'

He grunted.

I got stuck into my first breakfast and Emald into his second. I looked around Alia's – quiet at this time – and noted how varied those men eating and drinking here were. Looks and coloration showed them to be from all the different parts of these islands, and far beyond as well. All happily now rubbing along with each other.

'What do you think, Emald?' I continued. 'You have spent more time with these folk than me in recent years. Could there be one Kingdom forged in these lands, to make them all as one?'

Emald picked some bacon from a tooth and considered this:

'I have not travelled as far and as wide as you have, Chaucere, but in my experience people are pretty much of a muchness wherever you go. And most good folk simply want to be left alone to get on with their lives, raise their children to be strong and happy, and worship what gods they choose in whatever way they wish.'

'I agree. I have found much the same thing.'

'Good. Then perhaps there is a chance that we might yet have a Kingdom of Britain, where there will be nothing but Freemen and women too.'

I wanted to agree with him, but I had to add my own misgivings.

'The thing is this, Emald. I have also found that everywhere I have been there are more and more self-serving people around in each generation who are not happy to let others get on with their lives unless they first make the ordinary folk apply themselves to making the self-serving person's life better first.'

'Yes, my friend, as my father was fond of saying, there is the rub!'

'And I cannot help but think, Emald, that such self-interest will always scupper the chances of building a Kingdom of Britain in any land this side of Avalon.'

Emald moodily moved his food around the trencher.

'You are quite ruining my appetite, Chaucere.'

'Such was not my intention, I assure you.'

Emald considered the problem further. 'I believe, on the positive side, that there are also more and more people like your good self around every generation who are not willing to sit back and let these self-serving bastards get away with it! And that has got to be a cause for some optimism.'

'If you include yourself in that group, Emald, then I will agree with you!'

'Aye, then I will!' He raised his horn and I raised mine and we toasted the success of our venture to remove all those who despoil the world for others. We drunk deep and then set about devising our master plan for eliminating the threat of Lord Hudde and his band of brigands. First I had a trip North to get ready for. While I was away Emald would use the network of Camelot's smiths to find out what they knew about Lord Hudde and his activities. I still remembered that time he had turned up at Emald's forge with a shoeless horse. He had another life, of that I was sure.

21
THE NORTH COUNTRY

The itinerary for my journey North arrived from the Lady Ansithe after two days. I was pleased that she had assumed I could read, and I was grateful that she had at least written in a language I understood. I can speak some dozen, but my reading is less impressive.

With the message came as fine a piece of silk as I had ever seen. The colours glowed like a Kingfisher in the summer's sun. Rachel was beyond delighted, almost in tears.

'It's beautiful, Chaucere. I have never seen anything so lovely.'

I had to explain again that it was from Lord Petroc's friends in the Big House and not an actual present from me. Perhaps I explained too insistently, but I thought I saw a trace of something like disappointment flicker over her face. It was only fair though. I didn't want her to think I was buying her expensive gifts – did I?

I explained to Rachel and her father that I had been called away on important business. Isak was no fool, though.

'This business, Chaucere. Would it have anything to do with what has landed Petroc in my care?'

'It has, Isak.'

'Then you take care as well. I don't want to have you as a patient.'

I assured him that would never happen and went to say farewell to Sir Dace, but he was not living up to his nickname today. He was pale and drawn and not in good spirits.

'I don't like this, Chaucere,' he said weakly. 'You should not be undertaking my missions for me.'

'I would hardly call snooping about in the frozen north a mission, Petroc. Besides, with your perfect skin and bright eyes, you would stand out like a goose in the hen house in those parts of the Kingdom.'

'Not so bright-eyed now, Chaucere, I warrant. Not that Rachel will fetch me a mirror.'

'She just doesn't want you to spend your time fussing about whether your hair is combed correctly!'

Petroc went to complain, but lacked the energy even for that. And so I bid Sir Dace a rather light-hearted goodbye. He was still far too weak for my liking and I could see from his manner that Isak was also hoping for a more rapid recovery. However, as he had pointed out, every body gets better at its own rate. But it was now a rather sombre journey that I was undertaking. It was not just the weather that was uninspiring. The lands I passed through – when I was away from the fields surrounding Camelot – had little to recommend them either. Although no longer in the full grip of winter, the landscape had yet to completely surrender to spring: all was toad grey and bandage green. I wondered why I had ever thought to come back to this country from the sun-baked hills of Lusitania. Oh yes, I had no choice. That was reason, not if I ever wanted to sleep easily again.

This northern track was not a route I was familiar with either, and although the horse I had hired was sturdy, she was a little nervous and we did not make a great pace, even after we found an Old Empire road to ride along. A better road than many I had travelled, I had to admit, especially on my treks to the West. I put these thoughts away. The North occupied me for the moment; not the West.

The road was long, very long, and singularly lacking in places where one might find a roof and a hot meal. These were lands where people tended to stay where they were born and were still beholden to the same Lord that their fathers had answered to. To have ordinary men travelling to the next parish was rare enough, to find men undertaking the sort of journey I was on was almost unknown. Masterless men were looked on with suspicion. I found a few farmers willing to give me a meal and lodgings, after they had seen the colour of my money. Very few people say no to gold. I was concerned that news might get sent ahead of me to alert brigands of my movements – and my full purse. I was particularly worried about sleeping 'out of doors', as many people now called it. I did not want to be killed in my sleep.

I had solved that problem by taking Timothy with me. I had been feeling guilty about neglecting him and so decided that he would enjoy a walk. He did, and he enjoyed sniffing out and running down anything that wasn't fast enough on its feet. There would be fewer rats around to trouble farmers that year.

At night we would make our camp under whatever shelter we could find. And with Timothy tucked in next to me we were both soon comfortably asleep. Only once did Timothy need to apply himself in his guard role. Whoever was trying to creep up on my small encampment, where my rabbit was cooking on a small spit, hadn't been wary enough. They probably just saw the fire and thought their luck was in.

Their luck wasn't in.

It was the loudest I had ever heard Timothy bark. And the loudest I had ever heard men scream as Timothy went hurtling through the undergrowth, after my would-be assailants, like some monster from the Otherworld.

I actually heard one scream out 'Cù-Sìth' in a Caledonian accent as Timothy burst through the greenery. I thought this was rather a good name, as it certainly inspired a certain amount of dread. I considered changing his name, but overall Timothy seemed to say that he was used to Timothy now and didn't approve too much of change.

Slowly we approached the part of the North where Lady Ansithe's message had informed me that Lord Hudde was known to have his lands. It was low scrubby woodland for the most part, not suitable for farming, but lacking the splendour of the High Forrest and its abundant game. The occasional village and hamlet did little to break the monotony. Simple people, wary of strangers with little to spare or even sell to a traveller, I was glad to finally reach the Old Empire town of High Cross. There at least I could buy a decent meal and find a roof to keep the too frequent, and persistent, rain showers away.

'I have a hound,' I said to the Inn owner, as Timothy trotted into view.

'A hound is it?' the Inn Keep replied. 'I thought it was a spare pony for your saddle bags.'

They didn't mind Timothy at all and found him a bone that I coveted for a good while as I waited for my supper.

I knew I must be getting close to Lord Hudde's lands, but his name meant nothing to anyone I spoke to, certainly not the Inn Keep and he knew everybody, or so he said. So I continued north again through the woods and scrub.

Eventually I was aware of some signs of cultivation: sparse and poor though it was; fields barely ploughed and clearances half completed. Houses were simple huts with more leaks than an alehouse on a holiday night. Finally I found one local who recognised the name of Hudde, although he pronounced it very differently. I took him to be simple at first as he sniggered like a loon when I asked for directions to Lord Hudde's Great Hall, but I continued along the path he pointed out.

It wasn't until I arrived at Lord Hudde's 'Great Hall' that I realised why the man had been so entertained: what a hovel! It was of a good size, but the roof needed thatching, the walls needed daubing and the people, who were going about their chores in a very half-hearted fashion, needed feeding. And this was the Great Hall of the fabulously wealthy Lord Hudde?

A surly-looking, balding, knob end of an overseer came out of the hall as I rode up, wiping his hands down his filthy tunic, whether to clean it, or them, wasn't clear.

'Good day to you,' I said cheerfully.

'What would you be wanting?' the overseer came back, with an accent as thick and unpleasant as the crust on spoilt milk.

'Is this Lord Hudde's Hall?' I replied.

'Who's asking?'

'I was told that he might be a Lord on the lookout for good men.'

'Who told you that?'

This was not going well. I like a conversation where a question is followed by an answer not another question. The overseer had now been joined by a couple of younger versions of himself. They did not look like they had particularly good sword arms, but they looked like they didn't need them, not when they were carrying briar hooks that were a lot less neglected than their clothes.

'Perhaps I've come to the wrong place then,' I said, turning my horse's head ready to go. The overseer stepped forward and grabbed the reins.

'I asked who you were and why you thought to make Lord Hudde's business your own?' he said, pulling on my horse's reins. He was obviously not much of a rider, as he should have known that this is not something you do to an easily startled mare – not that he knew this horse was easily startled. He soon learnt though. I was prepared, he wasn't. The horse bucked and caught the overseer under the chin. He went down rapidly. I was away almost as quickly and I didn't look back until I was well clear.

There was no sign of pursuit, so I slackened my pace and whistled for Timothy. I thought it wise not to take him with me to the Great Hall, in case the locals had their own dogs that he might try to play with. Timothy is very playful and sometimes this can lead to other dogs getting just a little damaged.

Together we skulked and studied our surroundings more closely – a proper investigation this time. The lands and fields around looked no better than their Lord's hall, poorly cleared and badly maintained. The livestock looked sickly and what workers I could see working in the fields even more so. I was not impressed. Timothy was totally dismissive. This left us with a big question: so, Lord Hudde, where does all your wealth really come from?

I thought on this long and hard on the journey back to the Big House. One possibility kept putting itself forward. Lord Hudde and Cecilio, the man I believed ran the ring of bandits, was this where Lord Hudde's wealth was coming from? It seemed highly likely. That gave me a lot of food for thought on the long track back south.

22
THE OATH

Sir Dace was dead. The brave, noble and colourful Lord Petroc had breathed his last while Timothy and I were busy ferreting out the gods-knew-what in a foul-smelling miserable corner of the wet north country. I could not believe it and neither could Isak.

'I have seen many men in far worse general health make full recoveries from far worse wounds,' said Isak, his rage giving him fresh strength. 'There was no sign of a secondary fever setting in, as can happen to even the strongest of men. It was as if the initial wound carried something else with it.'

'Put it simply for me please, Isak.'

'I think he was poisoned, Chaucere.'

'How?'

'A taint on the blade. I have heard of it being done.'

'Really?'

'Putrefaction and foulness painted on a sword – then even the smallest cut can prove calamitous to the injured party, and it would seem as if his treatment was to blame. I swear it was not!'

I consoled the poor man. I knew that Petroc could not have received better care.

'As I said, Chaucere, I have heard of this being done in heathen lands, but I did not expect to see it in a duel between two Knights in Camelot!'

Self-reproach was written loud in the healer's voice.

'I did not expect such a deed either Isak, though now that I have learnt more about "Lord" Hudde I am perhaps beginning to believe that I should have.'

'What will you do?'

'What I must.'

'Think carefully on this, my friend.'

'I do not think such behaviour should go unpunished.'

'And neither do I,' the older man said, with metal in his voice. 'Yet these Lords are still powerful, despite how the King has curbed their excesses. And you have no proof, only the word of an ageing healer who some might even blame for your friend's fate.'

'Well, I do not!'

'Thank you. I truly did all I could. He should have recovered.'

Rachel also offered me kind words of consolation as I left their warm and comfortable house.

'He was a noble man, Chaucere. He did not once complain of the discomfort he was in. I have nursed sick people nearly all my life and in my heart I know that this was no natural death. There was base behaviour of the worst sort at work here. '

I could barely find the words to thank her for her civility. When the words failed me she held me, as I have not been held since childhood. I had to move on quickly, before I was totally unmanned. Somebody was going to pay for this and he would suffer before he died, and I would get to the bottom of the reason for his betrayal of everything Camelot was supposed to stand for. He was poisoning more than just a noble man.

I next had another woman to talk to and I knew the words I needed to speak to her would be even harder to find. The orchard entrance to the castle had two guards. The gold token that the Lady's maidservant had given to me was recognised immediately by one and I was escorted through the maze of corridors to a small waiting room. I was soon called into the room where I had met the Lady Ansithe previously.

I did not have long to wait. As before, her beautiful, unnamed, handmaiden also accompanied her. Her Ladyship took her seat, while the handmaiden lingered by the door, which was strange but it was not my place to comment.

Lady Ansithe's initial enquiry into the success of my investigation into Lord Hudde's household was stilled when she finally became aware of my countenance.

'Oh no,' she barely breathed, 'not Lord Petroc?'

I nodded, painfully aware of the sharp intake of breath from the young woman stationed now behind me.

'But you said this healer was skilful!'

'He was, and is, your Ladyship. I have no doubt of that. Lord Petroc could not have been in better hands. He suspects, and I – having seen similar wounds in the past and how they should heal – agree. Lord Hudde had deliberately corrupted his sword so that the slightest injury to his opponent would prove fatal. In a word, poison.'

The Lady was aghast. 'Can he even do such a thing?'

'It is probably easier than you might imagine, My Lady.'

'Then he must be punished!' She was furious. Her eyes flashed and her face grew red.

'I agree totally. There is something very wrong about Lord Hudde. His Hall is a joke and his lands are poor, there is no way they could support a Knight at Court. I also suspect him of all sorts of other foul deeds, including more than this one murder.'

'If I was a man I would cut his throat myself,' she exclaimed with real feeling.

'Then they would probably be obliged to stretch your lovely neck, M'Lady. The King has introduced laws to stop such behaviour.'

'I know!' She looked at her handmaiden, who I could sense was also very upset. 'We must have law or the King's Peace will not be maintained!'

'But actual proof of his foulness, that could be placed before the King to convince him of this taint will be hard to obtain.'

'Yet I expect you to find it, Chaucere. Find it for me! Please!' The woman's distress was written all over her face. The stifled sobs of the beautiful Lady-In-Waiting were breaking my heart as well.

'You have my word on it, My Lady.' I turned to include her weeping maidservant as I spoke. 'You both do. This oath I take, I will avenge Lord Petroc and bring Lord Hudde to the justice he deserves!'

'Then you will have both our thanks, Chaucere,' said Lady Ansithe. 'There are many here now in Camelot who call themselves Knights, but there are few I would trust to carry out this task as I now trust you.'

I bowed deeply. It seemed the right thing to do in such circumstances.

I turned and departed the room, leaving the two women comforting each other in a close embrace. I wasn't sure who was crying the harder or deeper – the lady or her maidservant. Both had obviously cared deeply for the man. I could understand it for I too was gripped by a cold fury the like of which I had not felt in an age.

As a rule I am not an angry man. An angry man does not live long in my profession. Well, my profession as once was. I am not exactly sure what my profession is now. I am not even sure it has a name. I must make one up. People are always impressed when you can give something a name. For the moment I was a most confidential investigator and, as such, I would get to the bottom of how this foul deed was accomplished and whatever else it was that I was convinced Lord Hudde was hiding. For I was sure of one thing, Camelot could only be spoiled by the presence of this rogue.

As a sword-for-hire, though, it does not pay to be angry. Angry does not win fights. Angry does not help you win battles, although it must be said that in a battle having a few angry men on your side does not hurt. Just make sure you are not one of them – their life expectancy is not to be envied.

A certain calmness is a better recommendation, you will find that the heat of conflict will supply plenty else of what you need to keep your fires stoked. In the meantime keep your wits about you and you will be more likely to keep your head on your shoulders and your lights full open.

I was certainly still too angry when I went to find Lord Hudde. That was a mistake. A good man had died. I know that good men die every day and many of them do so in fights that might be just considered ill advised, by the loser. This was different. This had not been a fair fight, of that I was sure.

Why this worried me, the survivor of more battles than I could remember, where fighting fair was simply what guaranteed your survival, I do not know. All I can say is that if this whole Camelot adventure was to mean anything, this new world of chivalry – and the rest – then fights such as the one Lord Petroc had taken part in needed to be fair. He had fought fair and his opponent hadn't. It was as simple as that.

So I went to find Lord Hudde as a silly angry man. I found him easily. Much too easily. Even that wasn't enough to warn me. He was in the alehouse I had followed Gipp to. He was also in the company of Gipp, which I really should also have considered further at that time, but angry men don't excel at thinking clearly.

'Good evening, Lord Hudde,' I began conversationally.

'It has come to my attention that you are in need of a lesson, Lord Hudde,' I continued, pleasantly enough – well, as pleasantly as an angry man can do when he is talking to the back of the source of his anger.

The table Lord Hudde sat at was not round, it was square, and his companions were hardly Knights either, although they looked to be of more substance than the weasel Gipp. Lord Hudde continued talking to them and they laughed as if he had said the funniest jest imaginable. Perhaps he had. I'd probably heard it. I've heard them all.

He ignored me.

'A lesson in manners is required as well it seems,' I added.

'Who are you who dares even talk to a Knight of the King's Table?' Hudde spat out, not bothering to turn.

'I am a Freeman in the land that same King has decreed is to be made fit for men such as me,' I replied with equal venom.

'You are a fleabite. Go back to whatever sty you wallow in "freeman" and do not bother your betters again,' Hudde said in a tone that indicated that, for him, the conversation was now over.

It wasn't.

My hand went for my sword and it was then that my anger went from being red-hot to ice cold. I became aware that Hudde's companions were not the only men in the alehouse taking a healthy interest in the proceedings. Out of the corners of my eyes I was aware of two more tables where men sat with their hands hovering over their swords like falcons ready to swoop.

I could see what the plan was. I was to be struck down as I attempted to attack from behind this most 'noble' of Knights. This is not the way this was going to be played out.

'Nevertheless, Lord Hudde, I will bother you. Unless you are not man enough to accept my challenge, I will meet you at first light tomorrow on the Field of Penitence. Miss this appointment and the world shall know of the full extent of your cowardliness. And I mean the full extent.'

I took my hand away from my sword and leant forward to whisper one short sentence: 'maleficent peddler of poisons.'

That made his ears prick up.

And with that I left the Inn and let the cold of my anger drive my preparations.

The Field of Penitence looked the same. It could have been the same morning, except these were autumn fogs chilling us now, not the lighter mists of spring. And it was Emald standing by my side, not me next to Lord Petroc.

'Surely the man is late?' Emald said. 'Can we not go home?' He yawned, unimpressed by the whole venture.

'He has a reputation for being tardy,' I replied sourly. I looked at the Justice. He was the same as well: same grey hair and same unpleasant aspect.

'I had not thought to see you here again so soon,' he said to me, with the same sour tone. 'Certainly not as the challenger this time.'

'I like it here,' I replied. 'Stops me lying around in my bed. Early to bed, early to rise and all of that nonsense.'

'I hope the Knight you seconded made a speedy recovery and is now well rested,' the Justice continued, ignoring my response.

'Oh, he's at his rest. That much is sure, but it is what many now call the Lord's rest and his recovery from that will only be at that Lord's pleasure.'

'But he was only scratched!' the Justice said, properly animated for the first time.

'Yes. Almost as if there was something wrong with the sword, but I'm sure that can't have been the case. You would have checked it.'

The Justice was suitably thrown off balance.

'I mean, you did check it didn't you? You wouldn't simply have taken his word for it, would you? Just because he's a Knight of the Round Table.'

The Justice's face went through all sorts of grimaces, frowns and scowls. He was about to give me his thoughts on the matter, when a boat finally came into view. Just the one this time, and not a party boat – no minstrels and only two ladies who did not seem at all happy to be there. Neither did Lord Hudde. He was standing at the prow looking very red-faced and harassed.

'Where's the fleet?' I shouted across the field. 'Only one boat? That's a bit of a come-down, surely? Maybe they all know the result isn't in any doubt?'

'I miss the minstrels. I like a good tune,' Emald observed dolefully.

'Really!' I said to the world in general. 'The lengths some people will go to make an entrance! I turned to the Justice, 'I really don't think any of this is in the spirit of a challenge, is it Justice?'

The Justice held his peace.

I looked away and gave my attention back to the boat and Lord Hudde. He was haranguing his oarsmen, who, undoubtedly anxious about incurring their master's displeasure, were making a real pig's ear of landing the boat. It finally pulled up next to the small pier and Lord Hudde impatiently reached out for the upright pole placed there for the purpose of aiding disembarkation. Unfortunately the planks of the pier gave way under him and his grip of the pole helped not at all as he fell backwards into the water.

It was quite a splash!

Lord Hudde thrashed and splashed about like some baby leviathan of legend, as he struggled to get out of the river. His oarsmen and most of his fellow passengers tried hard not to laugh. Emald and I felt no such compunction. Our laughter echoed over the field and did not seem to help Lord Hudde's mood at all. Even the edge of the sour-faced Justice's lips turned up – or maybe I just imagined it.

Lord Hudde's dunking had certainly cheered me up, despite the fact that I knew exactly what was about to happen. It was worth the effort that it had cost me the previous night to slip into the river and swim up to the pier and cut the ropes that held the structure together. Of course, at the time I hadn't been wearing heavy chain mail and armour plating, and I'd had a nice warm blanket to wrap round me as soon as I got out of the water and a flask of something warming too!

I didn't have a duel to fight either. I only had to ride back into the town and make holes in the bottom of Lord Hudde's other boats. At the moment, however, this Knight still had an awful lot left to do, including facing me on the field.

He had made it, floundering, back to his one boat and was trying to get back in – his second ineffectually presenting an oar for him to hold onto. Unfortunately the boat was already overfull and dangerously unstable. Lord Hudde's efforts only contributed to the inevitable – the boat went over, spilling the courtly Lords and Ladies into the drink.

Emald and I could not contain our mirth, but funny as it was, I felt compelled to remind Lord Hudde of the important matters at hand.

'If you have finished messing about, perhaps we can get on with this? I do have other appointments you know?'

This encouragement didn't go down at all well with Lord Hudde, who was finally clambering through the reeds and up the muddy bank to the field proper. He called for assistance from his bondsmen, but they were too busy righting the boat and saving themselves and the waterlogged Ladies of the Court.

'I do believe he has a fish caught in his mail,' Emald observed, as the Knight floundered further, gasping onto the field.

'Perhaps we can have it for breakfast?' I replied to my second. 'Oh well, shall I get on with it, Emald?'

'It would be a good idea. It's not getting any warmer.'

'Take your guard, Lord Hudde,' I shouted as I approached him, sword at the ready.

'I need time,' he spluttered, water still escaping from every hole in his assemblage. Lord Hudde looked for the Justice to intercede. The Justice kept his own council.

'Time, please!' Lord Hudde shouted again.

'No, I don't think so, Knight,' I responded. 'You treat this matter of life and death as if it is a show, to entertain your followers, a game to be played at your convenience. You mock tradition and break serious laws. You have had your time! Your time is now up.'

I was not Lord Dace. Fighting was my occupation and I had become rather good at it.

Your sword master will tell you: whatever else you do, don't stand still. This is not a game of seeing who can hit the other the hardest – not with these weapons. Be like the summer nectar collector, moving constantly from flower to flower. Do not caper or scamper though, ward off and answer back. Defensive never won the day – be aggressive, bold and brave they will tell you! Feints and glancing blows win points but not battles – not when lives are at stake and not when one of them is your own. Displace the enemy's strikes with counter blows timed to interrupt their actions. Don't just hit out without control. Use body leverage, bind on their sword. Do not receive their sword's edge on yours, but knock them aside with your flat or counter-hit with your edge.

So the sword masters will tell you.

It's all bollocks.

You do whatever it takes to win – to live.

If your enemy is wet and weighed down and does not have a hundred underlings stabbing at your back, you caper as much as you want. Scamper all you can. Wear him down. Wear him out. There is nothing noble in a sword fight, only a winner and a loser. You need to be the winner. Otherwise you will end up like Sir Dace, the lost and lamented Lord Petroc.

The Justice did not pull me up. Perhaps he had had enough of the man's posturing as well. I know I had.

Lord Hudde put up a pretty good fight considering how weighed down he was, as well as freezing near half to death. I didn't make the mistake of letting him find firmer ground, but kept him cornered in the swampy ground that would sap the strength of the heavier armoured man. I used my lighter weight and greater speed to my advantage.

He swung – I dodged. I thrust – he blocked, but he couldn't keep blocking forever. He soon tired. His followers now all safely, but damply, back on the boat, looked on in disbelief. They knew Lord Hudde was losing. This wasn't the plan at all. Well, not his plan, but it was most certainly mine. He waved his fancy dagger at me – like that was going to scare me!

When he was finally on his knees, his breath ragged and he couldn't raise his sword any more, I kicked it away from him. I then took his pretty knife for my own – a keepsake as I told him.

'You have no chivalry, Chaucere,' he gasped.

'I don't pretend to have,' I responded. 'Unlike some I could mention.' I picked up his sword and pointed it at him. 'I know you Lord Hudde, remember that.'

He looked up at me, his eyes – focussed anxiously on the sword – now regaining some of his cunning and guile. 'You know nothing of me.'

'Oh no?'

I struck quickly. The temptation was to run him straight through and send him to whatever rest his ilk can find, but that could wait for now. First I would destroy his honour and see to the rest later. He would be the laughing stock of The Big House by nightfall. So I cut him where he would remember it, drawing blood from his cheek with his own sword. He gasped and clutched at his face before calling for his second, who was still busy trying to find a safe mooring for their boat.

The Justice called 'first blood' and I walked back to the horses and Emald. 'Excellent entertainment. Can we go and find some breakfast now?' he asked, with a yawn.

'Sounds like a fine idea, Emald. I have worked up an appetite!'

I passed Lord Hudde's sword over to the sour-faced Justice. He took it with some caution, as if it might bite, which was true in its own way.

'Why did you wound him with his own sword?' he asked.

'Now, that is a good question,' I replied. 'Why indeed? Let us say that you should be careful to not scratch yourself with that sword's tip. The river has probably washed off whatever he chooses to corrupt his weapon with, but you never know, you might be unlucky. I hope Lord Hudde is.'

The Justice didn't add anything else. He looked very thoughtful though and examined Lord Hudde's sword very carefully.

Emald and I rode off. Camelot looked a great deal more cheery. News of Lord Hudde's humiliation would spread like wildfire, especially after I let it be known to everybody in every alehouse that I could visit in one day.

I intended to visit a lot.

Emald and I first broke our fasts in a very satisfactory fashion at my favourite alehouse; Alia's. Thick slices of ham with newly baked bread dripping sweet honey. We enjoyed it so much that before we realised it we had moved on and were enjoying a midday meal as well. I am partial to a fresh fish, especially for lunch. Three's the gift, as the saying goes and so we moved again and really got our teeth stuck into some good red meat. Three such meals meant that we were obliged to wash them down with something – and this was no occasion for small beer! Strong ale for starters, followed by spiced wine for the venison and beef. It was the least we deserved.

Of course, as we went, we spread good cheer, and the news of Lord Hudde's humbling. We soon assembled a good crowd, including many of Emald's fellow smiths. Now smiths are not the sort to spread idle gossip, but when asked to spread important news they can't be bettered. Soon the whole of

Camelot would be aware of what had taken place on The Field of Penitence that morning.

I would happily bet that it had already reached The Merlin's ears.

I realised that Lord Hudde was not the sort to take such a humiliation quietly. I imagined that as soon as he got himself home and dried out he would start plotting some response. I just didn't realise how quickly such an action might come into being.

We left the final alehouse in remarkably good spirits. Even Emald, whose capacity for drink was much greater than mine, was staggering. Somehow I mounted my horse and I was now considering whether this was really a good idea. I had just decided that walking the animal might have been the better option when the first arrow hit me in the shoulder. I barely had time, in my ale-addled mind, to realise just how much this hurt, before the second arrow hit my back. This arrow sent me sprawling forward to the ground, actually making me a far more difficult target, which probably saved my life.

Emald showed remarkable presence of mind and turned my horse to block me from the archer's view. Two more arrows bit harmlessly into the earth as our fellow drinkers, alerted by our cries, came rushing out of the alehouse. The archer, or archers, had escaped by then – or so I was told later.

At that time I had no awareness of anything.

I had fallen from a great height, far higher than the back of a horse. I had fallen from the top of the highest mountain to the deepest chasm, so long did my fall take. Maybe I had never stopped falling, perhaps I never would? The fall went on forever. And then, like a candle being extinguished by a sudden draft, I was dead to the world that mortals walk.

23
HECUBA

I was woken by a friendly kick to the head. I knew it must have been a friendly kick because any harder and I would probably not have woken at all.

'Wake up, Chaucere! There's a job for you to do.'

I recognised the voice immediately. It was my battalion leader Justinian. But wasn't Justinian dead? Evidently not, otherwise he couldn't be kicking me again.

'Stir yourself. Commander wants to see your ugly face.'

I shook my head and tried to bring everything into focus. Dawn had barely broken and there was still relief available from the daily onslaught of blistering heat.

I knew this camp.

I looked closer: familiar faces and familiar gear: Justinian's mercenaries, good men, all of them. We were a day's march from the provincial capital, forced to retreat after our army was routed – by whom exactly and what capital? So many enemies and so many cities, to be put under siege or to be relieved – to be raised to the ground or to be rebuilt? I couldn't remember.

'Come on, Chaucere! You don't get asked three times.'

I got up and followed Justinian, still bleary, to the commander's quarters. It was all as I remembered, except how could that be so? Our esteemed leader did not often consult me – well, never actually. He had only consulted me that one time, the time that changed everything. And considering that change, how could I be walking through the flap to his tent now?

I had done that walk before. A long, long time past.

I needed to get my head back to the here and now before I found myself losing same head, which admittedly had served me so well up until now.

'So, you are Chaucere?' said the commander, whose name I definitely knew: Cesar, Augustus? Something of the Old Empire, of that I was sure. A Latin name, when now it was mostly Greek being spoken. He spoke Greek to me. I think it was Greek.

He looked me up and down. 'My officers speak highly of you.'

'Thank you, Sir.'

'And you have the lighter skin that so many of these horsemen of the North also share.'

Horsemen, is that who we were fighting? Yes, I remembered fighting horsemen! Ferocious enemies, their cavalry could tear through our infantry like a scythe through summer corn.

'Can you ride, Chaucere?'

'Well enough, Sir. I was brought up on a farm.' If only I could remember his name. Surely I should know his name?

'Good, you may need to be able to ride. And where are you from?'

'Pretani,' I said, giving the older name for my island home.

The commander made up his mind. 'Justinian will explain the mission. It is important Chaucere. Do not fail.'

I was dismissed.

The city had been called many different things, depending on who considered themselves its current rulers. The names changed, the city didn't. It was old – some even said the oldest.

The city that begat all others.

Perhaps this was the first place where men assembled in such numbers that not only did you now no longer know your neighbour, but you no longer cared about him either. I do not know if this was true, but age was certainly ingrained into every brick and wall, every step and staircase, of that sun-baked labyrinth.

Age seemed to ooze from the mortar and plaster.

Just walking through the streets, your hands and face felt like they were coated with a residue. A balmy reminder of those uncounted generations; as if those men and women had left there an essence that a magician might collect and distil to tell their stories to all those with wit enough to listen.

I was a spy, not the first to walk these confined byways and given the primacy of this city, surely not the last. I was looking for a woman, again hardly an exceptional assignment. The woman I sought though was apparently something very much out of the ordinary. She was an augur, a fortune-teller of repute whose ability was such that even those savage horsemen from the North, who had displaced us, might seek her out.

At least that was my story.

It was a story that would hold no water with any of those savage horsemen, should I have need to speak to them, but my tale, my colour and stolen clothes, should be enough to satisfy those locals seeking to gain favour with their new masters.

I had little time for mystical women, preferring their kin with the more down-to-earth interests. But there I was, in borrowed clothes and armour, now seeking out one such, at my commander's insistence. Exactly how I had arrived there from our encampment was unclear to me, as was my progress past the guards at the City Gates. Even my name sounded a little wrong and how could that be?

I was there and I had a job to do. It wasn't a good idea to question events too closely. The here and now was what was important. I knew the here, but as for the now? When was now?

The door was ahead of me. That was the now.

Her door.

How could I forget it? A blue as dark as the night sea. But when had I seen it before? I had just found the house – the beggar with the one eye had directed me, his sight somehow able to see so much further than mine. The door opened, before I had even knocked, and a man beckoned me in. I thought I knew this man, or I would know him – it was all so confusing. He was a bearded, mysterious, figure and carried with him a feel of immeasurable age, even though he moved like a man in his prime. He was clothed in a gold robe, but sometimes it looked deepest blue.

I followed the man, who did not speak to me, and he led me to a room full of further strangeness. Such peculiarity it held, that it was as if I had actually stepped from this world into another, where everything I took for granted was now changed. Perhaps I had.

It was a room full of luxury as well. I had never seen so much wealth on display. Rich fabrics and intricate tapestries, both patterned and figurative. Polished metal ewers and statues reflecting lights coloured by stained glass of every conceivable tint. Plus precious gems that seemed to be scattered like so many pebbles on an exotic beach, leading to a sea of the extraordinary.

The sea was blue, of course – a deep rich satin blue material on the largest bed I had ever seen; waves of material overflowed onto the carpeted floor and around small islands of plumped-up pillows over which was draped a woman as extraordinary as the room itself.

I have heard that there are unnatural creatures in the oceans of the world that are so attractive that they can lure unsuspecting sailors to their doom upon hidden rocks.

This woman was their more attractive sister.

I have no clue as to her nationality or origins. Is there an island somewhere whose people all share skin the colour of molasses, with amber eyes and hair like a raven's wing? Oh, those ravens! If there is such a place and such a people, they must be a most remarkable race.

She was dressed in gold and her name was Hecuba.

Not only did she look more beautiful than any woman I had ever seen, but she smelt more wonderful too. The whole room was a delight for the senses. There was even music playing, the like of which I had never heard before. No simple tune or melody, this was the work of instruments I could not even name and the effect was like water for the thirsting and food for the starving. I was carried on a tide of music to that sea and the enchantress lying there.

Hecuba read my fortune.

This was not why I had been sent to find her. I was sent to fetch word on the fortune of my commander and of our battalion and the fate of our current conflict, not my own well being.

Hecuba wasn't interested. Their fate was all sealed. Mine was different.

I lay with Hecuba and took her as a wife. We had many fine sons and beautiful daughters and lived a fine life in this, the eldest of cities. The robed man became my mentor and advised me in the building of a mighty empire here in the East. It was an empire that included many different peoples who worshipped many different gods, but it was an Empire that brought peace and justice to them all.

I never learnt the name of the robed man and he never seemed to age, although I did, and eventually I felt my powers wane and knew I had lived well passed my three score and ten and so was grateful.

Hecuba, whose beauty was still untouched by age or ailment, smiled at me and spoke:

'It is time for you to go home, my love. Shed no tears, for we have had a wonderful life together.' I nodded. I had indeed lived a life unlike that of any other man and I regretted nothing.

'You must return to your island home,' she said in a voice that was now half song and half prayer. 'You have turned your back on destiny, but destiny has not finished with you, Chaucere. Your land still has need of you.'

With one sweep of her hand she offered me a picture of the lands I had grown up in, had loved, I suppose, in the manner of a much younger man. All looked well, the barley grew and the fruits ripened, but underneath – deep in the soil – there was something wrong. There was a poison here, unnoticed and, as yet, without effect, but if unchecked, it would grow, and the land itself would be lost along with all that depended on it.

Hecuba continued portentously, 'you will not be that which once you might have been, what was offered to you and you rejected, but you must play your part in a different manner. It will lack the glory and there will be no crowns to wear and you may yet go to a warrior's grave on a distant shore. I cannot tell, as that is still unclear to me, yet go you must, lest something more dreadful awaits you.'

So I left our bed and made my way out of the door as dark as the sea at night, to another place and another time, A different face, no less beautiful, but much less exotic, leant over me and wiped my brow. It felt good and so I relaxed and once again I was dead to the world. This time when I recovered, it was to a world that was much more familiar – yet I ached to return to Hecuba and the other place I had left behind, but I never would. Not this side of the veil. But Hecuba would never desert me.

24
THE KING'S PARADE.

That I did not remain dead to the world after the assassination attempt upon my person was thanks to the ministrations of Rachel and Isak, plus a certain amount of forethought on my part. Perhaps forethought is pushing it a bit. If I had gone home first I would have taken off the armour I had worn for my encounter with Lord Hudde and then my goose would have been well and truly, stuffed, basted and cooked to perfection.

Laziness, and a desire for drink, saved the day. As it can do.

My armour was not the heavy metal plating that Lord Hudde had chosen for protection, but a much more lightweight version that I had picked up on my travels. I say picked up, but I had actually taken it off a fallen comrade, as he had no further use for it. This lightweight protection was made from a series of lacquered plates of a ridiculous hard foreign wood joined by toughened leather straps. It is the perfect foil for arrows, especially when covered by a light chain mail. Arrows did not necessarily bounce off you, but the impact is considerably lessened as they embed themselves into the wood and, thankfully, flesh is seldom pierced.

This armour had not help my fellow sellsword as it does nothing to protect you from a bolt in the eye – nothing can help with that – however I knew he would not begrudge me its use. I like to think he would have been pleased to know that it did, in truth, save my life that day. The second arrow that struck my back had stuck firmly into the wood and thereby my life was saved. I still had the arrow in my shoulder to contend with though, and the poison that Lord Hudde and his bootlickers had taken to employing to tilt the battlefield even further in their favour. Coping with such a poison was by no means easy.

I'd had a fever that lasted nearly a fourteen night and came very close to killing me. But Isak had some knowledge of the poison now and had considered possible remedies – one of them worked.

In that time of delirium I revisited many places I had not been to in years and spoke with people I had never expected to see again among them friends, comrades-at-arms, lovers and the enemy: the missed, the forgotten and the dead; always the dead. The dead – ever present to remind me of my own mortality or perhaps waiting to welcome me to their new estate?

And Hecuba of course – too much Hecuba, but still not enough.

I had no control over where Laso, the goddess of recuperation from illness, led me. However, I had never fought with Justinian's men – though he knew my name – and I'd never walked through those narrow stall-lined alleys, rich with history and I had never spoken with Hecuba or led that life I had once dreamed of. Not in this skin. Yet she knew my name.

To say that this was all rather strange was a very serious understatement.

The only thing that mattered is that, after days of tossing and turning and muttering and cursing – in four or five different languages – the fever broke. I returned to the here and now and the first face I saw belonged to Rachel, which was not a bad welcome at all. I was back with the living, but death was still on my mind. Somebody else's death that is.

First I needed my strength back and that did not come easy. It was the work of many weeks and it took a lot of effort on my part, with Emald's help too. He was a good taskmaster. And, almost before I knew it, summer was with us again.

There was to be merry making on Midsummer's Day, by order of the King. A Midsummer Fair was to be held – not that the good people of Camelot ever needed much excuse to make merry. One could probably argue, quite convincingly, that rather too much of the good people of Camelot's time was spent making merry. Merry was a way of life that frequently prevented other useful activities like milking the cows, or ploughing the fields or walking in straight lines.

I was not in a mood for making merry. I had never felt less merry in my life. My shoulder was aching like I'd had an arrow buried deep in it, which was a reasonable feeling under the circumstances. I needed to get back on my feet and take some fresh air, though. I had missed the whole spring, laid up as I was, and summer was blooming around me. Isak and Rachel had worked wonders and the rest was up to me. It was not an easy task, but I had a great incentive. I had a man to kill.

I refused Rachel's offer of a shave and my beard was now of sufficient length to provide an adequate disguise for any of that proportion of the city that had not previously seen me so hairy-faced. I was also walking with a crutch, not part of the disguise, just needed to help me get from here to there. The total effect made me look twenty years older, mostly because I felt thirty years older.

'On reflection, I think it makes you look very learned,' said Rachel, helping me on with a summer weight kirtle and still eyeing up my beard.

'Then you must shave him immediately daughter!' said Isak. 'We cannot let the poor people of Camelot be so mislead.'

I tutted to great effect.

'To think a Healer would mock his own patient in such a cruel manner! And me still not a step from Death's Door, and still holding his invitation in my hand.'

Isak laughed and added something to Rachel in the language they shared that I could never understand. This didn't worry me as I often said things that made no sense to anybody – not even myself.

My main motive for attending the Midsummer Fair had nothing to do with merry-making. I was curious – curiosity having long been my downfall. It had been confirmed that the King's new bride was to be in attendance. Queen Guinevere had not been much in evidence since the nuptials, to which I hadn't been invited. The reasons for this were many and often contradictory – not the reasons for the lack of my invitation, which, though many, were blindingly obvious. Some said that Guinevere's beauty had been exaggerated and she was therefore loath to be seen. The more spiteful said that the young bride only showed up the King's increasing age. Others still talked about a lost child in hushed tones.

I didn't care.

I was just being nosy and I like being nosy. It shows that I am still alive for a start.

Which is good.

And capable of taking an interest in the world beyond and above simple concerns like where the next meal is coming from. I took my interest as a positive step after these weeks of incarceration. No matter how pleasant Rachel's company may have been, and it was very pleasant, I felt the need for a few new faces.

And, after all, I had never seen a Queen before either. In my travels I had seen all sorts of Caliphs, warlords, barons and potentates and, of course, a King or three, but I had never seen a Queen - not one with that title anyway. I had a feeling that they might well be over-praised as a commodity and I doubted that any women could live up to the reputation that went before them. Certainly I was sure that Guinevere could not be the epitome of all the womanly virtues that she was made out to be. Modesty, beauty and chastity can go hand in hand, I am sure, but I would say that if you managed two out of the three you were generally doing very well.

The gods (or God – I'm not well up on matters theological) overseeing Midsummer Fairs had obviously heard the proclamation from the King and were taking his order seriously. The sky was as blue as a blackbird's egg and the clouds that were present were only there to provide a moderate amount of shade for the pale skins of young maidens strolling with their sweethearts. Fair Meadow was bustling and full of colour, with flags and buntings fluttering cheerily, and the tunes from a clutch of minstrels blended tunefully as jesters japed and capered and fire-eaters decided against eating fire and tried to singe revellers instead.

As I entered the meadow from Fair Lane, I won't say I exactly gained a spring in my step, but I found myself wielding my crutch with more vigour. The crutch, naturally, was not required for my shoulder, but the damage done to my knee as I fell off my mount was proving equally bothersome. However, equipped with crutch and a beggar's beard I felt my anonymity was assured.

I certainly wasn't doing too badly for a dead man.

My funeral had been a quiet affair. Emald and his blacksmith friends, Rachel and Isak of course and Dale the King's Messenger were present. I would have liked to attend, but I understand it is not the done thing. And I was still prostrate on the sick bed in Isak's house of healing. Dale had actually done quite well out of my 'demise'. He had inherited my house and was taking care of both it and Timothy as well. I had decided to confide in him shortly after Sir Dace's murder. He had been furious at the news of Hudde's infamy. Lord Petroc was a well-liked man and Lord Hudde very much less so. Dale had been all for calling Lord Hudde out for his crime. I managed to convince him that proof was still lacking. In the meantime I would see to his comeuppance, with Merlin's assistance, although I kept that titbit to myself.

Still, it was very useful to have another contact in the Big House. At first, I had been concerned that the Lady Ansithe would believe I had broken my word to her. It was Emald who had been able to find Dale for me, and after our reunion, he then took my message and smuggled it to the Lady – along with her token. He had returned with a carefully worded note that wished me a speedy recovery and thanked me for 'my endeavour that has been appreciated by many'. Lord Hudde, apparently, had been a laughing stock for many a month. I hoped the news had given her Lady-In-Waiting some cheer. She had been very much in my thoughts during my convalescence.

I was delighted to have somebody take care of Timothy. I had grown fond of the monstrous hound. Dale's position as a King's messenger did not entitle him to better lodgings than a straw mattress in the Royal stables, so he was glad of the change of scenery. I knew I could count on Dale to take care of my house, and I was looking forward to sitting in it again and scratching Timothy behind his right ear in the manner I had learnt he was very fond of. First though I had something else to do.

I had a man to kill and for that I needed to be in fine fettle. So I took my exercises seriously. I was getting there.

I like a fair. I like the colour, the noise and the smiling faces. I like the foolish clowns, who are not really that funny, as everybody knows, but we go along with the joke, because it's good to laugh. I like the fire-eaters, although having shared a berth with a part-time fire-eater on a ship across the Middle Sea I can say I do not like their farts. I like the jugglers, although any idiot can learn to juggle if he takes the time, these idiots have certainly taken the time and thus should be applauded. I like the acrobats because they have taken the time to learn to do things that most people can't. I like the men on stilts in particular and I am not sure why. Perhaps we have all wanted to stride across the land with a giant's step, to see the world from up on high – present yet not present, involved but aloof. A stiltman must be a great thing to be.

One day I will get myself a pair of stilts, so tall that I will be able to stride across this land of ours and seek out where all injustice is being done and I will apprehend the wrong-doers. I will not hang them. I will not put them to the sword. I will simply pick them up and I will show them the beauty of this land set in the midst of a troubled sea. From my vantage point on high, I will show the distant lands of heat and wonder where adventures await any willing to take a chance. Then I will show them the people that they are wronging. People who, by and large, just want to get on with their lives and find love and what happiness they can. I will explain to the wrongdoers how they are not helping.

And after that I will drop them.

I like the sense of hope that always seems to accompany fairs, as if one day all of life might be like this. I like the smells of roasting hog and the sweetmeats and pastries. I like the pig so much I bought a big slice of well-seared meat on a chunk of bread nicely hollowed out to take the juices. I felt about as good as any man recovering from a nasty wound and a nastier poison has any right to feel.

Eventually, the King came. Once again I was struck by just how regal he held himself. He did the King business very well. One might almost believe the nonsense about Kingship being decided by Higher Powers. As he smiled and waved, I felt those pale blue eyes, so similar to the ones that I showed to the world, dart and flicker, as if seeking me out from amongst the crowds of people. As if he knew I was there and was just waiting to find me. As if.

The King's Parade was quite a small procession as these things go. It only took half an hour for the Royal entourage to ride past where I was standing, to where a Royal Pavilion had been erected at the top of Fair Field. There were courtiers, scribes and whatnots, followed by ladies and gentlemen and then the Knights and their Ladies. I saw Lord Hudde and was pleased to acquaint myself with the new livid scar he carried on his cheek. It looked like his wound had never healed properly – small consolation. I nearly broke the crutch, so tight was my grip as I watched him parade by in all his pomp.

There would be a reckoning.

I was much more pleased to see the Lady Ansithe in all her finery, seated on a litter carried by four sturdy men and I was disappointed that her doe-eyed Lady-In-Waiting was not present. I had been thinking far too much about her of late. In my more optimistic moments, I had even began to wonder what it would take to win such a beauty. Could an itinerant swordsman, albeit a Freeman with his own house, ever aspire to such a prize? Such flights of fancy – and there was I, not even knowing her name!

I didn't have long to wait to find it out – her name was Guinevere.

Arthur's carriage was a thing of beauty, with multi-coloured ribbons and garlands of flowers but the wife within was more beautiful still. How could I have ever mistaken her for a mere Lady-In-Waiting? But, as I looked at her in her bejewelled beauty, I realised that this was part of her allure, part of her appeal; she could be anything and everything to anybody – even a poor deluded clod like me.

I must admit I was shaken. What the subterfuge might mean as regards the relationship between the late lamented Lord Petroc and Arthur's Queen; I did not like to consider. I didn't really like to think about very much at all. I felt like leaving, but didn't. I stayed and watched as the King and his young Queen took their places on the pavilion stage. Close by, but somehow still veiled in shadow, was the Merlin. That man carried his own dusk with him. I shivered at the thought of being in his presence again, but I knew I would be, and soon.

I stayed for the entertainment, which didn't entertain me at all. The mock fights and jousts just made a mockery of the whole of my profession while the strolling players and their stories seemed tired and of no interest. I stayed for the same reason that you prod at a tooth that is giving you the toothache.

It is just what you do.

And all the time, when I should have been looking at what was happening in front of the crowd, I looked and looked at the beauty that was Queen Guinevere. I looked so hard that every detail of that perfect face was burned forever in my mind, and then I turned away and stared instead at Lord Hudde. I stared and hated and planned and plotted. There is nothing like a little revenge to assuage the hurt of heartache and misery.

25
MERLIN AGAIN

Another way to cure heartache is to find yourself being quizzed by a man who, as common belief had it, was the centuries old spawn of one of hell's own. A man who had seen the Men of Rome come and seen them leave again; a man who you might just have met before in another country, speaking another tongue, with a different type of Queen, in a different age. If such things were possible, which of course they weren't. Were they?

I should not have been surprised that Merlin found me with no trouble, despite my beard and limp and looking two score years older. I was a little disappointed though. I didn't bother arguing with his men and, as meekly as a baby, put on the blindfold they offered. I followed them by what I would swear was a very different route. The room was the same though and the sword hung in the same place and still scared me down to the marrow.

'You have been busy, Chaucere.'

'I have.'

'You do not look too bad – for a dead man.'

'I've looked worse, it's true.'

'Busy giving our Lord Hudde a wound he will carry with him for the rest of his natural days – one that is very loathe to heal.'

'Well, it would be a lie if I said that didn't give me a great deal of comfort at nights as I drop off to sleep.'

'I don't believe I mentioned that you should actually scar a Lord who sits at the King's Table?'

'You asked me for evidence.'

'I did.'

'There you have it. Lord Hudde corrupts his sword points. Surely not the act of any Lord that sits at the King's Round Table?'

'He says the scar was from a dirty nail.'

'Oh yes? A nail that was his own weapon. Ask the Justice.'

'I have.'

'Well then, good.'

'Some think Justice Hobby surly. It is not actually the case, but he has seen a lot in his life and most of it has disappointed him. This matter did not restore his faith in chivalry.'

'Our duel had a just result, considering.'

'You ruined the pier at the Field of Penitence and sunk Lord Hudde's boats.'

Now I was getting annoyed. 'So what if I did? The man was not fit to lick Lord Petroc's boots and he made a mockery of single combat – which is not a sport.'

'Lord Petroc? He jousted with him I know, but….'

'Never mind,' I replied testily, forgetting for the moment that I was addressing the second most powerful man in the land and I had plenty to hide from him as well.

'There is no – evidence, not as you would understand it.'

'That's the problem Chaucere. I need proper solid evidence to put before the King and his Knights. Lord Hudde has made himself a popular man and his largesse is well known.'

'Yet what is the source of this largesse?'

Merlin looked at me quizzically. 'He has lands in the North, a Great Hall.'

'His lands are poor and his "Great Hall" is no better than a midden hut. His rents must barely pay for his new linen!'

'Now that is interesting. You checked this?'

'Yes, I checked it!'

'You should have told me, Chaucere.'

'It is hardly evidence of the sort you requested.'

'No, but it is very – interesting, very interesting. Find me further evidence, Chaucere, and you shall have a better revenge than a scar.'

I sighed and nodded my agreement. 'I am looking. Still looking.'

Merlin paced a while and then started on a new track. 'You are local are you not, Chaucere?'

I nodded, not liking the direction the conversation was now taking.

'But your name is not of these islands?'

'No, my mother said my father came from across the Narrow Sea – he made hosiery apparently – before he died.'

Merlin's face betrayed his doubt: 'Oh, really?'

'So she said.'

'But you have travelled?'

'Yes.'

'And earned your money by your sword?'

'Mostly. It paid better than other "metal work".'

'And when did you first leave Camelot for your adventurous life?'

'With great respect, Merlin – does it matter?'

'I am interested in you, Chaucere. As I said, I don't think you are everything you would seem to be at first sight.'

I sighed: 'I am far less than the sum of my parts, Master.'

'Perhaps.'

I shifted uneasily. 'Now can I get on? I have evidence to find after all, and must get myself fit after my travails.'

Merlin looked at me and then glanced up at the sword that hung on the wall – the sword that I still tried so desperately not too look at. The sword that drew me like a moth to a campfire.

'Yes, yes. Get on then. Find me my evidence!' He called for his men and they blindfolded me again, but before the cloth was pulled over my eyes I muttered one last word: 'Hecuba.' I was delighted to glimpse his previously controlled and expressionless face break into something very much like surprise, before they led me out.

26
THE ROUND TABLE

I needed to ask Dale for a favour. It was a difficult one to explain, as admitting to my reason meant touching upon areas that made me uncomfortable. The previous night I had dreamt of the Round Table and the figure behind the rat, that I was now sure was Sir Hudde, was growing darker and more menacing. I thought the King was looking a bit peaky too. In fact there was something like a shadow on his face. That couldn't be good, surely?

Ever since my first dream of the Round Table I had wanted to know if it really was just a dream or something more akin to a prophecy? Could one of the King's much lauded Knights really be such a traitor? Were others involved? I felt that only by seeing the Table itself could I gain the insight I needed, so, I went ahead and asked him. He was most amused:

'What are you now, Chaucere? Some school boy who would boast to his friends of having seen the famous Round Table?'

We were drinking in Alia's alehouse, which was thriving, even after my departure. I was happy about this, honestly. I know I'm not indispensable, although occasionally it is fun to believe so.

'You know I wouldn't ask if it wasn't important,' I said, in a serious tone.

'Chaucere,' he said in the voice he had adopted after getting to know me better, and realising half my supposed inspired ideas were actually anything but. 'You have to realise that the Round Table is the most important symbol of King Arthur's rule. As such there is a Guard stationed, day and night, at the door to the Great Hall, where the table is located.

'Who are these guards? Do you know them?' I asked eagerly.

'Well,' he took a deep breath, 'the guarding of the Great Hall is considered a great honour and so only the King's Messengers are allowed the duty.'

He waited a moment or two for this to sink in, before adding, 'Oh, and one or two Lords occasionally.'

I finally grasped the full import, 'You mean you are actually one of the people who can get me in to see the Round Table?'

'Next week as it so happens.'

'Oh this is too good!'

It was as straightforward as it sounded. It wasn't that security was poor in the Big House, but, in my opinion, too much of it relied on guards simply recognising one another. It was like the possibility of people turning traitor had never occurred to those in charge.

Dale was on night duty, which made life even easier. Holding torches, we entered through one of two doors, and my first sight caused me an involuntary intake of breath.

'It is impressive,' said Dale, mistaking the reason for my reaction.

It wasn't that I wasn't impressed – I most certainly was – it was more that it was exactly as I had imagined in my dreams. The Table, easily the width of three tall men, was divided into four and twenty segments, each demarcated by what appeared to be different woods, or maybe tints and stains. Dale was right – it was very impressive,

'That I take it is the King's seat?' I asked, pointing to the only chair with arms.

'Yes. It is said that the King actually wanted all the chairs to be the same – to show that all were equal at his Table. However, the craftsmen weren't having any of this, and not being allowed to make a throne, did at least manage to put some arms on his chair.'

I laughed at this. It did indeed sound the very least wood-workers would have insisted upon. I walked around the Table to the chair I had seen in my dream.

'Is this where Lord Hudde sits?' I asked Dale.

'Yes,' he said, surprised. 'How did you know that?'

'It's a long story Dale, for another time.' I kept walking round to the chair where I had sat in my dream. I took a breath before asking, 'Who sits here?'

'Now it's interesting you should ask that,' Dale said, walking to join me. 'Although there are seats for four and twenty at his table, the King only has twenty three in his immediate circle.'

'What is the reason for that?'

'The King has said he leaves a seat free to show that any man worthy might join him at his Table.'

Now wasn't that just a little scary and didn't it send a shiver down my spine?

'Here' said Dale, let me name who currently sits with the King.' And with that he walked round the Table naming who would normally sit there in a quiet reverential voice:

'Sir Gawain, Sir Percivale, Sir Lionell, Sir Tristram de Lyones, Sir Hudde you know, Sir Gareth, Sir Bedivere, Sir Bleoberis, Sir Lacotemale Taile, Sir Lucan, Sir Palomedes, the Knight to come, Sir Lamorak, Sir Bors de Ganis, Sir Safer, Sir Pellea, Sir Kay, Sir Ector de Maris, Sir Dagonet, Sir Degore, Sir Brunor le Noir, Sir Lebius Desconneu, Sir Alymere and our youngest Knight, the valiant and much missed Sir Petroc.'

We both went quiet for a moment in memory of the departed Sir Petroc.

'And there you have it Chaucere! Now perhaps you would be so kind as to tell me what is so important that you need to see the King's mighty Round Table?'

I considered this. Sharing my concerns seemed the least I could do:

'I believe the King is in mortal danger and for reasons not clear to me the Fates have chosen me to prevent this.'

Dale unsheathed his sword and held it out to me. 'Then Chaucere, my friend, you have my sword and my life, if necessary.'

I nodded my acceptance. 'I sincerely hope it won't come to that Dale, but you have my profound thanks.'

And with that we left the Great Hall and I left Dale to his vigil, while I went back to Rachel and Isak's and to my cogitation.

27
THE SHEPHERD'S HUT

I needed solid proof of Lord Hudde's baseness for Merlin to take to the King. If, as I suspected, he was in league with Cecilio supplying him and his company with intelligence gleaned from his position in the Big House, or probably even leading the band, then such an accusation could not be made casually. I needed to catch him with blood on his hands. Red handed or nothing.

Cecilio was the key – of that much I was sure – so I became Camelot's expert on Cecilio. I learnt where he lived – a surprisingly nondescript doss house run by a woman with an expression that could curdle milk at four hundred paces, and a tongue that could strip the hide from an ox. I learnt Cecilio's drinking haunts, which were varied and well spaced and not at all the dens I would have expected.

I got to know his associates and they were not all as base as I might have expected either. Yes, there were lowlifes like Gipp and Ham, but a lot of the others were men with a position, although, as I learnt from my inquiries, they shared one thing: they were all men with ambition. Possibly also men who thought that advancement was their natural right.

There are a lot of men in Camelot at this time who believed they had been born beneath the station nature should have provided for them. In a world where power can be gained by freeing something sharp from something hard, why not? Not me, of course, I should add. I distrust Fate when she puts such things before you, and I tend to run a thousand miles. At least I have in the past.

Little by little, I began to put together a chain of corruption that I suspected ran right through the Kingdom of Camelot. From the highest to the lowest there were men taking advantage of the sudden growth of the Kingdom to find a place to prosper in the cracks. Sometimes it doesn't pay to grow too quickly.

Nobody suspected that they were being followed. Of that I was sure. There were, unfortunately, for the city, but fortunately for me, a host of other beggars and cripples on the streets of Camelot. I changed rags frequently and sometimes had my crutch, or a stick, or then as my knee improved, no aid at all.

I learnt one thing I did not suspect – how little charity many of the good people now had for those less fortunate. The number of times I was told to move on, and even had clods of earth and stones thrown at me, gave me food for thought. This new religion might not be such a bad idea if it does indeed encourage us to look more favourably upon our neighbours down on their luck.

Finally, after many days of shadowing Cecilio, I learnt of the places where he met Lord Hudde. First on the list was the Bath House! Of course, I should have looked there first, although I was hardly dressed to undress in such company. That first occasion was no coincidence, this was a regular meet.

It was never the same place twice in a row, thoughown and not ever in the expected bawdy houses, alehouses, and out-houses either. A lot of thought was given to their meets. They did not want to be seen together, and they were careful not to be followed, but, as the saying goes, nobody notices a beggar. Sometimes I blended in so well I almost forgot what I was doing there. The more clandestine their arrangements became, the more convinced I was that it was Hudde's hand that was forging the links of the chain of corruption and rattling it for his pleasure.

It's strange to think now, that I was actually wrong. There was another's hand involved as well and they were pulling the strings.

A connection between the King's Knight, Lord Hudde, and the outlander Cecilio meant nothing. They could simply be associates, with a habit of meeting up to share an old tale or two in the more interesting corners of Camelot. There needed to be more. There needed to be evidence of the thievery. There needed to be proof of the conspiracy and the rot in the Big House, so I reminded myself of the oft-quoted adage "follow the gold".

I suspected that Lord Hudde was using his cut of the booty to fund his life in Camelot and keep his manor from going to ruins. However, as Abram had first pointed out to me, there was a lot of wealth being lost in and around the Big House at the moment, yet Hudde had not been gilding his own Manor House with gold. Was I missing something?

In the meantime, surely these bandits needed a place to meet to divide the spoils after their thievery: a stronghold, a fortified keep or sturdy, safe, farmhouse perhaps? Or perhaps they met in a shepherd's hut in the middle of some scrubby heathland? The hut's innocuous appearance definitely worked to their advantage. Such a building was surely not the headquarters of a nefarious gang of brigands?

I had found the hideout almost by accident. I was following Cecilio on foot, but had lost my quarry when, outside an alehouse, a companion had turned up with a spare mount for him. I sat and waited. The two men came back a few hours later looking very happy with themselves and went into the alehouse.

My interest piqued, I then fetched my own horse and some fresh clothes and decided to investigate where their destination may have been. It was very long odds, but I saw that Cecilio's mount had old-fashioned hipposandals, which some riders still prefer if their horse is prone to hoof rot – although other riders claim they are the cause of it. The boots made a horse easy to trail, but I still was not optimistic about achieving anything by this. However, we'd had a light rain after a dry spell and so the ground was very co-operative.

I found the trail of Cecilio's horse and his companion and then found that they were overridden by first one, then two, then three and finally four other horses. The last horse made good deep impressions in the mud. It was a fine mount with good shoes and a large rider. I would put gold on it belonging to Lord Hudde.

The trail led me to the shepherd's hut. Not the normal meeting place for a collection of rogues, although I knew that many a ne'er-do-well would take refuge in such place. Their steeds had been tied up in a thicket that was conveniently hidden from the nearest trail. Whoever had been there was long departed. The floor of the hut was scuffed up, but sadly there were no convenient coins or jewels left lying around. A shame, but I had no doubts in my mind that this was where they had met.

It was ridiculous to believe it I know, but I swear I could even smell Lord Hudde's rankness – or perhaps it was just the sheep shit.

The next time news reached Camelot of a party waylaid on the road I made straight for the shepherd's hut. I was not alone. I had organised a small company of concerned citizens, including many who had lost goods or gold to the bandits. We approached the shepherd's hut quietly. The weather had been dry and there were no new tracks to follow, but as I hoped, several horses were tied up in the thicket behind the small ramshackle building.

My men spread out. Emald had a large smile on his face and a very large hammer in his hands.

'I think we may have the sprats in our net,' he whispered to me.

'And one large fish I hope!' I whispered back.

Emald grinned as he snuck off. He was enjoying himself far too much on our little escapades. I think perhaps his heart wasn't as set on 'blacksmithery' as it once was.

When everybody was in position, the hand signals were exchanged, and I cleared my throat. Now was my moment.

'Men inside the hut!' I shouted. 'Lay down your arms and come out with your hands in plain sight! We know what you are and what you have done and the gold that you are now dividing is all the proof we need.'

As speeches go it lacked motivation, but I thought it did the job.

There were raised voices within the hut. Time to offer some more incentive.

'We are many times your number and, to be honest, all now ready for some supper and not above setting fire to a shepherd's hut to get home quicker.'

That should do the job.

There was a further commotion from inside the hut – there was little doubt that we had taken everybody by surprise. The plan could not have gone better. I unsheathed my sword. They were not going to come quietly. We approached, using what cover we could find. There were no windows or slits for an archer, but it pays to be cautious. We had archers aplenty.

And then the door to the shepherd's hut flew open and out strode Lord Hudde, divested of his travel cloak, now with gleaming mail and the King's crest for all to see.

He was smiling. He shouldn't have been smiling:

'I, Lord Hudde, have found and defeated the brigands that have preyed upon our travellers and traders. They will steal no more!' And with that he held up the severed head of Cecilio, which to my eyes at least still had a look of surprise on his face – as well it might.

'Shite,' said Emald to my right.

'Through my network of spies,' Hudde continued, 'I tracked them to their lair and by professing to be interested in their ill-gotten gains I have, single-handedly, put them all to the sword.'

'Shite,' echoed Dale, to my left.

'Put down your swords, good men of Camelot!' Hudde continued. 'Today has seen a famous victory for the Knights of the Round Table and the King's justice. Rejoice!'

Apart from Dale and Emald I had not told the rest of my militia of my suspicions concerning the venal Lord Hudde, lest they be intimidated. The men's reaction, upon seeing one of the King's Knights, in all his Knightly glory, holding the head of an obvious villain was as one might have expected.

They cheered.

They cheered even louder when they saw that the rest of the band was slain as well, as this meant they did not need to fight and end up similarly bloodied.

Lord Hudde was a hero.

This had not gone as intended at all.

Dale, Emald and I exchanged confused words while the rest of my company congratulated Lord Hudde. Emald nodded at me: 'You'd best be gone, Chaucere.'

Dale agreed. 'I will be the spokesman for our party. I will say we had an informant, but his information was given too late to notify the King's men. We will keep your name out of it.'

So, in what should have been my moment of triumph, I crept away with my tail between my legs, as my men continued to mob Lord Hudde with compliments, but not before he caught a glimpse of me. From the brief, surprised look on his face, he quickly realised I was not actually as dead as his erstwhile-colleague Cecilio, whose head he now held in his hand. He lifted it in my direction – a warning or a promise?

Lord Hudde had slaughtered the rest of his thieving band without hesitation, taking advantage of his speed of thought and falseness. This was a man who knew nothing of loyalty or trust. He was as dangerous an individual as I had ever come across and I realised then that I had underestimated him and was lucky to have bested him on the Field of Penitence. I had hoped to put an end to matters today, but I now knew our blood feud was only just beginning. There was only one way it could end. One of us must die.

I was not a happy man as I rode steadily back to Camelot, but already my mind was racing. How could I reveal the truth about Lord Hudde? I dare not involve the Lady Ansithe or Queen Guinevere, so what other options did I now have? Merlin? I still did not have the evidence he required to take to the King.

The one good thing to come out of a dire situation was that I was now permitted a spectacular return from the dead. The reasons given for my subterfuge were long winded and enough to bore anybody mildly interested in knowing why I was not six feet underground, as previously proclaimed. These reasons involved a widow woman and an inheritance and a scheming stepson whom, apparently, I had known in a previous life. Solving this situation required me to play dead. All very involved and complicated and actually nobody asked for long explanations anyway – not to my face.

I was pleased that more than a few of the good folk of Camelot were actually quite pleased to see me – or at least pretended as much. It was also pleasant to be back in my own house with Timothy. He was delighted to see me. Not that it hadn't been a pleasure to be with Rachel and Isak, but I could feel myself becoming more attached to my nurse than a man in my profession could afford to be. Being taken care of will do that to a man. Regular food, kind words and the feeling that there was somebody in the world that cared whether you lived or died, was not the way to strengthen the sword arm and refine the killer instinct.

I was not the marrying sort, I told myself, but I was concerned about how badly I was reacting to the discovery of my doe-eyed maiden's true identity, and that wasn't fair to Rachel – my dedicated nurse, only a nurse.

Dale was also quite happy to be back in the Royal Stables with his fellow Messengers, but I warned him to be wary of Lord Hudde. Dale, thinking cleverly, had been quick to be first among the many cheering Lord Hudde's discovery of the bandit ring, but I knew that Hudde was not a man to be easily fooled twice. As for myself, I bought new bolts and extra locks for my doors, was particularly pleasant to my neighbours and made sure the local children acted as extra eyes and ears for me. They enjoyed doing this as Timothy was a great favourite locally and could even be found giving rides to the smaller children.

Life settled back into something like a routine. I met up with Dale regularly, my eyes and ears in the Big House. He did not have the high-level access of a 'Sir Dace', but he was my best source for information about what the Lords and Ladies were saying and thinking – if not providing insight into the Queen's state of mind. I put all thoughts of her far to one side.

The news from the Big House was not encouraging. Lord Hudde was in particularly good odour in the nose of the King. His single-handed uncovering of the 'bandit ring' and speedy dispatch of those involved was greeted with delight at court. These attacks had become an embarrassment, with the miscreants regularly managing to evade the King's patrols. Of course, nobody questioned how exactly the bandits had found it so easy to elude capture – why would you when the problem was now solved?

28
A WEDDING

Emald and Rachel were to be married. Was I surprised? To be honest, I wasn't sure. They were both good folk, and attractive and pleasant as well, even taking into account Emald's brusqueness, which did little to obscure his essential decency. They were also both of an age when society would have expected them to have been long wed. It had never occurred to me to question why this was the case, which is rich coming from the life-long bachelor.

What did surprise me was how Emald had come and practically asked my permission for her hand. I almost joked and said he must have mistaken me for Isak, but fortunately I spotted the seriousness of his expression and said I was delighted for both of them, of course, and said as much.

So, why exactly was he asking me?

It wasn't as if I had any intentions towards Rachel. She was my nurse, and friend too, of course. He wasn't butting in and my troth remained unplighted. Not that Rachel wasn't attractive – she was! Her hair, when it was out of her coif was lustrous and a warm shade of chestnut that put me in mind of perfect autumn days. She was good company and had a figure that was very agreeable as well. But even if I was the kind to settle down, which I wasn't, I was probably actually the sort of fool that went mooning after doe-eyed, supposed Ladies-In-Waiting with actual royal pedigrees, instead of eligible spinsters.

But was there something on Rachel's side? That had never occurred to me. Rachel was a marvellous, caring nurse, but she had never expressed anything other than a general regard for my well-being.

How much more would a modest woman like Rachel have expressed though?

Had I been a total idiot?

This would not be the first time, but what exactly did I feel now the matter had come up? I felt totally fine about it all. Fine enough to agree to be Emald's Groomsman – although fortunately, I wasn't expected to pay for the wedding. I did try to insist but Emald wasn't hearing of it and I think Rachel would have been cross and Isak livid.

So, everything was fine.

At least that's what I thought – wasn't it?

Having my own house had given me plenty of time and space to do this thing that hasn't always come as second nature to me: thinking. I sat at my table, with my feet up on it and caught up with this unnatural estate. It wasn't easy.

As a fighting man, I had always done most of my thinking on my feet. A lot of that involved ensuring that I could continue to be a fighting man and the best way to achieve that was by doing as little fighting as possible. Any fighting man who tells you anything different, who tries to impress you with tales of his bravery and valour, is a liar. An arrow in the back has no respect for the elegance of your swordplay – as I now knew, to my cost. And a heated battle is the best place to get an arrow in the back – apart from occasionally innocently mounting your horse outside an alehouse! For your long-term survival it is best to stay as far away from battles as possible.

Thinking on my feet was fine – thinking with my feet up was a new thing.

Timothy looked at me with some concern, before turning round a few times and settling, with a sigh, in front of the cold fire. I didn't get very far with my thinking at first. If I could have afforded parchment I might have even made a few notes. Perhaps I should get myself a slate and some chalk as I had heard the children of the Lords and Ladies of Camelot now use to learn their letters. I had learnt mine using a sand tray, while I recovered from a scimitar wound, in the palace of a sultan, the name of whose country I never could pronounce properly. I had saved his daughter from certain death. I did a lot of that in those days.

I had saved the sultan's pride and joy and he was properly thankful. She was properly grateful too. She taught me to read and write. Big disappointment there, but it probably stood me in better stead than any relationship could conceivably have done. Not that there was much opportunity, given the two huge eunuchs who accompanied her everywhere. Certainly reading and writing did not make her father inclined to kill me. He treated me very well and his thanks made me a wealthy man, for a while. Wealth just doesn't seem to stick to me. However, since then, I have collected languages like an old hound does fresh fleas and I always try to get at least some idea of how they are put down.

There was a knock on my door and Timothy stirred, interested. I realised that night had fallen while I had sat musing, with my feet up, at the table. Was I getting old?

'Are you at home, Master Chaucere?' said Mistress Gunnhild, knocking again. 'Only it's as dark as the grave in there.'

'Please do come in, Mistress Gunnhild! We are indeed at home.'

She entered, and the smell of something very tasty wafted ahead of her. Timothy stirred, as did I. Mistress Gunnhild and I had recommenced our arrangement after my recovery and eventual return to my house. It suited us both very well and Timothy certainly approved. Not that he seemed to have gone hungry during my absence.

'Wonderful news about Master Emald and the wise woman Rachel,' she said.

'Oh, yes! I'm sure they will make each other very happy.'

I hope my enthusiasm didn't sound forced. Truth be told, I was rather preoccupied with the contents of Mistress Gunnhild's basket, which was making my stomach rumble in a very undignified fashion. She unpacked her basket onto the table and unwrapped the dish therein from the cloth that was keeping it warm.

It was a pie!

I love a pie. In all my journeying I have never found a people who can put together a pie like the women of my native land. Mistress Gunnhild's pie was a thing of beauty. Mutton, if my nose wasn't mistaken – as good as Aila's pork pie! Timothy thought so as well. Timothy came quickly to attention by the table, quivering slightly from wet shiny nose to partially erect tail. His mouth dropped open in eager pie-induced anticipation.

Timothy was out of luck.

Yet would I be able to resist those pleading big brown eyes? Fortunately our friendship was not put to the test as Mistress Gunnhild also unwrapped a bone that must surely have come from a cow the size of a carthorse.

'And has Timothy been a good boy and guarded his master well?'

Timothy assured her that he had been an excellent guard hound and he received his reward, which he took back to the fireplace for the serious attention it deserved.

I thanked Mistress Gunnhild on both our behalves and I got down to some serious pie eating. It was a pie to really get your teeth stuck into. Mutton that had been slowed-cooked until it fell apart like the tenderest of lamb and mixed with the best of spices and onion and garlic, which I am very partial to, as she knows.

I was enjoying my pie far too much. A thought suddenly hit me – although I was back walking again, I was not yet, after my injury, the fighting man of old. With my house and regular meals, I had got soft again. I might as well have been married! I was as good as, and all without the other benefits a Goodwife brings.

This would not do at all. Action was required. From now on Hudde's every move outside the Big House would be watched. When he even sneezed out of turn, I needed to be ready.

That meant I also needed to speak one more time with Lady Ansithe and the Queen – if that was possible. I took the token Dale had returned to me to that small door. The guard spoke no word, but I was allowed entry and taken to a different room. Lady Ansithe was waiting for me, but she had a new gentle-woman with her. She was very attractive but I could barely look at her after what I now knew. She in her turn did not know what to make of me.

'Lady Ansithe,' I bowed – a respectful nod.

'Chaucere, I am so pleased to see you well recovered. Healthy even.'

I glanced at the gentlewoman. 'Is it safe to talk, M'Lady?'

She laughed before speaking, 'Oh yes, a sweet thing from relations across the Narrow Sea, who speaks not a word of English as yet.'

'Then I would update you as to the actions of a certain party so that they might be passed further up the House.'

'I see and I should say that persons up the house are also much relieved at your recovery and would be here, if it was possible, to thank you in person for all the trouble you have been put to. However, it is not an easy time.' She paused, considering her next words very carefully. 'The King has not been in the best of health recently.'

My face registered my shock.

'It is nothing of import, I am sure. And word of this obviously must not leave this room, Chaucere.'

'Of course not, M'Lady.'

'Simply some digestive problem.'

I nodded. 'I understand, to rule cannot be easy.'

'Indeed.'

'But she, who we both hold in high regard, should know that the one we have discussed is even more base than we thought and far from being a hero, he killed his men in order to save his own neck.'

'Then this adventure at the shepherd's hut, was what?'

'A sham M'Lady. A chance Hudde took to regain favour and escape our trap by savagely slaughtering his own men without warning or remorse.'

She was stunned, as well she might be.

'Then he truly is a devil,' she said, woefully shaking her head.

'And worse.'

'You think?'

'I am sure. He has some scheme that is now only just beginning to unfold. He means Camelot no good.'

She sat back, considering. 'But proof?' she said finally.

'Aye proof,' I sighed. 'He is clever, or he works for somebody cleverer still.'

'You suspect that he has another Master, Chaucere?'

'I do, M'Lady. It feels as if he works to a closely thought-out plan and does not perform well when he must respond at speed. The killing of his own men was not the cool-headed action of a clear thinker. It was the desperate act of an animal forced into a corner and could easily have been his ruin if his men had only realised how truly foul he was.'

'I see. That is worrying.'

'You should both also know that he has come to the attention of another man of great power and influence here in the Big House. This man, to whom you do not say no, has requested my assistance – if request is not too weak a word.'

Lady Ansithe's eyes grew wide with realisation. 'But you have not mentioned…' she began.

'Of course not,' I interrupted, to put her mind immediately at ease. 'And neither will I, but this powerful man is no fool.'

'Oh no, a fool is one thing he most certainly is not!'

'However, he too is suspicious of Lord Hudde and requests that I find proof of base infamy to bring before the King and this I am attempting to do. My first attempt was not wholly successful.'

'No, it was not.'

'Your friend should be informed.'

'She will be, and you should know, she too considers you a friend – a good friend – and she is sorry for any deception. She did not intend to cause … distress.'

I bowed, partly to hide what seemed to be happening to my eyes, and partly because I now found the Lady Ansithe truly worthy of such respect as well. We said our quick farewells and a new guard saw me out.

I quickly made my way back down the hill, conscious of my mood. I needed to cheer myself up; after all I had a wedding to go to, which, it occurred to me as I walked away from the Big House, was the first time I was going to be a bridesman. Technically not the first time I had been asked, but certainly the first time that the man that had asked me had lived to make it to the ceremony.

On reflection, perhaps I was not the best person to be asked to be involved in such festivities. Yet asked I had been and as such I had duties to perform.

We had celebrated the groom's last night as a single man in a modest fashion, by which I mean that nobody had required the attentions of a Physic. There was a dinner – many toasts were made and I delivered a speech of sorts. Dale, the King's Messenger, turned out to have a fine collection of filthy jokes that he had collected on his travels around the realm and was only too happy to share them. Many involved blushing milk-maids and amorous young squires and did not exactly rely on subtlety, but were none the less funny for all that. Some I actually hadn't heard before! Even Timothy was invited and he had his own bone, which surely had belonged to an ox of prodigious size. Aila's **cuirim** was as good as I have ever tasted, and we all had plenty, but not too much. It had been a fine evening, but as Timothy saw Emald safely to his house, there was part of me that was not as relaxed as it should have been.

I sometimes felt like an onlooker observing my own life and I wasn't sure why. Was this truly the life I was meant to lead? I had chosen it for sure. There was no doubt about that. Yet, there was now rarely a day that went by when I didn't replay my life's most momentous events and question whether I had I made the right choice? This was not like me. The revelation of Guinevere's true identity had perhaps unsettled me more than I realised.

As did my thoughts on unfinished business and there were certainly a lot of them. I was keen to see current matters settled and Lord Hudde to meet the end he deserved, but was that truly all that ailed me? Would Hudde's demise settle the questions playing around my head and solve the mystery of what had made me return to Camelot? I asked Timothy, newly returned from seeing Emald home. Timothy had no answers for me. His stomach was full and he had a warm bed to look forward to, as soon as I got into it, and that was enough for Timothy. Perhaps he was telling me something after all.

The day of Emald and Rachel's wedding was full of joy and sunshine – nothing less than they both deserved. A long wet spell had broken and summer was now ready to make amends and start to go about her business of growing enough crops to get Camelot's burgeoning population through the next winter. The 'churchyard' was full of wild flowers – kingcup, columbine, cornflowers, water avens and forget-me-nots, and enchanter's nightshade – and the guests had done their best to add more gaiety to the occasion.

Emald was almost unrecognisable, handsome with trimmed hair and beard. Even I had taken an extra trip to the baths. I took my duties seriously and, as we waited for the bride's arrival, I could see one or two of Rachel's unwed women friends looking at me with an appraising eye.

As Groomsman I had Emald's best blade strapped to my waist. I was conscious of him shuffling besides me.

'It's too late to run now, Emald, and I would be obliged to hobble you if you attempted it,' I told him.

'Don't be soft, Chaucere! Only a fool would turn down the opportunity of marrying with a woman like Rachel. It's just these new shoes the cordwainer made for me.'

I looked at the source of his discomfort. They were indeed shoes and they were indeed new. I had no other comment, as I cannot ever remember wearing such items of footwear myself.

'Rachel said she wouldn't marry with me if I wore my boots,' Emald explained further.

I looked down at my own boots. It had never occurred to me that they could be the source of any discussion, let alone dispute. And that was possibly why, along with a host of other reasons, that it was Emald getting married here today and not me.

The bride arrived. As she had no younger kinsman to carry the new sword, Dale had volunteered to step in and very gallant he looked too, striding ahead. Rachel wore a beautiful blue dress to symbolise purity and it suited her well. Truly she was a picture. Isak, there to give her away of course, looked as pleased as a cat that has not only eaten the cream but the cheese too.

Do cats eat cheese? I didn't know much about cats, but Isak's cat certainly would have on that day.

The priest officiating first blessed the site, which considering that it was the garden outside Aila's alehouse wasn't such a bad idea. The handgeld and brýdgifu were then exchanged, but given Rachel's background, and bride and groom's ages and situations, this was mostly symbolic, especially as Isak would be coming to live with them both at the Smithy.

Then came my part! I took off Emald's sword and handed it to him. He cleared his throat and, turning to Rachel, said, very forthrightly, 'I give you this blade that I cherish to hand on to our sons to have and use,' before handing her the sword, hilt first.

Dale then gave Rachel the new blade and she handed it to Emald saying, 'To keep us safe, you must wear a sword. Wear this new sword to keep our home and children from harm.'

Emald took the new sword (which of course he had made himself) and held Rachel's hand as a knotted rope was laid over both their arms to symbolise their union. Finally they exchanged rings. A difficult feat I always thought, with a rope over one hand – but as countless have done before, they managed it well.

A great cheer went up and I found I had led it! We then all went into Aila's alehouse for the Wedding Feast, as that was conveniently close and full of fine drink and food to boot. Aila had done them both proud. I doubt if the King and his Knights in the Big House ate better that day. The drink was plentiful of course, but I did not over indulge myself. It was as if I was waiting for one more event, unplanned but not unexpected, to take place.

In the afternoon of the wedding feast I received the news from one of the young lads I was currently paying to be my eyes and ears on the streets. Hudde was on the move! I left a message with Dale to pass on to the happy couple and slipped quietly out of the back of Alia's alehouse. I had a man to trail.

29
WESTWARD

T railing a horseman under most conditions is not an easy
task. That is why trackers earn good coin. In an open landscape it is too easy to be seen. In wooded countryside, unless
there happens to be just the one track, it is far too easy to lose
your quarry. Tracking is a skill that needs patience and lots of
practise. I am very good at it.

The best way of tracking a horseman is to not trail him at all,
but to just happily be going in the same direction, either that or
perhaps to become invisible. Given that Merlin had not endowed
me with any powers or a magical talisman, and I had no idea
where Lord Hudde was heading, I needed to make the most of
all those skills that I have mentioned – or cheat, of course.
Cheating is good. Cheating increases both profit and the chance
of survival.

Cheating, or as I preferred to call it: careful pre-emptive
preparation and intelligence gathering, by Emald and his smiths,
had identified the ostler where Lord Hudde, as well as the late,
very unlamented, Cecilio, kept several horses. These were not
horses used for the King's business and so were not shod in the
King's Smithy. Talem shod them.

Lord Hudde was a man who seemed to think that his position
in Camelot entitled him to talk down to those who services he
procured and to endless credit as well. This made him no friends.
Talem the Smith, however, was a good friend of Emald's and
was at the wedding. Given how much Lord Hudde owed him,
Talem had had no objections to us adding a nicely distinctive
scratch to one of Lord Hudde's horses' shoes. The very horse I
had nearly reshod as it so happened.

Trailing a horseman under these conditions is child's play, especially if the going is good and soft. It had rained for five days straight before the wedding, before the sun came out, and Lord Hudde made his move.

Talem had actually notified Emald that there might be something in the wind. Hudde's man had asked for two animals to be checked over – the sure-footed mount with plenty of stamina that I had previously seen and a pack pony.

Lord Hudde was not ill prepared either. He left when there was still plenty of daylight and any 'shadows' on his trail would have been spotted by the various low lifes that he had now signed up to his cause. They didn't spot anybody though, because there was nobody following him at this time. I had simply placed men on every road out of Camelot. They looked like herdsmen, and shepherds and indeed many were, but all were ready to tell me which way the now disguised Lord and his horses went. Then, thanks to a muddy road, I was easily able to pick up his distinctive tracks and follow him – destination still unknown – but he appeared, at first, to be heading north. His own dilapidated Hall and meagre lands the most likely objective. Simply a Lord attending to lordly tasks.

Hudde carried on like this for two days and, on the third day he turned off westwards. It was a small track, not well travelled, but I knew that in another two days it connected to a larger road of the Old Empire that was the main artery to the West. I knew this for I had travelled this very track myself many years before, on my way to meet my Tinker Master. It seemed I was heading back again to the sunset lands. The Ordovices and Deceangli, the Demetae and Silures were beckoning – shite, I was going to get properly wet again. At least this time I was better prepared at least.

I didn't recognise the House of Morgen an Spyrys at first. For a start, there was now a small village at the bottom of the hill, where once there had been a few scattered houses, and at the top of the hill there was now a very different dwelling. It was large and made of stone, a rarity in this time and place, and it looked vaguely familiar. There were still the three rings of fences and ditches, but the fences now contained large gates and the roadway was paved. Morgen the Enchantress was doing well. Perhaps this big house was even the reason why there was a hamlet here now?

Even as this thought crossed my mind I realised what Morgen's abode reminded me of – Camelot, of course! For some reason the Enchantress had decided to build herself a smaller Camelot on a hill in the lands of the Silures. And this was where Lord Hudde was heading, of that there was no doubt. Lord Hudde and the Enchantress in the Little Big House, now there was a thing. A thing I needed to know a lot more about.

I was in something of a quandary. I couldn't pay a visit to the Lady of the House, with Hudde still there, so I needed to know when he departed, but I didn't want to alert any inquisitive villagers in the employ of Morgen the Enchantress. I reckoned Hudde would not have visited her only to leave within a day or two and so I circuited the village and made my way to the other, slightly larger hamlet called Blaenavon that I remembered from all those years before.

Along the way, I packed my sword carefully in a waterproofed wrapping, and swapped my travel cloak for something a little more beaten-up and stained. I placed my sword way up high in a tree fork, where the wind couldn't dislodge it and casual eyes couldn't see it. Then, with my old cloak wrapped tightly around me, Alwin the Tinker rode into Blaenavon.

Blaenavon means "source of the river", or something similar. As there are a lot of rivers in this part of the world, there are a lot of Blaenavons. This one hadn't changed, not that I had been expecting it to.

There was nothing much that needed fixing in the rudimentary huts, bar a single venerable kettle that was owned by a grandmother who was probably old when Beryan and I first passed this way. She might have even been a previous customer judging by the knowing look that she gave me. I couldn't ask her of course, as with many in this part of the world our languages were foreign to each other. Yet we communicated for all that and she got her kettle fixed and I got a meal and a warm place to sleep.

In the morning I was on my way heading to the hamlet that sounded like it was called Hendref, the village below the stronghold of Morgen the Enchantress. There wasn't an obliging grandmother in Hendref – there was an alehouse though, to my surprise. The building was quite large and had a fine, welcoming, well-ventilated open fire over which something beguiling was simmering. The place seemed to be run by a rather rotund bald man called Godwin, who wasn't local, which was unusual. He was very jolly and friendly, which was also pretty unusual. It didn't occur to me to wonder about either of these things at the time.

'Well, pots and pans? I wouldn't know about that,' said Godwin.

'Perhaps your Goodwife?' I asked, with the right hint of civility. 'I have just come from Blaenavon and the pickings were thin there, I have to say.'

'Never mind,' Godwin continued, not answering my question. 'I have some wood that needs splitting. If you can see to that it'll be worth a beer and some stew tonight.'

I nodded enthusiastically. I have never had any problem with a spot of physical labour. After all it is good exercise, builds muscle, and if you get paid for it, so much the better.

There were a lot of logs to be split, but the axe was sharp and I had nothing better to do. I took my shirt off, for the day was becoming hot, and went to it. So engrossed was I that I didn't notice the attention on me – not immediately at least. When finally I turned, it was to see a rather startling pair of violet eyes and a mass of uncoifed dark chestnut hair examining me as a very full cat might look at the mice lurking near a grain store; tempting but perhaps for later.

'You have a lot of muscle, for a Tinker,' the woman said finally.

'I used to dig the tin before I started to shape it,' I replied, having got my story well prepared.

'That would be it,' she continued, not bothering to conceal her interest as I continued my axe work. When I had finally completed the task and slipped my shirt back on she turned away, saying, 'You can come and get your beer now. It is hot and there is a storm coming.'

I followed her in, intrigued.

She had the beer poured, for both of us. Of Godwin there was no sign. I sipped the beer. It was excellent and I said so.

'Thank you,' she replied. 'I am the alewife.'

'Then you know your beer and are to be congratulated. And Godwin?' I left the question hanging. She shrugged and said, 'he takes care of the place while I am otherwise engaged.'

I wondered what these engagements might be and gave them an indulgent moment's thought. She was a remarkable-looking woman – not young, and certainly not doe-eyed. This was a woman in her prime and she knew it.

'Godwin did not think there were likely to be any tinkering jobs around here for me?' I said.

'Not that I know of,' she replied.

'How about the big house on the hill?'

She curled her lip. 'Her? You'll get short shrift there!'

'Really? It looks very prosperous. Surely they might have a holed pan or two?'

She laughed loudly, displaying fine white teeth. 'Haven't you heard of Morgen the Enchantress who lives within its walls?'

I shook my head. She leant forward and whispered conspiratorially, 'an aged filthy hag, who can appear like a beautiful young maiden to trap unwitting men in her web!'

'What, really?'

'So they say! She's not the kind to dirty her feet in my place.'

'Doubtless she is afraid of the competition, even when magicked as a maiden!'

She laughed again. 'You have a clever tongue, Tinker.'

'So I have been told.'

She laughed and went to fetch us more beer.

I lost track of how many beers she fetched in the end and I never once noticed how few other customers the alehouse was attracting. I only had eyes for the remarkable violet eyes that were fixed on me across the table. There was nothing else worth thinking about.

Eventually she took my hand and led me to a back room.

I was carried away on a cloud of pleasure, as I did not so much take as was taken. This woman knew what she wanted and was not shy about getting it. I had not experienced anything similar, not since I had laid with Hecuba many years past – if indeed I had ever achieved that in what we call the real world. Indeed, for a moment, I thought I saw Hecuba's dark eyes looking down at me, her face a mixture of disappointment and concern. And then it was the alewife's violet eyes, rolling back in her head to show the whites in her female ecstasy.

When finally I was spent, the face firmly fixed again as that of the woman with violet eyes, I laid back enjoying the movement of the body still astride me, her magnificent hair falling across her face.

I wanted to speak, but my tongue felt thick and refused to obey its master. Finally I managed to croak out. 'I don't even know your name?'

She looked down at me, her face now very far from ecstasy and coldly replied:

'Why Morgen of course, you silly man.'

To my horror I found myself incapable of movement. Then to my further dismay I saw Lord Hudde look over Morgen's shoulder. He spoke coldly, 'Yes, that's him. Calls himself Chaucere. Nothing but a jumped-up arse ache! It was blind luck that I saw the mark on my horse's shoe.'

'So, resourceful.'

'Let me finish him now!'

'No,' Morgen barked. 'I want to question him first. There is more to your Chaucere than meets the eye.'

'But..?'

Morgen barked again angrily, 'Do not question me, Hudde. Know your place!'

'Yes, Majesty,' Hudde said sulkily. 'When will that be then?' he continued, 'that you question him?'

'A day at least. The potion I dosed him with should have laid him flat out hours ago. I had to add yet more to his beer. Still, he proved an entertaining diversion, I'll give him that.'

She got up, unashamed of her nudity. Hudde's eyes followed her hungrily as she walked away. 'Take him up the hill,' she ordered.

Hudde nodded his compliance.

'And I don't want him hurt, Hudde! Not until I say so. Make sure of that.'

Hudde didn't like any of this. I could tell that much at least as he picked me up and carried me naked out of the alehouse and chucking me in a cart that smelt strongly of cow shit; my clothes and possessions being thrown in after me.

So now at least I knew who pulled Lord Hudde's strings. Small consolation I realised, as I watched him mount a horse much finer than that he'd ridden all the way from Camelot.

Godwin got on to drive the cart. A storm of some ferocity now broke around us. It seemed only right. Thunder rolled and lightning flashed. We headed out of the yard and up the hill and that was the last I knew for what seemed like an eternity.

30
ANOTHER HOUSE ON A DIFFERENT HILL

Hecuba came to me again, in my drug-induced slumber – fully regal but thankfully without a trace of the doe-eyed Guinevere this time. Hecuba was very upset with me, but also concerned.

'Honestly, Chaucere, to be taken in so easily! I am very disappointed.'

I tried to apologise, but I had yet to regain control of my mouth. It felt like I never would, not if I lived a thousand years, which at the moment seemed very unlikely.

We were in Hecuba's private quarters and the morning light was already pouring through the light curtains, promising anotherr scorching day. She got up off the bed and made towards the window to get some air.

'You know I am hardly the jealous sort, and doe-eyes, although duplicitous, did not, I think, set out to ensnare you.'

I said something like 'ungh', which was meant to indicate that it has been a long time – I think.

She sighed and turned back.

'I appreciate that, and myself having passed from the corporeal realm I can hardly blame you, Chaucere! But honestly, she was so obvious! You should have seen her coming from miles away.'

I couldn't argue. Literally and also on a more philosophical level.

She turned back to look at the bed on which I was laid out before she spoke again, very carefully.

'So now we have to do something very difficult, Chaucere. We have to get you off this bed and out of here, as I do believe Morgen and her lick-spittle intend you no good at all.'

I agreed, but could not move so much as nod.

Hecuba sighed and shook her head, 'Now, in order to save your skinny self, Chaucere, I am going to have to borrow your body for a while. I will take the best of care, I promise. I have many happy memories of it.' She smiled, not unkindly.

She stepped forward and began to climb onto the bed and, at least so it felt, into me.

'Oh,' she said, finally. 'You must not scream, there are guards. This may hurt a bit, but no screaming – remember that!'

And with that every fibre of my being burst into flame.

I was in an agony the like of which I had never known, yet somehow my legs swung themselves off the bed and my eyes now properly opened fully wide, thanks, presumably, to the red-hot pincers that had hold of my eyelids. They didn't see Hecuba's brightly lit, luxurious, bedroom, but thankfully neither was this some dark and dank dungeon. It was a rather ordinary storeroom, presumably in Morgen's Little Big House and I had been dumped somewhat unceremoniously on a pile of sacks that my super-sensitive nose told me had once held roots of some description. The room was cool but not freezing – they obviously did not mean for me to die that way – not yet anyway. Heightened senses told me there was even a small fire somewhere close – probably behind that rather shoddy door.

Hecuba found my clothes and she dressed me carefully, as many times before she had unclothed me. I was then walked across burning coals to check the door, conscious now of voices outside. Guards perhaps?

There were indeed guards, two in fact. They were in another room – along with the fire. They were drinking, I could hear them clearly.

'That one in there's going to be out another day they say.'

'Oh yes, Her Majesty's brew knocked another out for a week once!'

'Blind me!'

'It would'.

They laughed. I did not join in.

'Who is he?'

'Buggered if I know. I didn't get an introduction.'

'Not much point now. He'll be swimming in the cesspit to-morrow. We just need to make sure he doesn't croak before she gets what she needs from him.'

'I imagine she has already done that. Lucky sod!'

'Call that lucky? She may be a looker, but bear wrestling is less dangerous.'

'True.'

I heard them moving chairs.

'Time we took a stroll around the walls I think.'

'Why not, I need some air.' An enormous fart ripped through the air.

'So do I now!'

I heard their laughter as they departed. I tried the door. Or rather I felt what I took to be the spirit of Hecuba move my hand to try it. Locked of course. I looked around the storeroom. In one corner they had dumped my pack – along with my tools! They really weren't expecting me to be going anywhere, which just goes to show you that you shouldn't put all your trust in spells and potions! Says the man who currently owed his ability to move to a dead Queen who just might have been a goddess to boot.

I got out my tools, and together Hecuba and I made short work of the lock. It wasn't a good one. I wouldn't put such a lock on the doors of my house – not either of them!

The guardroom was warm after the cool of the storeroom. There was an outside door that was closed and another inside door similarly shut. Not wanting to meet any returning guards I chose the inside option. I did not have my sword of course, so Hecuba and I picked up a poker from the fireplace, hoping it

would not be missed. Even with Hecuba leading me, I felt
ridiculously ill-prepared. Sword or no sword, I don't think I
could have bested a child with a pointy stick. However, I had
little choice so, poker to the fore, pack over my shoulder, I went
forth into the house of Morgen an Spyrys.

It was very quiet, still dark outside and I realised that far from
days, it must be scant hours since Morgen had laced my beer.
Without Hecuba I would still be unmoving and unthinking, of
that much I was sure. I walked through corridors that had
strange echoes of the Big House I had visited very various
guards, until I heard voices talking in a large hall ahead of me.
My Hecuba-guided footsteps made not a sound as I followed the
source of the conversation.

I was on something like a balcony and it was Morgen and
Hudde sitting eating and drinking off full platters of meats and
cheeses in front of a large fire down below me. Hudde was
eating with his pretty knife. I missed it and thought I would have
it back. I tucked myself in behind a pillar and listened. Hudde
was on the defensive, 'I can't act any faster. It's not often that we
all sit with him. I am on guard duty even less.'

'You must find a way. The greater my little brother's hold on
this Britain he seeks to create, the harder it will be to replace
him,' Morgen insisted.

Brother!

'When Camelot is lawless and kingless again, the people will
welcome the strong saviour that is his sister to succeed him.'

Morgen's voice took on the air of a teacher addressing a slow
pupil. 'It is not as simple as that, Hudde. I wouldn't expect you
to understand, but there is a link between ruler and land that
transcends anything as simple as occupancy of a throne. A
relationship develops whereby the land works for you and you
must work with it as well. In that way land and monarch become
truly a reflection of each other – they are one. One land, one

ruler and then one people. This link Arthur is creating can't become too strong or even a sister will not be readily accepted and the land will not flourish.'

With a start I realised that Morgen and Hudde were handing me everything I needed to know – and on a platter as well! Morgen was the King's sister! I thought there was something about the eyes I had recognised. The ramifications of this were too much for me to take in at this time.

'I will need more of the potion then,' Hudde continued. 'Are you sure the Merlin will not suspect?'

'The arrow poison is not something the Merlin will be familiar with. It is from places he has no knowledge of and accumulates in the body by simple touch. He will not be prepared for such a threat. It only needs be given in the minute amounts you apply, over time, but time is running out. Even a weakened Arthur will be a threat. We must do everything we can to humble him further.'

'I will, Majesty – don't worry about that. Although this Chaucere has destroyed an important source of income for us both, I have never been in better odour with the King and his ridiculous Round Table. As if men could ever all be equal!'

'It is exactly the sort of idea my brother Arthur would have. Yet, him and the Merlin are an affective team. I will admit that much.'

'What of the boy?' Hudde asked, spearing himself a choice cut of mutton.

'The boy is none of your concern, Hudde.'

'But he could be very useful…'

Morgen slammed her tankard down, and eyed Hudde, well displeased. 'He is more than useful! He is my son and the throne will be his one day. But this is not of your concern, Hudde!'

Chastened like the lowliest servant, Hudde occupied himself with his late supper. Looking at him I realised what his ambition was – to see himself with a crown, sitting next to Morgen as her husband and the new King. My limited experience of Morgen told me in an instant just how unlikely this would be. But who was this boy they spoke of? Morgen's son it seemed, but who was the father? If he truly was Arthur's nephew he could have a claim on Camelot while Arthur still lacked an heir. Hudde found his voice again, 'When can we start on the cur in the lock-up?'

'Not for a good half day yet. He will not be sensible until then, not with all the potion I plied him with. Eat your meat. He's not going anywhere.'

But he was going somewhere, as quickly and quietly as possible. The news that the King himself was being poisoned must be brought to Merlin's attention – proof or no proof – along with the falseness of Hudde and the threat of Morgen the Sorceress.

'I am off to my bed,' said Morgen. 'Alone.'

She stalked out of the room without a further word. This seemed to displease Hudde, judging by the way he banged his dagger into the table and stomped off. This was a very stupid thing to do and within a matter of minutes I had myself a weapon.

Thanking Hecuba for her continued invaluable assistance, I went to look for the stables.

There were a number of fine horses in the stable of Morgen an Spyrys, but none so fine as the one Hudde had ridden up from the alehouse where the Sorceress had bewitched me. This was a splendid mare as dark as night with a confirmation ideal for both speed and endurance. I had seen horses like her on my travels in lands to the east of the Middle Sea, but none of her ilk in our gloomy isles.

I rubbed her elegant neck and spoke softly into her ear. 'You are a beauty, ' I said. 'Do you mind if I call you Fallow, in praise of another beauty whose eyes are a match for yours? She is a

Queen, but I see a great tenderness and a great strength in both of you.'

Fallow did not have a problem with this, so she was the one I took. All the horses were remarkably well behaved – perhaps Morgen really was a sorceress after all. I had no trouble saddling Fallow and no trouble cutting the tack for all the other horses that I found. Nobody would be following me – not with any ease at least.

Departing Morgen's fortress on the hill was not going to be so straightforward. There were men stationed on a platform above the main gate and being so clearly visible they had not given in to the sleep they must have craved. How to get the massive gates open was my immediate concern. I doubt I could have lifted the crossbar, even when in the best of health. It was a two man job. So I needed to get the guards to do it for me. That wasn't so hard. The stables had a couple of old horseshoes awaiting the farrier's arrival, I imagine. One thrown over the new stone wall made enough of a satisfying noise to attract their attention, and the second was enough to make them do something about it.

'We should maybe check that out?'

'It's probably just a pig rooting.'

'It sounded more like a horse shoe on stone to me.'

The guard had good ears; I'll give him that. Very little between them, though.

'Help me with the crossbar then.'

'Are you sure?'

'Come on. Some exercise will keep us awake at least.'

They lifted the bar and opened the gates just enough – just enough for the mare and me to push our way through the gap. Morgen's house was built to keep people out, not guests in. We were away before a single arrow could be notched, a spear or even a curse, thrown.

I gave the horse her head. I didn't have a lot of choice. It felt like Hecuba was riding me, and I was riding Fallow – or perhaps Hecuba was riding us both now. Either way we sped down the hill as if driven by a tremendous wind blowing from sacred Avalon itself. I lost track of time and I lost track of distance. There was just the wind, the sound of Fallow's hooves and, of course, the rain. Always the rain.

Did we stop to drink or to eat? I have no recollection. Presumably Fallow must have. Not even a horse as fine as she could make it from the House of Morgen an Spyrys to the tree where I had hidden my sword some days before. That is where I next remember finding myself, with Hecuba's assistance ebbing away like water draining from a leaking bucket.

Somehow I climbed the tree and found my sword still safely wrapped against the elements. I had forgotten just how high it had been placed. I looked back in the direction of the House of Morgen and Spyrys. To my surprise I saw a beacon burning brightly on what must have been the hill top. With trepidation I looked at the road ahead. There, closer and brighter, was another lit beacon.

Whatever else Hudde was, he was nobody's fool. I judged this was his idea. He had some sort of warning system in place. Presumably the main threat to Morgan en Spyrys was going to come from the road east, but it worked just as well for alerting her people regarding anybody escaping her clutches.

I climbed wearily down from the sword's hiding place and considered my situation. To the north I knew the going was difficult – all uncleared woods and bothersome streams and rivers. The south would not be that much better, but at least there was less of it and eventually I would arrive at Mor Hafren – the sea separating the land of the Celts from the people of Kernow.

There were a lot of vessels that traded across this dangerous stretch of water and they weren't cheap to hire, but I had just inherited a jewel-encrusted dagger that wouldn't miss a gem or two. The disadvantage was that I am sure this is the route Morgen and Hudde would both expect me to take – after they realised I wasn't going to walk into the arms of whoever they had positioned to watch over traffic on the Old Empire road.

What I could do was make my way along the coast and find a ship to make landfall in Britain further west. This would take me nearer to the Summer Sea and would be more costly – but then again, these weren't my gems! First I needed to reach the coast.

And so I went north, a route that would eventually lead me to the distant Black Mountains. What I would do then – well, I had no idea.

Fallow and I took off, but Hecuba was once again in the saddle and time became as malleable as clay upon a potter's wheel. But even Hecuba could not find us an easy path through the tangle of scrub and woodland that clung to the sides of the deep, flat-bottomed valleys, that made east-west travel so difficult.

Fallow was a horse built for the open road or heath – she did not enjoy trying to get through the undergrowth that scratched her flanks. I did not enjoy it either, or the waking dream that soon became a nightmare. A nightmare that now was filled with the barking of dogs – dogs? Dogs were not good, even in my stupor I knew this. Locally they bred a scent-hunting pack hound that was well adapted to the rocky mountainous terrain and were renowned for their perseverance. And how they persevered.

Sometimes I managed to get ahead of them, but other times they were so close I could hear Hudde's gruff, hoarse tones, urging his men on. Fortunately this country was riddled with streams, perfect for confusing our scent. I also had Hecuba riding me and she had eyes that could see more and further than mortals could.

Yet I was still mortal and I could feel myself slowing down. I was like a marvellous large cat I once saw in a large city around the Middle Sea. It roared and seemingly walked of its own accord, but was only a construction of gold leaf, leather, wood, glue and lacquers, variously coloured. It was enough to scare me almost shitless until whatever motive power gave it life ran down.

I was running down. I was also fed up with this. It was far too wet and I would much rather be back in Camelot in front of a good fire with Timothy by my feet. I missed him and the people I now thought of as friends.

Enough! It was time for the hunted to become the hunter.

Much easier said than done of course, but I had one advantage. They would not expect me to go looking for them. I did not have many tools at my disposal, but I had kept hold of my pack during my escape and in that pack I had a rope.

Very useful, a good length of rope. I strung it between two trees on either side of something that was reasonably close to being a track. Then I made some noise.

Three of them came hurtling along. They really should have been taking more care. The rope missed the horses – I don't like to hurt horses, but caught all three riders on the chest, sending them flying backward onto the ground. One man broke his neck straight off. The others had their throats cut before they could get their breaths back. Sadly, none of them was Hudde. After this, his men went on foot.

I managed to retrieve a bow and arrows from one of the riders. There were only five arrows in his quiver. Very soon I had four less pursuers – yes, I missed one but I am out of practise.

I needed to take care though. Trying to get ahead of my pursuers and their dogs I nearly came unstuck when I rode Fallow down a track, where a stream, newly formed by the heavy rains, had already dug quite a deep channel. Fallow and I had been lucky – such a stream could easily break a horse's leg. This gave me an idea. Forgive me, horses.

I looked around the woodland and found plenty of debris left by the storm – some large branches and plenty of leafy twigs. I rapidly covered the stream where it crossed the track. In the poor light the stream was now invisible, especially to a rider riding swiftly. And I was going to be riding very swiftly indeed.

I scored a white mark on a tree to mark the nearby stream. I then went to find Lord Hudde.

I was lucky. I found him still on horseback lecturing his motley company that was laid out before him, nursing their wounds and taking a much-needed drink. Their horses were tied loosely as they drank and ate. Hudde wasn't happy.

'This is just one man! There is no time for eating!' he shouted. 'I was told you men knew these woods!'

'Not in these parts,' one man replied, surly, in a voice so heavily accented I could barely understand him.

Hudde rode forward and kicked him from the saddle. As incentives for getting the best out of your men I have never found that useful.

'Do not answer me back, cur,' Hudde thundered, 'or I will have that ill-mannered tongue ripped from your head! And you address me as M'Lord!'

That started general muttering which pleased Hudde not at all.

'Quiet all of you! I won't have this!'

'Our loyalty is sworn to the Lady Morgen, not to some stranger from the Lost Lands!' replied the surly man as he picked himself up off the ground.

This was going so well, I hardly liked to interrupt – but I did.

'Ha, Hudde – you arse-licker!' I shouted down the track. 'Aren't we going to do this? I told you before, I have places to be.'

Then I threw the branch I had cut like a spear into the group of horses. They spooked nicely, which meant it was only Hudde close on my trail as I headed off at speed. I stayed far enough ahead of him to make sure he never saw me jump the covered stream. As soon as I saw my mark I urged Fallow on and she cleared the stream with room to spare.

Hudde was just too over-excited. The horse went down, a foreleg broken. For that at least I was sorry. I set upon Hudde before he had a chance to get his breath back. He had hurt something. I didn't care.

'You have no honour, Chaucere,' he screamed at me as we clashed swords. He could scream all he liked. I wasn't going to be distracted. I needed him dead before his men regrouped. He was many things I despised, but he could use a sword when forced to. We exchanged blows and I could see that he too was playing for time. I didn't have time and that meant taking chances.

Feigning initially to the left I went back to my right, but then swapped sword hands with a quick transfer. This left me too exposed on my right side and I felt his blade cut me deep. However, with a swing of the sword now in my left hand, powered by my equally strong left arm, I cleaved his head from his body. A pleasing result, it was a shame it could only be done once.

Hudde's head fell to the ground – a look of surprise fixed permanently now on his features. I clutched my right side, trying to staunch the wound, then I looked up to see the company now arrayed before me.

'You were right to call this scum out!' I said to them. 'I saw him, with my own eyes, slaughter his men – men who had ridden with him and shared his food and drink – rather than engage in a fair fight with those who would call him out for his treachery.'

The surly man, who had now taken on the role of a leader, looked at me evenly. 'He has caught you with a telling blow.'

'You can tell your mistress that, as I judge she instructed you to bring me back alive.'

'She did. It was his idea to end your life against her orders.'

'That is the sort of man he was – no loyalty and no honour.'

The surly man nodded and as one they turned and left Hudde's body to the beasts of the forest.

As much as I disliked the business, I searched his body for anything that might prove useful. He had on a clean doublet that I cut to make bandages to strap my wound. It helped, but I knew I needed proper treatment before I joined Hudde wherever it is that men who fall in battle truly go. As I mounted my horse it started raining again. I had no idea where I was, but this track looked as good as any other.

I left Hudde's head where he had fallen; the look of surprise still fixed on his face.

I grew weary as I rode and realised that my time must also be close. Fallow was leading now and the rain was more like a fine mist. I became aware that the valley had flattened out and ahead of us there was no longer an unbroken line of trees but what appeared to be a lake. There were lakes in this land I knew and perhaps it was just a trick of the light, for this particular lake seemed unending and hence impassable. I thought about finding a nice place to sit down and die.

As I stared through the watery curtain I thought I saw a woman, clad in the finest silks, rising from the lake surface. As she got nearer I realised that she was actually standing in a boat. She was close enough now for me to see she was extraordinarily beautiful. At first I thought this was Hecuba, come to spend time with me again. On closer examination I realised that she was as different from Hecuba as it was possible to be – pale and delicate with the blue green eyes of a Northern Spring – yet there was something that said they were two sisters at a much deeper level. There was no doubt that they were both of equal beauty.

She looked at me closely and cocked her head, as if judging me. I didn't feel as if I had passed whatever inspection she was carrying out, but neither was I found wanting. Perhaps she was just a little disappointed, however she held out her hand and smiled. I tried to dismount, but decided that falling was easier.

I lay there, enjoying my last dream and what I hoped was to be a glimpse of the heaven I was going to. But heaven wasn't ready for me yet. The lady leant over me, her perfect brow now puckered by concern.

Once more she offered her hand and this time I took it. New strength flooded through me as she drew me up. Unbelievably, my legs held and I was able to walk. Still holding her hand, I led Fallow onto the Lady's boat.

31
AVALON

Without the slightest trace of wind we moved across the water. I could hear the rain fall far behind me but that sound was coming from another place and perhaps another time. All lost – lost and forgotten. Here it was a warm twilight on a summer's evening. No clouds disturbed the blue of the sphere above and we floated on. I was lost in the eyes of the Lady and so I was totally surprised when she spoke to me. 'Three times he struck me, Chaucere. Would you strike me so?'

'Never!' I replied, with the last of my energy! 'What man in his right mind would do such a thing!'

She smiled sadly. 'Perhaps it is the very essence of man to hurt the thing they love the most?'

'Only some men,' I insisted. 'For others of us it is abhorrence to hurt the one you love.'

'Perhaps,' she replied, her voice now full of doubt. 'But he said the same thing and he said he loved me as no man had ever loved a woman.'

'Then he was no true man.'

'No Knight then? Are you a Knight, Chaucere?'

'No.'

'Are you a King?'

'No! Never that.'

'Then what are you?'

I paused, unsure what to say, as if I was aware that lying now might make all the difference – the difference to everything.

'I truly do not know.'

'Are you a hero?'

'No. I am a common man.'

'Really? Then who do you call Master?'

'None. I am a Freeman.' I smiled, 'I now have the house to prove it.'

'Will you kneel for a King?'

'I will kneel to no man simply for who he is, but I will respect all men that deserve respect.'

'So, a common man and yet an unusual man. A man of honour? A Freeman?'

'Yes, a Freeman.'

'Perhaps the best in his world and good enough for any world?'

'I could not say that.'

'No, but perhaps I could. I am Nimue.'

I was taken aback for folk such as what I knew she must be, did not give their true names lightly. She turned then and looked ahead to where an island rose suddenly from the water – higher than one might have expected, with a building at its top.

'Where is this?'

'This is Avalon, Chaucere.'

'Truly?'

'I could not lie to you, Chaucere. Truly, I could not lie at all. We cannot.'

'Then, this lake... where...'

'There is only one Lake, Chaucere, and all lakes are that one lake – for us at least.'

She smiled at my obvious confusion.

'We must stay here a while and you must heal.'

'Thank you.'

I looked down at my wound. It still gaped, but there was no blood. I knew that couldn't be right, yet here it was.

The boat pulled alongside a small pier and we disembarked. The moment my foot touched land I was aware of being somewhere different. The hairs on my arms and neck stood up, but this was not goose flesh. This experience was different in the same way as the time I had lived with Hecuba. Yet, if my time spent with Hecuba was strong spiced wine, this was the sweetest of cool water on a summer's day. Different but somehow the same – both fed the soul. I have no other words to explain myself.

I led Fallow from the boat and she gratefully set about eating the grass of Avalon, which I assumed was not a sacrilege as the Lady Nimue said nothing against it. Nimue then led me up the steep slope to the building on the summit, a single Tower. We passed two streams – one ran white and one red, which seemed perfectly normal in such a place. All around us grew plants of every shape, size, colour and perfume. Some I knew, some I had no name for. Even Ansaldo would have been amazed by what I saw and smelt.

The Tower, when we reached it, had no door and so we went straight inside. I was amazed to find it was much larger on the inside than it had first appeared as we had climbed the hill. She noticed my surprise and with a smile on her lips explained. 'We are in Annwn, Chaucere. The rules are different here.'

We walked through the Tower to a large room with a blazing fire where a meal had been laid out on a large round table. I knew the table, or its like.

'The King has been here,' I stated rather than asked.

Nimue smiled again. 'Did you think you would be the first man I had shared a meal with at my table, Chaucere?'

I shook my head, but could not help but feel a surge of jealousy. Guinevere and Nimue – benefits of the job, a cynical voice inside me said.

'Please sit, Chaucere. You are making the place look untidy.' She gestured me to a day bed. I was taken aback for a moment. I wasn't ready for humour from this Lady, but who was I to even begin to guess what to expect?

I did as I was told.

'Now let us see to that little scratch. It would not be seemly for you to die here.'

I did not watch her ministrations. If I have a choice I prefer it that way. I have been stitched enough in my time. She did not have a needle though. First she rubbed a potion on and covered it with a clean cloth – though what good that would do to such a wound I did not know. I soon found out as a numbing cold spread around the sword thrust. This in itself would not staunch the blood flow, but it was not unpleasant. It was what she did next that surprised me the most. Fetching a pot, she took off the lid and pulled out a large beetle with great pincers. This she then placed under the cloth covering me. She noted my surprise. 'Just relax, Chaucere. This is Avalon, remember.'

I did my best to do as she said as she placed a further handful of the large insects under the cloth.

Leaning back I felt myself becoming sleepy. If I was to die here it would not be too bad at all. I closed my eyes only to feel Nimue press a goblet into my hand.

'Drink this first, Chaucere.'

I opened my eyes and put the goblet to my lips. It was good – not wine or ale, but something stronger and yet more thirst-quenching.

'Good,' I managed. 'Very good. You must give me the ingredients.'

'You could not find them, Chaucere.'

'How long will I take to heal?'

'You will know when it is time to leave.'

'I could not imagine ever wanting to be anywhere else.'

She laughed, like the ringing of glass bells and then I was asleep.

When I woke up nothing had changed. The light was the same, a permanent warm twilight it seemed. It smelled the same too, like a wonderful summer's day. The only difference was that now there was music.

I have never had much time for music. I like a good tune and a bawdy verse but I have never had the opportunity to contemplate the complexities of real music. Now, though, I really concentrated. The music tugged at some part of me that had laid dormant for too long. It sounded like a mixture of bird song and a soft wind in leafy trees, accompanied by tinkling fountains and bubbling streams. Listening closer I realised it was birds and trees and the various movements of water, but how could they all connect together so harmoniously?

I was disturbed.

'Nimue?'

'Yes?'

She was sitting nearby, but so quietly I hadn't even noticed her before. She came and sat next to me.

'What are these sounds? They are beautiful.'

'It is the Music of Life, Chaucere,' said Nimue.

'Life?'

'It is around you all the time, present if you only stop and listen.'

'Surely not?'

'Yes. It is always more noticeable here in Annwn – and because you were close to being removed from the song altogether.'

I started uncomfortably. 'You mean I was that close to death?'

She nodded. 'Mere moments more and you would have been beyond even the ability of Avalon and myself to save.'

'Then I must thank you again.'

'No thanks are necessary, Chaucere. Each of us has a role to play and yours is not played out yet, but you have already done well.'

'Have I?'

She smiled again and the song sounded even louder. 'Oh yes, better than you yet realise. Ever since you were young you have made choices, the right choices, even if they weren't necessarily the easiest ones.'

I sat back. 'I don't understand.'

'You will. For now you must eat to replenish your spirit.'

She helped me up and led me to the table, which was spread with foods that I had no names for – fruits and cheeses that were at once familiar and strange – and instead of bread there were crisp wafers liberally buttered. We ate and it was delicious, as I might have anticipated. And all around the Music of Life played on.

I do not know how long I was in Avalon. Long enough for my wound to heal and my spirit to recover I judge. I walked the seemingly endless woods and observed the hind and hare that lived there unmolested. Fallow grazed contentedly, although as far as I could see there were no other horses in Avalon. I could have remained there at peace indefinitely, although I was concerned that as I recovered my health so my desire for Nimue grew as well. I judged that making unwanted advances towards the Lady of Avalon would not be looked upon kindly, as well as breaching every rule of hospitality.

She must have been aware of my attraction, for one night she came to my room. She stood there lit only by the moon and I thought my heart would break just to look at her. This was not what I had felt for Hecuba, which had been all fire, this was a slow burn, but it burnt none the less. She moved forward and sat on my bed and for a moment I felt my heart skip a beat. Then she smiled sadly. 'I am sorry, Chaucere. I am not for you. It might have been so once, but that was not to be our destiny – our paths were not so aligned.'

'And that is fixed, is it?' I asked, trying not to sound too peeved.

She nodded. 'It is. Besides I think my sister Hecuba would be rather cross with the both of us and it's not a good idea to get her cross.'

I was surprised, 'she is your sister? I didn't realise. I thought you were one of the Fay folk and she was... something else.'

'The names you mortals give us are not our own names for ourselves and neither do they describe our actions or intentions. They are not for you to hear and you would really not understand them anyway.'

'I see,' I said. I didn't.

'However, a sister is as close a description as I can give to you. You have met my younger sister Ēostre as well I know and you did her a great service. She thanks you and says she is more wary of men's traps now.'

'Ēostre?'

'Come on Chaucere, surely she is not that forgettable?'

My mind went back to the hill outside of Wellan, and a young girl with amber eyes, which surely was an age ago.

'I didn't realise.'

'She sends her best wishes for your continued health.'

'You are all so different.' I looked at her in amazement.

'Distinct maybe, but we are really not that different. Not when you look close.'

I looked at her and for a minute her face was that of the woman who had thanked me for saving the hare, and then it was Hecuba chiding me, before the Lady of the Lake was in front of me again.

'Do you understand now?'

'I am not sure,' I said. And I wasn't, I'm still not, in case you are interested.

'Besides, Hecuba is still cross with you over Morgen Le Fay.'

'Is that what you call her?'

'Oh yes! For she has dual heritage.'

'Is that even possible?' I asked, very interested to know how the worlds of man and this other realm interacted.

'Of course, Chaucere. After all, where do you think Merlin has gained all his wisdom?'

'It hadn't occurred to me. I thought he was just the Merlin.'

'Just? There is no just to him, Chaucere. You know enough to be careful in his presence I take it?'

'Of course. He scares me.'

'You are right to be scared of him. He scares many even in the land of the Annwn.'

'Really?'

'Oh yes! He has something very dangerous. Something we lack here.'

'What is that? May I ask?' I was wary now, unsure of the ground on which I stepped.

'He has a plan, Chaucere, and there is nothing more dangerous than a man with a plan, less it is a half-breed with a plan.'

I considered this. Was Merlin's plan so dangerous? And what exactly did I know of his plans – only what he told me, and I did not believe he was someone to share confidences readily.

Nimue rose from the bed. 'You must be careful of her too, Chaucere. Morgen Le Fay is a powerful foe and she has a hold on you.'

I sat up and shook my head. 'She has no hold on me.'

Nimue smiled that sad smile. 'Those who sleep with the Fay do not escape their clutches so easily. Remember what happened to Lord Hudde. It is a powerful drug.'

'Well, I have forgotten the incident already.' I was adamant.

'I imagine Lord Hudde said much the same, before he realised just how deep the hook was buried.' And with that she left and for the first time since I arrived in Avalon, I did not sleep easy.

The next day, after I'd woken and seen to the necessaries, we broke our fast together as had been our routine. Yet, even as we ate, the Music of Life filling the air all around us, I knew something had changed.

'It's time for me to go,' I said – a statement rather than a question.

'It is,' she replied. 'I must say I will miss your company.'

'And I yours.'

'Arthur is in danger.'

'He is and I will save him.'

'Yes,' she nodded wisely, 'that, I feel, is ever your duty.'

We left shortly after. I collected my pack, which had miraculously survived my adventures and buckled on my sword.

Nimue looked at this with something like amusement, before saying: 'It does have a name, you know, your sword. All works of such magnitude are imbued with a name as they are crafted. I know its name.'

'Then please keep it to yourself. It is just the tool of my trade.'

'If you insist, Chaucere.' She smiled again and I tried to smile back but I was actually a little cross for I now knew that the sword without a name would now forever be known as 'The Sword with No Name' in my mind. For all their beauty, and for all their wisdom, there was no doubt that sometimes these Fay folk could be a right pain in the arse.

We collected a very happy Fallow and once more embarked on her boat across the still waters of the lake. I was concerned about my journey back to Camelot and finding a route that was free from any men Morgen might have set on my trail again. I said as much to Nimue.

'Do not be concerned, Chaucere,' she replied. 'There will be no foe to cross your path here.'

I wished I had her confidence. I did not think Morgen the Sorceress would take kindly to the death of her Lord Hudde, her inside man at Camelot's court.

Yet as our journey continued I found myself disconcerted. A line of hills appeared before us, but these were not the densely wooded slopes of Powys. They were familiar though.

'Surely these are the Mendip Hills?' I cried out loud.

Nimue, of course, was amused by my surprise. 'There is just the one lake, Chaucere. Did I not tell you that? My boat can travel every aspect of it.'

I looked back, and instead of Avalon rising through the early morning mist, I now saw the hill of Glestingaburg standing proud from the waters. I had seen the images of it in Camelot and had passed at some distance once before. This made me think of Dale. I never did get an apple for him. I knew Glestingaburg was considered special by many and I now knew just how special it was. It was a gateway to Avalon for those that knew the way.

This meant we were now crossing the Summer Sea, which are the wet lowlands south of Mor Hafren. Although there was always drainage underway, to provide more pasture for farming, these lands were very prone to flooding, leaving small island villages, like Glestingaburg and Brenten Knoll, standing proud. The hairs on the back of my neck rose. In Nimue's company, on Avalon, it was too easy to forget that one was in the presence of somebody who far transcended what was normal for ordinary men and women.

Nimue was able to guide her boat for a good way, cutting down the distance I had left to travel. She found us a small pier and I helped Fallow off the boat and onto the slippery planks. I then turned, wondering what words of thanks and farewell I could say to someone like Nimue. She knew my difficulty.

'We never say goodbye, Chaucere for truly we are never parted. It is just an accident of how the world is ordered for mortal men and women that makes it seem that way.'

'Then we will meet again?' I asked hopefully.

'We will never be apart will we?' she said, and with one swift motion she reached over and kissed me once on the lips. Time stood still again and then she was gone.

I shook my head, knowing the truth of what she said, but still feeling her loss in my heart. I watched until her figure in the boat grew small and she returned from whence she came, wishing I might tarry there longer and be at one again with the Music of Life.

I led Fallow off the pier and back to dry land. The second my foot touched soil I was overcome by a wave of exhaustion such as I had never felt before. I could barely mount Fallow. I was aware of a great hunger, as if I had not eaten for a month, and my limbs were as heavy as if they were made from the lead that was mined from these hills.

This wouldn't do at all. I still had many miles to travel to Camelot. I needed to make haste, for although Hudde was no longer a threat I had no idea of Morgen's plans, and the source of the poison being given to the King needed to be found and eliminated.

I urged Fallow on. Fortunately she was well rested and keen to run. The route I took to Camelot? I have no idea, and although my body was healed I felt as light-headed as a youth after his first beer and more exhausted than after my first battle. The day passed in a blur. The next thing I truly recall is the Merlin standing before me in the moonlight in the centre of the road, in front of the gates of Camelot, staff raised as if ready to see off daemons from the foulest depths of the Earth. I doubt if a dragon, should it have decided to walk out of the tales of old and threatened the walls of The Big House itself could have seen him more prepared.

'Halt!' he shouted and Fallow came to an immediate stop, almost throwing me. His eyes narrowed and he seemed to draw the night around him, while the light of the moon became a beacon in his hand. 'I do not know what manner of creature you be, but you shall not enter within these walls or do harm to any under my protection. Be gone!'

'Merlin,' I croaked, only now realising just how thirsty I was. 'Really? Do piss off.'

The old man's brow – if man he still was in any measure – puckered at this unexpected answer. 'I was hoping for a beer at the very least, Merlin.'

The Sage looked at me as if I was speaking in tongues.

'Give me respite this time, please Merlin. I've come rather a long way and we went the scenic route, which seems to have taken its toll on me in a most unexpected way.'

'Chaucere?' Merlin said, surprise now colouring his threat. 'Is that really you? Then who rides with you? I see two beings of great power that cloud your semblance.'

'Yes, well they're both leaving now.'

I had no more time or energy for niceties. 'Morgen an Spyrys – the Powys Sorceress, she's Arthur's sister and Hudde's mistress. He was poisoning Arthur, an arrow poison – I don't know how. They seek the throne. He is dead now. There is a son.'

And with that I fell off Fallow and slept for two days.

32
GOOD BROTH

There were no dreams of Hecuba this time, or Nimue either, as I lay insensible. Fortunately my thoughts were also free from Morgen as well, but sadly neither did I wake up to Rachel's tender administrations. How could I? She was another man's wife now; I recalled with something like regret. I think the Lady Ansithe visited – I seemed to remember her kind face looking down with some concern. Guinevere might have been there too, or more likely I did at least dream her presence.

However, when I finally properly opened sleep-glued eyes, it was to be greeted by Merlin's chilling features. 'There is broth,' he said. 'I suggest you eat slowly. You are nothing much more than skin and bone.'

'I have eaten – I ate wonderful food – a marvellous banquet on Ava-.'

Merlin quieted me with one hand.

'Best not to speak of what happens across the divide without proper precaution, but let us say that such meals eaten there are better for the spirit than for providing what the body needs. For the moment, eat the broth.'

There was indeed broth. I could smell it now and it smelt very good and I was very hungry. First I needed to make sure the importance of my message was understood.

'Lord Hudde,' I began.

Merlin interrupted. 'The content of your message was clearly understood. Do not fret on that score.'

I went to push myself up and failed. My arms couldn't manage this simple task.

'What? How am I so weak?' I managed to splutter.

'I'll fetch the broth,' said Merlin, getting up.

259

I was in a room I hadn't seen before; a bedroom, but no cheerier than his other rooms. I don't think the Merlin worried overmuch about cheerfulness. It was at least warm and dry and although not exactly Avalon, I could not complain about the treatment.

Merlin returned with a large bowl of broth. He put it down. Then he moved me forward until I was sitting upright and put a bolster behind my back to support me. Next he fetched the broth and I had the embarrassment of being fed like a baby by the second most powerful man in the land. He spooned a few mouthfuls down and I immediately felt better.

'I don't understand,' I said. By way of explanation he brought me a looking glass. A rare silvered one as I had seen in lands by the Middle Sea. I looked in it and a stranger looked back – gaunt and drawn like a starving man on a slave ship. Merlin could see my lack of comprehension.

'It is an effect of possession.' he explained. 'Mortal bodies are not expected to host beings of divinity. Most mortal bodies should not even be able to host beings of divinity.'

'Is that what happened?' He looked at me with an attention that sent shivers everywhere that can shiver. 'Perhaps you could explain to me how else you were able to ride some considerable distance in a remarkably short time with a wound that really should have ended your life but now appears to have completely healed. By the way, your mount is in much better shape than you are.'

'Good. She's a fine mount.'

'The finest, and not yours I take it?'

'Lord Hudde's or perhaps Morgen an Spyrys's. Mine now.'

'Hush, Chaucere. We do not mention that name in this house either. Drink your broth.'

I managed the spoon myself this time.

'There seems to be no permanent injury, Chaucere, but you have been burnt up like a Smith's forge running with too much air and not enough coal.'

I did as I was told and ate deeply and was soon asleep again.

The next time I woke up I was questioned more closely. First I asked for further reassurance regarding the impact of my news. Of Hudde, Merlin told me, there was no sign. I explained to Merlin that even Lords rarely go anywhere without their heads. There would be no further signs of him at all. Take that for proof!

All of Hudde's belongings in Camelot had been seized and searched. Traces of a powerful potion were found, hidden in a false compartment in a travel chest. The King was now in his chambers being treated with suitable purgatives by Merlin and he was already much recovered. The poisoning, it seemed, had been stopped before there was permanent damage.

'However, we have no idea of how this poison was administered, so we cannot be sure if the threat is completely removed.' Merlin mentioned, still concerned, and also angry about how he had been outwitted.

'I see,' I said, thinking hard.

'We are sure it wasn't his food or his drink, or others would have become ill as well,' he continued. He shook his head in frustration. 'And they never mentioned how they were going about their nefarious business?'

It was my time to shake my head. 'It was never mentioned, just that contact was involved. He had touched the poison somehow.' My dreams of the Round Table came back to me, as did the shadow I had seen hanging over Arthur's seat. I suddenly knew the answer.

'The poison, it is on the arms of Arthur's seat at the Round Table!' I exclaimed excitedly. 'Hudde must have been applying it while he was on guard duty!'

'Yes, yes!' said Merlin, jumping up excitedly. 'That is also why the King was better when we were away from Camelot! I will see to this immediately.' He dashed away while I lay back and considered everything I had learnt about the forces that move, both seen and unseen, on our island home.

'What about the Sorceress, Morgen?' I asked as soon as Merlin had returned. 'Surely she is still a threat?'

'She is,' Merlin replied. 'But she is a threat we now know about and we can make preparations and take suitable precautions.'

'Her house is well guarded but it is no Camelot. I could devise a way in.'

'Her House is also in Powys, which is not Britain – not yet. It would not be the done thing for Arthur to send a sizeable force into a neighbouring Kingdom. And we don't have the supply line established for a siege anyway.'

I considered this. 'Then what do we do?'

'We do nothing,' Merlin answered, with some amusement. 'The King is considering what action to take and will inform me in due time. Whether you hear anything, well that's a very different matter.'

Seeing my cross expression he at least conceded.

'There are complications, Chaucere, about which you know nothing. And need to ask nothing either.'

'She has a son…'

'Enough!'

'Whose son is it?'

'I said enough, Chaucere! Shut up!'

I was about to ask more, but was further dissuaded by a scowl that could have flattened armies. I shut up and ate my broth. I was eating a lot of broth.

'In the meantime, Chaucere, there are questions that still surround you as well.'

'Questions?'

'I mentioned previously that I had found you an "interesting" man.'

'You did, and I think I said that there was little about me to interest a man of your standing, Merlin. I am an ordinary man.'

'I disagree. The old gods do not form alliances with ordinary men.'

'Then that is their business and you will have to ask them, when you next make their acquaintance,' I replied flippantly.

'I might just do that Chaucere,' he fired back. I was forgetting that it does not pay to be flippant to a Mage with the gift of prophecy and, according to many, the ability to turn himself into any animal he chooses. A man of such subtlety even Nimue had warned me: *he has plans,* she said.

I would not forget that in a hurry, or cease to worry what my part in his plans might be. In the meantime, I let the second most powerful man in Camelot, and Britain, feed me broth. Let him have his secrets, I had my own secret as well. And that secret he would never learn, nobody ever would.

EPILOGUE

I was only fourteen. Tall for my age, but with a lot of filling out still to do. All I knew was encompassed in Spring Farm and the village of Wellan. To me even Wellan seemed like a noisy and packed place. Camelot growing almost magically on the hill on the horizon was like another country. I had been there once with my step-father. The whole experience had left me in something like shock.

There was a rumour going around Wellan that a number of the Lords of the land were to visit that day and accompanying them would be the Merlin and a young man, hardly more than a boy himself. But this young man had a destiny it was said – a destiny that the Merlin was preparing for him.

We all knew about the Sleeping Man and the impossible sword. We were all told by our parents to keep away from the stone and the dell in which it lay. Of course, being young men, my half-brothers and I would make secret furtive visits to test ourselves. As the youngest, my older brothers Jeb, Sam and Ethan wouldn't let me near the sword itself – buried in the heart of the stone. They sneered and batted me back, warning me of the daemons that would come and eat my liver if I so much as touched it.

As we grew older my stepfather made sure our chores left us no time for such tomfoolery. I will say this for him, although I was but an extra burden taken on when he married my widowed mother, after he too was left without a spouse following the Winter Sweat, he treated us boys all the same. By that I mean harshly but without favour. He didn't hire any labourers except at harvest time. The rest of the time we had to more than pull our own weight. We grew up quickly, and tough. The sword was always there though, in my mind's eye – even when I slept I could see it.

Today all this might change – there might be a new King for our divided land. One to bring all the people together and 'herald a new age of peace and prosperity'. So it was said.

I rose early while it was still dark, although the moon shone so bright there were clear shadows on the floor. I knew the way to the Sleeping Man so well I could have found it blindfolded.

There he was, in the moonlight – the Sleeping Man – and he really did look like some lumbering giant in the weird light. The hilt of the sword protruded strangely, casting the shadow of a cross upon the body of the stone. I realised I was holding my breath and it felt like I had stood there for an hour at least. Time had taken a different track. My fourteen-year-old mind didn't know what to make of it. My body moved of its own accord. I jumped forward and gripped the sword hilt and pulled. It moved as easily as if I had lifted it from butter. I felt a cold chill run through my heart, as if I too had been pierced by that very sword.

I stood there, mouth open, staring at this old, old sword that barely glimmered in the moonlight yet was somehow also shining with a brilliance from another place and another time. It was there in my hand.

What did I do now?

I was suddenly afraid. No good could come of this. My step-father would be furious for a start. The Lords would be furious and as for the Merlin! I looked down at the sleeping man and he looked back up at me. I could see his every feature, the crown he wore, his strange long gown. He blinked and put his head to one side questioningly. My mouth was dry and I could find no words.

Just then I heard the sound of approaching horses down the drover's path – a whinny and a cough coming ahead of them.

I knew what I had to do. I was not fit to bring all the people of the land together and 'herald a new age of peace and prosperity.' I was barely fit to watch over the livestock, or so my stepfather insisted. I plunged the sword back into the stone and it went back as easily as it had been freed.

Voices were approaching now. I dived into a nearby bush with no thought for my own safety. The Lords filled the dell, amongst them was a mysterious, robed figure that carried with him a feel of immeasurable age. That could only be the Merlin and next to him, I could see by the first light of dawn, a tall strong young man with a bearing that could only be described as regal. He looked suddenly in my direction and I saw his pale blue eyes, so similar to my own, trying to peal back the undergrowth. The Merlin spoke and he turned away.

I had seen enough. I crept back through the undergrowth and then ran down the Drover's Lane to Spring Farm. Halfway home I heard the sound of a loud cheer. Something flashed through me again – my heart skipped a beat – and then the feeling was gone. I felt saddened but somehow free. I could see a light in Spring Farm, but I knew I could never live there again. There was no point in disturbing my mother or getting into long discussions. I had a rough bag hidden in an outhouse containing the few bits and pieces that had some personal significance to me and the few coins that had come my way. And so I left Wellan, and never once looked back. I knew I would never return but, as with so many things in my life, it turned out I was very wrong.

Milton Keynes UK
Ingram Content Group UK Ltd.
UKHW010643041223
433752UK00005B/322

9 781909 295278